DARE TO LOVE

The Maxwell Series - Book 3

S.B. ALEXANDER

Raven Wing Publishing

Dare to Love
Book Three: The Maxwell Series
Copyright © 2016 by S. B. Alexander.
All rights reserved
First Edition: February 2016
E-book ISBN-13: 978-0-9969351-1-1
Print ISBN-13: 978-0-9969351-2-8

Visit: www.sbalexander.com
Editor: Red Adept Editing, www.redadeptediting.com
Cover Design by Hang Le: http://www.byhangle.com

This is a work of fiction. Names, characters, places and incidents either are the product of the author's imagination or are used fictitiously, and any resemblance to locales, events, business establishments, or actual persons-living or dead-is entirely coincidental.

Adult Content Warning: The content contained is the book includes adult language and sexual content. This book is intended for adult audiences 17 years of age and older.

DEDICATION

To all my readers, fans, and bloggers, thank you for taking this journey with me.

DARE TO LOVE PLAYLIST

- "Jealous" by Labrinth
- "Always Be You" by Matthew Mayfield
- "Love is Hell" by Theory Of A Deadman
- "When You're Young" by 3 Doors Down
- "Sexy and I know It" by I'm Sexy and I know It
- "Tennessee Whiskey" by Chris Stapleton
- "Easy to Love You" by Theory of A Deadman
- "Better Or Worse" by Theory of A Deadman
- "Girl Crush" by Little Big Town
- "Yours" by Ella Henderson
- "Better Than Me" by Hinder
- "Waking Up The Dead" by Hinder
- "One Last Breath" by Creed
- "Love and Memories" by O.A.R
- "I Miss You" by blink-182
- "One Grain Of Sand" by Ron Pope
- "What's My Age Again?" by blink-182
- "Want U Back" by Boyce Avenue
- "Trouble" by Ray LaMontagne
- "Your Body is a Wonderland" by John Mayer
- "Good Man" by Devour the Day
- "Picture" by Kid Rock, Sheryl Crow

PROLOGUE

Kelton Maxwell

I'm a knight in shining armor, I'm Prince Charming on a steed;
I am Superman and Rocky; Hell, I'm all you'd ever need.
I'm a lover AND a fighter, even angel from above
But I won't be your ever after, 'cause I don't do love.

No matter how you spin it, I'm not willing to commit.
There will be no soulful promise, only sarcasm and wit.
My family is my focus and of course, there's getting paid.
I'm running all the bases; modeling and getting laid.

Stand in line and wait your turn, there's lots of me to share.
Baby, you're a booty call, I ain't got time to care.
This lifestyle was made for me; it fits like hand in glove.
I told you when we started that I don't do love.

I have seen my older brother fall, a victim to romance.
The girl he's got is a keeper but I can't take that chance.
I know that I'll be tempted. It's hard to beat that rap.
But every day I need a different lady on my lap.

Short and curvy, long and lean, brunette, ginger or blonde;
The women keep on coming, I've got the magic wand.
Many chicks will try and fail, but when push comes to shove
They'll walk off broken-hearted, 'cause I don't do love.
Consider this a warning, in time you all will see
The only way that I'd do love, is if it's doing me!

CHAPTER 1

KELTON

My nuts were about to freeze to my groin as I hurried across campus.

"Kelton!" Chloe Pitt's voice carried on the breeze. "Wait up."

I closed my eyes briefly, not wanting to deal with her. We'd broken up well over a month ago when the words *I love you* fell from her lips. Not only was that my cue to get the fuck out, but it sobered me up. She wanted the big house, the good-looking husband, kids, and someone to boss around. I certainly wasn't that fucking guy.

She walked up wrapped in a parka and a thick orange scarf. February in New England can be brutal with below-zero temperatures, and today was one of those days. I guarantee that if I'd taken a piss right then it would have frozen before it hit the ground.

"I've been calling you. Why haven't you picked up?" she asked, licking her lips.

Because I didn't want to get married. "What are you doing at BU?" I asked through lips so cold they were having a tough time moving. "Aren't you supposed to be in class at Harvard?"

"It's Friday. I don't have classes on Fridays." She rolled her eyes like I was supposed to know her schedule. I could barely keep track of my own. "Are you on your way into Mr. Brewer's art class?"

She knew my schedule. I'd bet she even knew when I took a shit.

"Chloe, we're not getting back together." She'd been trying every possible angle, including having her cousin, Lacey, talk to me anytime she was home from college.

"You're an ass. I need a date tonight for the art benefit my father is hosting, and you owe me." She pulled her hood up over her blond hair as her nose started running.

"Owe you?" The only thing I owed her was a big fat *no*. She was definitely a sweet girl, and we had loads of fun in the sack. But she wasn't my future.

Two people ran past us and into the warm building that was calling my name.

"That's right. I kept you from getting killed by my bodyguard," she reminded me in a snarky voice.

I vowed every day to stay away from women who wanted more than I could give—the women who wanted my heart in the palms of their hands, the women who wanted a life of forever. I didn't do forever, and I wouldn't open my heart to anyone. I'd seen how torn up my brother, Kody, was over the loss of his girlfriend and how my old man hurt when my mom fell apart after the death of my sister, Karen. The door to my heart was shut so tight that it would take someone with superpowers to pry open the lock. I bit my tongue. She wouldn't leave me alone until she got what she wanted, and right now I didn't have the patience to deal with her.

I glanced around. "Where is the jerk, by the way?" Chloe always had a bodyguard on her ass, compliments of her father, Jeremy Pitt, head of the Russian mob in Boston.

She shrugged. "I ditched him."

If anyone was good at fleeing the confines of her father's hold, it was Chloe. I flipped up the collar of my leather jacket. "I didn't ask you to fight my battles for me."

Chloe had shown up at a recent frat party. She'd scowled when she saw a girl sitting on my lap. Before the girl had had a chance to move, Chloe had her hands in the girl's hair, pulling her off me. Needless to say, we got into an argument even though we weren't dating, and her dense bodyguard had come in and tried to manhandle me. I was about to punch his lights out when Chloe maneuvered her curvy body in between Scar Face and me. My fists shook so hard with the need to hit the fucker. Not only for trying to rough me up but because the jerk had held a gun to my head once, and in the three years since the incident, I hadn't had a chance to show him my gratitude for him almost shooting me.

"Regardless, you owe me." Chloe touched her nose with the back of her gloved hand.

She wasn't going to let this go, and I was about to become an ice sculpture. "If I take you to this artsy crap, then we're done. No more trying to trap me into your love web. I'm not that guy. I've told you that."

"Fine." She smiled as though she didn't believe me.

She knew I didn't pass up sex. I stalked closer to her, my breath steaming as I exhaled. "I'm dead serious. You will not come between me and any of my dates. We will not sneak off and have sex." Like we had the day after we'd broken up. I was a moron for leading her to believe I wasn't serious about our breakup. Since then I've kept my distance. "And we sure as hell aren't getting married." There, I said it. Not in this fucking lifetime and not with a mafia princess.

Her smile vanished as snot slid out of her nose. "I said fine. Besides, Mr. Brewer will be there, and I'm sure he would want you to see some of his students' artwork."

I sucked in my bottom lip, the ice beads melting on my tongue. "We're through after tonight." I hesitated for a moment, drilling my gaze into her, then headed toward the building.

"Eight p.m. Malia's Art Gallery on Newbury Street. It's black tie. So wear your tux."

Fucking penguin suit. I hated it. I had one tailored for me last year when I attended a few of her father's charity events. He was always donating money to some cause. For a mob guy, Pitt wasn't a bad dude. He was fiercely protective of family, a good businessman, and in the three years I'd known him, I still didn't know what he did for the mob. I wasn't about to pry either. The last thing I wanted was to get involved in anything illegal. Not when I wanted to protect and defend the law as a future lawyer.

I jogged into the classroom. A myriad of perfumes bombarded me. The scent of lilacs, lilies, clean rain, and jasmine seeped into my nostrils. The last one almost made me stumble. That scent was imbedded in my memory and took me to a place I wanted to forget, yet remember, but didn't dare. I rubbed my nose lightly as I blew out some air, trying to rid my senses of a girl with dark hair, blue-gray eyes, and lips I could kiss all day long.

Fuck.

"You're late," Mr. Brewer said as he tried to quiet the whispers filling the room. "Undress and get on the platform."

The whispers all but died when he said to undress. Thankful for the undivided attention, I grinned as I scanned the room. Four men sat among the sea of women whose gazes were riveted on me. Some women shied away when I set my eyes on them. Others stuck out their chins, while others licked their lips. I'd bet my life half the women in the room weren't even artists. They were horny twenty-year-olds attending a class to get a glimpse of Kelton Maxwell. It always amazed me how women reacted to the male species. Maybe that was the reason I took the job. Maybe I should have majored in psychology rather than math. But I dumped that thought. I wasn't there to analyze anyone. I was there for the adrenaline rush. I was there because I loved the attention. My brothers thought I was way beyond crazy. But I was never the cautious brother. Fuck caution. "You're hiding behind something," my old man, the psychiatrist, had once told me.

Maybe so, but posing and showing the world the physical side of Kelton Maxwell was a high like bungee jumping, and I needed that rush like a junkie needed his next fix. Because I sure as hell wasn't about to reveal my fears or secrets.

I sauntered over to the makeshift dressing area in the corner of the room. Once behind the wooden wardrobe panel, I toed off my boots then peeled off my clothing right down to nothing. The room was warm, and my body began to thaw. Mr. Brewer always kept the temperature high. He'd mentioned something about the warmth keeping the body at its natural state and coloring.

As I wrapped a large terrycloth towel around my waist, Mr. Brewer doled out instructions to the class then added, "Since a couple of you are new in here, I also want to point out that we're all adults. The human body is a beautiful specimen. I'm certain that most of you ladies have seen a naked man before. Therefore, refrain from giggling and talking and concentrate on the model."

"Oh, we will," a girl with a high-pitched voice said.

"Ms. Davenport, I warn you."

Ugh! Trudy Davenport was an uppity bitch who thought her daddy's money could buy her anyone and anything. I had to give her props though. Once she'd heard Chloe and I were no longer an item, she'd tried to get in my pants on several occasions. She struck out each time. Sure, I could get off on screwing a beautiful redhead with legs that went on forever, but I knew my limitations. One night with her and she'd dig her claws in and not let go. Or maybe I was afraid I'd want more. Either way, I didn't want to find out, especially since her father owned one of the biggest law firms in Boston. The same law firm I'd applied to for a summer job. The job I needed to add to my résumé for my Harvard Law application. Sure, several other law firms in the city would suffice, but none had the clout Mr. Davenport's did.

I walked around the partition and over to the platform in front of the room.

"Drop the towel, Kelton," Trudy shouted.

"This is your last warning, Ms. Davenport," Brewer said as he circled his desk. "One more and I'll give you an *F* on this assignment." His long stride ate up the space from the back of the room to the platform, and he tapped on Trudy's desk twice as he passed.

Trudy mumbled under her breath, and the crimson-faced girl next to her giggled.

I winked at an auburn-haired girl who was sitting in the first row. When I did, I got a strong dose of jasmine, and my heart sped up. Suddenly, I had a strong sense that I knew her.

"Mr. Maxwell, let's try a different pose today. I also want you to leave the towel on for now." He waved long, thin fingers at the velour chaise longue on the platform.

"Sorry, ladies," I said as I scanned the disappointed faces, finally settling my gaze on the auburn-haired girl.

She peered up at me then looked away. She must have been one of the newbies since I didn't recognize her, and most who took this class were shy on the onset.

Mr. Brewer climbed up on the platform and spoke in a low voice. "Sit. And don't make the new girl nervous. And keep your dick from making an appearance." His voice dropped even more as he shifted his back to the class. "I don't need you with an erection when I have twenty-five females with raging hormones ready to attack you. Even though you're one lucky bastard."

"That would be difficult since I think it'll be shrunken for a week after standing out in the cold."

He chuckled.

I eased down onto the soft fabric. "Besides, that only happened once. Over a year ago." Since then I'd learned how to control myself.

Fuck. With beautiful women, flowery scents, porcelain skins, long hair, thick lips—the list went on—they made it difficult for me not to get a damn hard-on.

"Kelton." Mr. Brewer's gaze dropped to my dick.

"Sorry. You started me thinking about... Never mind." I closed my eyes and thought about who was going to win the Super Bowl. The Patriots or the Panthers.

Mr. Brewer went over to the far end of the platform, lifted the wooden screen, and brought it over to block us from the class. "Take the towel off. Then I want you to sit up against the back of the chaise and angle your body toward me."

I went through the motions. "I thought you said towel on."

"Extend both legs then raise your left knee. Drape your left arm casually over your leg."

After several more instructions about positions and angles, he moseyed over to a small round table next to the chaise longue and collected a cowboy hat.

"I don't do bright-blue cowboy hats," I said. The accessory was downright ugly.

"It will bring out your blue eyes against your black hair. And it will also showcase the colorful lizard tattoo on your abs." He set the hat so it covered my dick.

The tat was inked in blues, reds, and greens with a hint of brown.

He scanned my body. "This pose should be perfect." He rubbed his unshaven jaw. "I think you're ready." Slowly, he slid the panel open. "Don't move or sneeze. Or the hat will fall."

"Thanks for the warning." Not that I cared. Most of the people in here had seen me naked already. Still, sometimes the poses were hard to hold for the entire class, but sitting wasn't as difficult as the standing ones.

"Come on, Brew," a female student piped up. "Don't keep us waiting."

Mr. Brewer moved the panel. "I want you to put all your effort into making this piece your best," he said to the class.

*Ooob*s and *aaab*s and swear words were muttered by just about every person, except my little friend in the front row. She lowered her gaze, her long lashes fanning out into the shape of a perfect crescent moon.

"Get to work," Mr. Brewer said as he returned to his desk.

Given the wide eyes and excitement on people's faces, Mr. Brewer must've outdone himself.

As the students went to work, I kept my face relaxed and concentrated on something in the room. Usually I stared at the windowless door, but today the shy girl drew me in. Her throat worked so much she seemed to be swallowing an elephant. Her cheeks flushed a bright red, but this time she didn't shy away from my gaze. Her light-green eyes met mine, and I refrained from letting out a groan. Her bottom lip was slightly thicker than the top, and they had a pinkish color to them, reminding me of the girl I once knew.

The more I studied her, the more I was taken back to that hot summer day in Texas seven years ago.

The ground burned beneath my bare feet. I ran as though I was fleeing a serial killer. I pumped my legs and arms as fast as I could, my breath coming out in short gasps. I'd be surprised if I didn't die of heatstroke. The hot Texas sun beat down, adding to the sweat pouring off my body. But I couldn't stop. I had to see her one last time. I didn't know if I would ever see her again, and that thought pierced my heart, sending waves of pain shooting through my body.

A car sped past. The driver honked his horn and spewed cuss words at me. I threw him the finger as I darted out of the road, in between two cars, then up on the sidewalk. Small rocks embedded in my feet, and I welcomed the pain. Pain was a sign I was alive.

One more block. One more chance. One more look before the one girl I loved walked away with my heart in her hands.

The moving truck came into view on the tree-lined street. Large men swarmed the lawn. Some were hauling huge appliances. Two others were moving boxes around.

I stopped across from Lizzie's house, wiping the sweat from my face with my sweat-soaked T-shirt. I gulped in air as an elderly man walked past with his dog on a leash. The dachshund paused to lick my foot, the sensation a rather calming contrast to my racing pulse.

"Harvey." The old man scolded the dachshund as he tugged on the leash.

I kept my eyes on the two-story stucco house. Would she come out? Was her father home? He'd forbidden her to see me. We'd had to sneak around for the last month. My mom even said it was best if I broke ties with Lizzie. How could she say that? Lizzie was my best friend. We did everything together. She'd loved to throw the baseball, play tackle football, and climb trees. She was beautiful. She had blue-gray eyes and a distinctive square gold speck in her left eye that I would always tease her about. I'd dubbed it the pot of gold.

"You just want to kiss her," my big brother Kade had said. "Girls are trouble, especially at your age."

I was a teenager. Okay, I was thirteen, and puberty was hitting me hard. Sure, I wanted to kiss Lizzie, but only because she had the prettiest lips I'd ever seen. The bottom one was slightly thicker than the top, and they always seemed to have a pinkish color to them.

A horn blew, shattering my thoughts.

Mrs. Reardon came out of the house, carrying a suitcase. "Elizabeth, get moving. Your father will be home any minute." Then she disappeared behind the moving van.

At the sound of Lizzie's name, my heart beat even faster than when I was running over there. I scanned the neighborhood in both directions. The coast was clear. So I hurried across the street. As my feet touched the burnt grass on the front lawn, Mrs. Reardon spotted me.

"Kelton, young man. You shouldn't be here. If Mr. Reardon catches you, he'll call your parents."

He could call the National Guard. I didn't care. I wasn't leaving until I said good-bye to Lizzie. I tilted my head slightly, trying to put on puppy-dog eyes. It always worked with my mom. "Two minutes." Hell, I wanted more than two minutes. I wanted a lifetime to say the things I needed to say but didn't know how.

"You're young, Kelton. It's infatuation. You don't know what love is," she said as she pulled out a small cloth from the pocket of her shorts and patted it along her neck.

Tell that to my heart. Lizzie's voice always turned my insides to mush. I knew her tomboy personality made me love her more. I knew her touch gave me butterflies. Most of all, I knew when we were together the world around us didn't exist. I knew without a doubt that the minute she drove away, the minute I didn't get to talk to her, the minute I didn't get to touch her, was the minute I would die inside.

"Kelton." Mrs. Reardon snapped her fingers in front of my face.

I blinked away the hurt that was engulfing me.

"One minute," she said softly.

I was about to dart around the house and slip in through the side door when Lizzie walked out of the front.

I drew in a breath as our eyes met. She had on a tank top, battered jeans shorts with the insides of the front pockets hanging out at the bottom, and a bandana around her neck. Her brownish-black hair was pulled into a high ponytail, which gave me the opportunity to stare at her satiny skin.

"Kelton, what are you doing here?" She searched the road. "My father will be home."

Screw her father. He could beat me until I was blue. He'd chased me one time when he caught us kissing.

"I had to say good-bye. You've been ignoring me for a week." It was summer break, so I didn't get to see her every day like I did when school was in session. I shuffled closer to her, desperately wanting to touch her but afraid if I did I wouldn't let go.

Her mother went inside.

Lizzie climbed down the steps, adjusting the pink bandana on her neck. "I'm sorry. I thought it would be best." Tears clouded her eyes, but the pot of gold in her left eye shone through. She dropped her gaze to the ground.

With my thumb, I caught a tear. "Please don't cry." I couldn't see her cry. It broke my heart even more. "We'll talk on the phone."

She lifted her watery eyes to mine. "It'll be too expensive from England."

It was going to kill me not to hear her voice. I leaned down until a tiny space separated our lips. "Then we'll email each other."

The sound of an engine drifted toward us, and as she moved to check out the oncoming car, her lips touched mine. I had to kiss her. I didn't care who was around or if her father was the one in the noisy car. I had to taste the sweet bubblegum lip-gloss she wore. I had to inhale her jasmine scent and imbed the essence of Lizzie Reardon into my memory well enough to last a lifetime.

She stiffened when I pushed my tongue through her lips.

"Please, Lizard."

She melted into me as she always did when I called her Lizard. I took her in my arms as she trembled, and I tentatively kissed her. Her tongue slithered out until the roar of the engine slowed.

She gently pushed away. "You better go," she said, almost out of breath.

Suddenly, a cold shiver gripped my body even though I was sweating like a pig. A car pulled to a stop in the driveway. Her father grimaced in our direction. But if he didn't want me near his daughter, he would need to chase me with an ax before I moved. "Why does your father hate me?" I had to know why he didn't want us to see each other. Every other time I'd asked her, she'd changed the subject.

"He doesn't. He's just torn up over what happened. And every time he sees you or any of your brothers, he can't handle it. He blames himself."

"It was an accident." A pain shot through my heart at the still-too-vivid image of seeing Karen on a stretcher being wheeled out of the garage just over a month ago.

"That may be, but we're all mourning, especially Gracie. You know how close they were as friends. She's so distraught that she's barely talked since the accident. My dad feels that keeping our distance from your family is best."

Gracie and Karen had somehow gotten into my father's gun cabinet in the garage. One thing led to another, and Gracie accidentally shot Karen.

I tried to push out the pain. I tried to erase the images of my mom crying and the sounds of sobs and screams coming from her bedroom in the middle of the night.

"Is that why you're moving?" I asked.

The car door slammed shut, sounding like a cannon going off and making us both flinch slightly.

She nodded with sad eyes. "I'm sorry, Kel. Even if we stayed, I'm not sure I could be with you anymore without seeing the hurt in your eyes or you blaming me and my family."

The blood rushed out of me. As I stood in front of this girl, all I saw was her beauty and warm heart. I choked back tears. "I could never blame you."

"But what about Gracie?"

I looked past her to Mr. Reardon. His short stature was unassuming, but his narrowed gaze was anything but. I didn't know the answer to her question even though it was an accident. Maybe even my fault.

"I got to run." She started to leave.

"Wait." I dipped my hand into the pocket of my shorts and pulled out a chain with a half-heart charm. "I want you to have this." I handed her the necklace I'd bought with my allowance.

She glanced at it then up at me, tears streaming down her face. "Where's the other half?"

I grabbed her hand and flattened her palm against my own heart. "Right here."

She drew in a sharp breath, her bottom lip trembling.

"I'll find you one day, Lizard."

She smiled weakly.

"You'll always be the other half of my heart," I said as she walked away.

In the art class, a chair scraped along the floor. I blinked away the past to find the auburn-haired girl hurrying from the room while the rest of the students were still absorbed in their sketchpads.

"You're free to go," Mr. Brewer said, standing in front of the platform. "You did well. You didn't move a beat, although you made the new girl, Emma, a little squirmy by staring at her the whole time."

"Did I scare her that bad?" I asked jokingly as I covered myself with the towel and pushed to my feet.

"She had to leave early. I'll see you next week." He ambled around the desks, checking the students' artwork.

I was about to tell him I would see him at the art gallery tonight then decided not to. I didn't need the girls in this class knowing my schedule. I stalked behind the partition and made quick work of getting out of the towel and into my clothes. I had a math class I had to get to on the other side of campus.

Once I was outside, the frigid February air hit me like a girl I'd once dumped had slapped me. It was a welcome relief at the moment from the heated room and the crazy trip down memory lane. I zipped up my leather jacket then pulled out my knit cap and covered my head. I made it a few steps before I spied Emma talking to a dude with shoulder-length hair next to an old, beat-up Camaro. He looked my way, causing Emma to do the same before she said something to him. The dude studied me.

I shoved my hands in my pockets and strutted over to them. I wanted to at least apologize to her if I'd scared her.

They scurried into the car like I was a criminal about to shake them down. He peeled out. I stopped in my tracks and winced at an oncoming SUV about to crash into them. At the last second, the SUV swerved, narrowly missing the Camaro. The driver in the SUV honked his horn as he slowed.

I watched the Camaro fade into the distance, wondering what I did to scare them.

CHAPTER 2

LIZZIE

I spun around in my seat and glanced behind me as Dillon dodged
cars on the streets of Boston. My pulse was racing, and I couldn't
get it to slow down. What were the odds that I'd find Kelton
Maxwell after all these years, and of all places, posing for an art class in
nothing but a darn cowboy hat? His Greek godlike form made my
mouth dry, but what had me doing everything I could to hold back
tears was the lizard he had inked on his abs and his left arm. He used
to call me Lizard. If it weren't for the itchy red wig covering my dark
hair and the green-colored contacts masking my blue-gray eyes, I
swore he would've recognized me. Then again, I wasn't sure he hadn't.

*Get a grip, girl. You're in Boston to find the man who stole your inheritance,
not pine over Kelton.* I almost laughed at my subconscious. I was sitting
in the freaking front row, admiring the boy who'd graced my dreams
every night for the last seven years. He still had those piercing blue
eyes that contrasted so well with his black hair, and that scar on his
chin brought back wonderful memories of playing with him in his tree
house. The one difference now—Kelton was all man. An extremely
handsome and well-toned man. I was certain he made all the girls drool
or squeeze their lady parts. Yikes! *I* had to squeeze my legs. Not to
mention, I had to swallow several times to quell the nerves, excitement, and fear that had coursed through me.

Dillon's deep baritone drilled through my brain. "You want to tell me what that was all about, and why you were in such a hurry to get away?"

"You can slow down now." I righted myself just in time to see we were hurtling toward the back end of a dump truck before Dillon cut the wheel hard to the right and into an alley, slamming on his brakes.

I lurched forward slightly, thankful I'd managed to strap myself in. Otherwise, I would be sailing through the windshield right about now.

He threw the car into park. "Who was the pretty boy?" He stabbed a thumb behind him as his thick eyebrows bunched together. "Is he your boyfriend? Tell me. I want to know who you're messed up with."

"Fuck off. Who I know or who I'm with is none of your fucking business. I'm paying you to get me a gun and ammo. That's it. One that can't be traced."

His nostrils flared, shifting his skull nose ring. "Sweetheart, I need to know who my clients are. Just because you partied with my cousin twice removed doesn't mean I trust you. That dude back there looks like the guy who dates Pitt's princess."

I scrunched up my nose. "And that means what exactly?" I'd only been in town a week.

"That means I'm not getting involved with the Russian mob. Start talking." He mashed his lips into a thin line.

I wasn't about to tell Dillon that Kelton and I were childhood sweethearts. Or how I'd cried my eyes out, locked myself in my room, and didn't eat for a week after we moved away. Or how I dreamed of him every night. No matter how scary a vibe Dillon gave me or what type of illegal business he was running, my business was my own. Sure, he could probably hurt me, even make me disappear, but I had to choose my battles at the moment, and sharing my childhood with him had no place in this conversation.

Dillon reached over the console and grabbed my arm. "Do you know him?" he asked, his tone dripping venom. "If it's Kelton Maxwell, I'm not selling you shit. Rumor is he's about to marry the daughter of the head of the Russian mob. I value my miserable life. If the mob gets wind my crew is selling guns under their noses, I'm dead. As well as my crew. Plus, if that isn't enough, his older brother is mixed up with a gal who's the granddaughter of some Italian mobster out of LA. You get me?"

My heartbeat dipped drastically at the thought of Kelton getting married. Actually, my stomach suddenly hurt as though I'd been sucker punched. I rolled my shoulders back. After I'd had a meltdown over moving away from Kelton, I'd put my life back together, sealing off a part of my heart that Kelton had stolen. I had to in order to help my sister, Gracie, overcome the tragic incident. Even more so when she committed suicide after two years of a life worse than hell. After her death, I focused on the positive things in life like she would've wanted me to.

"Chill, all right? I get you." *And you don't want to get on my bad side either.* I shrugged out of his hold.

I'd been on my own for two years. Protecting myself and handling thugs like him became second nature to me after I was attacked on the streets of Miami.

"You sure are confident and cocky for a chick. Maybe you should be working on my crew." His features softened. "The guys wouldn't know what hit them with someone like you."

I laughed. "You want me to sell guns for you?"

He sat back against his seat. "Your arms are well-toned, you seem like you can kick ass, and there's an innocence about you. Yet I can tell you're far from innocent. And I get the feeling you're pissed off at the world. You have fire in your eyes, like you're ready to kill someone. I like that. I could use that on my crew."

I *was* ready to kill someone—the trustee of my father's estate, if I could find him. First, I had to get my life savings back. The law was of no help until I could prove the trustee stole my inheritance. But if working for Dillon meant I could have access to a gun, then maybe cutting a deal with him wouldn't be so bad.

We studied each other as if we were two lions about to do battle. Dillon hardened his strong, square jaw, flaring his nostrils.

I sucked in my cheek. He was right. I was more than angry at the world and all the turmoil I'd been through. Regardless, I wasn't about to feel sorry for myself. I'd been on that emotional rollercoaster. It was time to buck up and get back what was mine.

"Who are you hiding from?" he asked, breaking the thick silence. "Don't tell me no one. You're wearing a wig. And you still haven't told me why you wanted to run from that dude."

The Caribbean could freeze before I'd tell you.

"Look, Emma, if that's even your name. Whether you work for me or not, you still want a gun. Which means I need to trust that you're not going to rat me out to the cops. If it's trust you're worried about, let it go. I stand to lose more than you."

I could argue that point. I had a million dollars in my inheritance that I had to get back. "Are you going to sell me a gun? If not, I'll find someone else." I opened the door. With my luck, the landlord in Miami I owed back rent would find me and hold me hostage until I could pay him. Not to mention, I owed the University of Miami a semester of tuition that I'd thought had been paid.

"My cousin tells me you lost your family."

"I'm out of here." I was about to jump out of the car when he took hold of my arm once again.

"Wait. I'm sorry. I hate when people pry into my past too."

I sat back. "Listen, sell me a gun, and you'll never see me again." I didn't want to research another dealer or get caught up with someone who didn't seem as nice as Dillon. Or with my luck I would find that one person who was connected to the mob. Given what Dillon had mentioned about the mob, I wanted to stay away from them.

He kept his brown gaze glued to me as he seemed to be mulling over something. "I'll text you a time and place to meet me tonight." He shifted the Camaro into gear.

I dove into my own thoughts as he drove through the busy streets of Boston. I contemplated whether to at least tell Dillon what I was hiding from. I could use a guy like him, a guy who knew the city, in the event I got myself into a pickle.

"I'm not hiding. I'm disguising. I'm looking for someone who stole from me. Let's just say what he stole was very valuable. And that man back at school, he was posing for the art class I'm taking. He was staring at me the whole time. He gives me the creeps, that's all." It wasn't a total lie.

The way Kelton drilled those blue eyes of his into me—the same blue eyes that had hooked me from the moment we'd met back in the fifth grade—gave me a cold chill instead of the warm feeling I'd always gotten when he'd looked at me before. Maybe because I could never go back to the past. We'd been kids with a pipe dream—a dream of love, family, and happily ever after. But given what I'd been through, I knew nothing was forever.

"Is the person you're searching for in college?" Dillon asked.

"Yes." It was better to keep some information private until I could totally trust Dillon.

Terrance Malden, the trustee of my father's estate, always bragged about his son Zach and how skilled and creative he was with a paintbrush. He'd shown me drawings Zach had painted, which hung in Terrance's office. He'd also mentioned how Zach had been trying to get into Mr. Brewer's art class at BU. So I'd enrolled, trying to get close to Zach to discover the whereabouts of his dad. But I hadn't seen Zach in class.

"And this dude isn't the one we left standing on the sidewalk?" He flicked his gaze from me to the road.

I huffed. "For the last time, no." Surely, Dillon wasn't afraid of Kelton.

"What are you going to do when you find him? Shoot him?" he said in a mocking tone.

I lifted a shoulder. "Maybe."

CHAPTER 3
LIZZIE

The kitchen was a good size for an art gallery. It housed two side-by-side wine refrigerators, as well as two full-sized refrigerators. The room was also equipped with a stove, two ovens, two sinks, several cabinets, and a large dishwasher. If I wasn't mistaken, the gallery had been a restaurant at one time.

I inhaled the light aroma of what smelled like chicken warming in the oven as I checked myself in a compact mirror. Since Dillon had figured out I was wearing a wig, I decided to put on dark-green eyeliner to highlight the light-green contacts followed by two coats of mascara, giving my eyes that smoky look. That way people would be drawn to my eyes and not my hair. I couldn't risk being noticed by Terrance, who might be able to recognize me since he'd hung out with my dad at our house quite often. Until I could find him or chummy up to his son, I wanted to stay incognito. Then when the time was right, I would unveil the real me. Hopefully by then I would know where my money was and how to get it back. Satisfied, I dumped the mirror in my purse and rummaged around for my lipstick.

"What are you looking for?" my friend Peyton asked as she tied back her pinkish-blond hair into a ponytail.

"Lipstick," I said as I continued to search my bag.

"You don't need any. Your lips have a natural pink color to them, and I told you to go natural tonight. You're prettier without the wig and contacts."

"I like the color. Besides, it's fun. Remember when we used to wear different color wigs and contacts every weekend?" We loved keeping the frat boys guessing our freshman year at the University of Miami, even going as far as changing our names.

"What do you mean *when*? My sorority sisters still do it for the BU frat parties."

I laughed. "Unless I look hideous or ugly, what's the harm?" I was wearing a white blouse and black pants. My red wig was short enough to frame my face, and my makeup was artfully done—not too much, not too little.

"I'm sorry. You look great. I guess I like your long, dark hair better."

I did too. But until I got my money back, I was Emma with red hair and green eyes, and not Elizabeth or Lizzie with dark hair and blue-gray eyes, although Peyton had always called me Emma. Before our first frat party we came up with names. I'd always liked the name Emma, and since she'd said I reminded her of an Emma, the name stuck with her.

She donned an apron she'd removed from a cabinet. "Anyway, you okay with this art gig? I know it was last minute, but I promised my mom I would help out, and you said you need the money."

I mainly took this gig when I learned that Mr. Brewer was show-casing his students' artwork. It was my chance to get closer to Zach. And without my monthly deposits from Terrance, money was tight. "Yeah, it's fine." Since I hadn't seen Zach in class, I wasn't sure if he was or had been a student of Mr. Brewer's or if he would even make an appearance that night. Either way, I had to find out. I spotted my lipstick.

"Did he have Kelton posing today?" Peyton asked excitedly.

My hands stilled around the lipstick.

Her face paled to a shade matching her white blouse. "Oh my God. Was he naked? Did you sketch him? I bet Kelton will be here tonight."

The lipstick fell from my hand, clanging to the floor. I'd been so wrapped up with Dillon and figuring out the train system in Boston to get here that I didn't think of Kelton attending an art gala. After all, he wasn't a student. Thoughts of fleeing danced in my head. But I wasn't one to let someone down, especially if I gave my word. So, I collected my lipstick, dropped it into my purse, then moved to the cabinet and plucked out an apron.

"You know him?" I hadn't shared much of my childhood with her, and when she moved back to Boston to help her mom with the catering business, we'd only spoken a handful of times.

"What girl at BU doesn't? He's a god. Every girl wants a piece of him. Every girl wants to marry him."

After seeing Kelton in nothing but a cowboy hat covering his manly parts, I wanted a piece of him, too. But I wasn't in the class to swoon over Kelton. I was there on the off chance that I would find Zach. Peyton thought I was in Boston for family reasons, and while I sort of was, I couldn't tell her the truth yet. I didn't know what I was up against, and I didn't want to involve her if things got ugly.

She walked over to the sink. "You're one lucky bitch. That's all I got to say. I wished I had the option this semester for an elective."

I wouldn't call myself lucky. In my mind, running into Kelton was a distraction. He was all I kept thinking about since art class, when I should've been thinking about my next move to find Terrance or Zach Malden.

She washed her hands. "What position did Brew have Kelton in? And you never answered if he was naked." She rubbed her hands together slowly.

Yep, my work was cut out for me. If she continued talking about Kelton, I was burnt toast. I tied the apron around me and joined her at the sink.

"Tell me before I wet my panties."

Mine were already moist. I busted out laughing. "I'm definitely not telling you. You'll have your soapy hands down your pants."

She moaned. "Damn straight I will."

A phone rang to the tune of "Better as a Memory" by Kenny Chesney.

Peyton swiped a paper towel from the dispenser. "That's your ringtone? Can you get any sadder?"

I snagged the towel from Peyton, quickly wiped my hands, and retrieved my phone from my back pocket. "Hello?"

"Emma, it's Dillon. I have to be in Cambridge tonight. Meet me at a club called Rumors at 11:00 p.m. And if you want to do business, lose the wig. I want to see the real you." Then the phone went dead.

No way was he seeing the real me—not in public anyway.

"Who was that?" Peyton asked. "Are you making friends already? His voice sounds yummy."

Dillon did have a soothing voice for a scary-looking guy. "You heard that?" I had barely heard him.

"Only when he said your name. So, spill. Who is he?" She anchored her body against the counter.

I tensed.

"Okay, we need to get moving," said a short, middle-aged lady with a bob as she glided in, carrying shopping bags. "You must be Emma. My daughter hasn't stopped talking about you." She set down the bags on the counter. "Thank you for helping out. I understand you've served before?"

I thought Peyton would have at least told her mom my real name. But I wasn't complaining. The less people knew of the real me, the better the chances of me staying incognito. "Yes, ma'am. Applebee's and The Olive Garden."

"Good. Good. Oh, and call me Wendy." She went over to the fridge and pulled out trays of shrimp cocktail and empty lettuce cups. "Let's get started. The quiches and chicken are in the oven. Let's start with the champagne and wine."

Peyton and I moved to the bar adjacent to the door that spilled into the gallery. The bottles of bubbly and red and white wine had already been opened. So we poured and prepped four silver trays of alcohol. Then we collected a wad of napkins before inserting half of them in our apron pockets and placing the other half on the trays.

"We should have a packed house. Let's start with alcohol," Wendy said. "And be sure to smile. I'll have the hors d'oeuvres ready shortly."

Carefully, Peyton and I each grabbed a tray of glasses and made our way out. The gallery had a warm atmosphere with just the right amount of lighting showcasing the art pieces displayed around the room either on stands or hanging on the walls. A soft hum of chatter filled the room. People dressed in elegant evening wear mingled around the geometric paintings, landscape portraits, and photographs of people of all shapes and sizes. If this was a showing for Mr. Brewer's work and that of his students, I was impressed with the perfection of some of the pieces.

I served, moving from one group or couple to another. I worked one side of the room while Peyton worked the other. My pulse jumped every time I offered someone a drink. I was nervous about the possibility of bumping into Kelton. I was also apprehensive about confronting Mr. Brewer. I'd told him I'd left class early because I had to pick up my cat from the vet before they closed. He'd arched an eyebrow but hadn't questioned me. He'd asked for my sketchpad before I left, but I'd ripped up the drawing of Kelton so fast Mr. Brewer didn't have time to stop me. It wasn't a good way to start my first day, but I'd panicked. So I thought about a cat, her name, her breed, and what was wrong with her. Guilt rode me since I didn't own a cat, although I imagined petting Kelton as he posed on that stage in art class. Though nothing about him resembled a cat or the silky coat of one. Heat shot through my belly as I pictured my fingers running along every hard angle and ridge along his abs, biceps, and thighs.

A dainty voice severed my porn moment. "Miss." A green-eyed brunette met me eye-to-eye. "Do you know where the ladies' room is?" she asked, fingering the polar bear charm hanging around her neck.

"I'm sorry, I don't. But you can try the hallway." I turned to point behind me, and my tray of glasses wobbled.

"Thank you." She dashed into the crowd.

I watched her for a second before a lump formed in my throat. The brunette stopped to chat with none other than Kelton. The lump seemed to grow as I tried to swallow. At any second, I was afraid I was going to choke.

Peyton came up beside me. "You should lower your finger. It's rude to point." She giggled. "I see Kelton has the same effect on you as he does on the rest of us women."

You don't know the half of it.

"He's delicious in his tux, isn't he?" She cooed as if she was about to have an orgasm. "I wonder where his girlfriend is?"

As though cold water had been poured over my head, I snapped out of my trance. "Is that his girlfriend?" I asked.

A guest came up to us to exchange an empty glass for a red wine.

"No. That was Kelton's potential sister-in-law. Lacey Robinson is dating his older brother, Kade. She's a big deal in this part of the country. She's been in all the newspapers for her outstanding pitching for Colby College. I have to say she's good at the game. Girls around here revere her. But she's also the cousin to Kelton's girlfriend, Chloe Pitt."

Suddenly, my heart sank. Kelton was getting married, he still had a tight-knit family, and I had nothing. Two years ago, my parents had died in a boating accident, reducing the only family I could boast about to an aunt on my father's side and an uncle on my mother's. I didn't consider either of them close family. I shook off the self-pity. I wasn't in town to reminisce, get married or start a family, or even feel sorry for myself. I was there to get what was mine, no matter what I had to do to accomplish that.

Lacey had her hands on her hips as she peered up at Kelton, who was shaking his head.

"We should get back to work before my mom starts ranting," Peyton said. "Come on. Let's refill our trays. I'm sure it's time for the finger foods."

I kept my head down as I passed Kelton and Lacey. With my hand on the door to the kitchen, his smooth, deep voice caused my limbs to lock.

"Emma," Kelton called.

"You know him?" Peyton stopped short, almost losing her tray of empty glasses.

Yes. "No." I pushed in the door and deposited my tray on the counter.

"What do you mean, no?" Peyton gently placed her tray beside mine. "He seems to know you." She scurried back to the door to peek out.

Please don't let him recognize me or come in here. Otherwise I might throw myself at him before I run.

"You're sweating," Wendy pulled out a tray of quiches. "Everything all right?"

"Emma is being chased by one of Boston's most eligible playboys," Peyton teased. "You're clear," she said to me. "Kelton is talking to Trudy Davenport."

I remembered that name from art class. Mr. Brewer had to keep telling the redhead to quiet down. I'd wanted to stick a sock in her mouth.

"Is Kelton's girlfriend with him?" Wendy asked. "I need to talk to her. She called to ask if we could cater her graduation party."

"I haven't seen Chloe," Peyton said. "Emma, dish. I want to know how you know him." She glided back to me at the chest-high table where more trays of alcohol were ready to go.

I was tempted to gulp down a glass or two of champagne. "I don't. The first time I saw him was in class today, and we didn't talk." I wiped my sweaty palms down my pant leg. I was probably going to hell for lying. I wasn't ready to tell Peyton that I knew Kelton. She would have questions that I wasn't prepared to answer, especially since Kelton was such a celebrity. My scalp itched like crazy underneath my wig. I scratched it, wondering if maybe I should get out of there before I dug myself into a bigger lie.

"Let's keep the food and drinks flowing," Wendy said. "You two can gossip about the handsome man later."

Considering I did need the cash and was hoping to see Zach, I brushed off my escape plan.

"Emma, keep serving drinks. Peyton, start serving the quiches and shrimp cocktail," Wendy ordered, spooning a meat-and-rice mixture into the small lettuce cups.

Peyton picked up a silver platter of finger food. "I'll just ask him how he knows you." She stuck me with a glare.

"That's a great idea." I would like to know how he knew my name, and what else he knew about me. I grabbed a fresh tray of drinks.

"Peyton, send Chloe in if you see her," Wendy called as Peyton and I exited.

Voices droned through the packed room. Peyton and I split up again. My pulse was still on overload as I served alcohol. Knowing Kelton, he wasn't going to let up until he got my attention. I scoped out the exits just in case I needed to hide. One sign was lit up at the far end of the room. I'd remembered an exit located in the kitchen, and the other one was the main entrance off to my left.

"Are you about to make a mad dash for the exit like you did earlier today?" a male voice asked.

I peered up at the skinny man on my right. "No, Mr. Brewer. I'm trying to find the other server." Another lie.

"Uh huh. Why don't you tell me something that's true?"

"Brew!" someone called.

A blond guy with curly hair and dressed in a blue suit, white shirt, and satin purple tie waved at him. My hand shook, and the glasses dinged on my tray.

"You sure are jumpy." Mr. Brewer's long fingers wrapped around the stem of a glass of red wine.

The closer Zach Malden got to us, the more I broke out in a nervous sweat. I'd seen pictures of Zach in his father's office in Miami when I had been visiting my dad at work. I'd only met him once briefly three years ago when he was visiting his father for a weekend. Apparently, he'd lived with his mother in Chicago until he started at BU. I took in a quiet breath. It was time for me to shuck the nerves and get in the game. My hand steadied, as did the glasses. I scanned the room for a hefty, older version of Zach and came up empty. The ray of optimism that had gripped me vanished. At least Zach was here.

"Sorry I couldn't make it to class today." Zach puffed out his scruffy jaw. Then he slowly released his breath as he snatched a flute of champagne from my tray.

"Rough afternoon?" Mr. Brewer asked.

Zach gulped down the champagne then replaced the empty glass with a fresh one. "It always is when my old man blows into town for the afternoon then leaves like the city is about to blow up." He downed the entire contents of the glass.

I felt my eyebrows come together, and I silently screamed *fuck*. "Your father is missing a great event," I said coolly.

"He'd never show his face at an art function, even if he was still in the city," Zach said, sounding dejected or wanting of his father's approval. "He couldn't give a shit about my artwork or the fact my masterpiece is on display tonight."

I tipped my head to the side slightly. His dad had spoken proudly of his son, at least the one time he'd told me about Zach.

"Zach, meet our newest student, Emma," Mr. Brewer said as he sipped his wine.

I smiled and batted my eyelashes as naturally as I could. Somehow I had to befriend Zach in the hopes I could learn the whereabouts of his father, although I never considered myself good at going out of my way to get a guy's attention. My mom had always told me men were sometimes more attracted to the art of the chase. "You said you had a masterpiece. I'd love to see it." God, I prayed I wasn't coming across as fake.

With his bottom lip between his teeth, he sized me up.

"Maybe you can teach her some of your tricks of color and light," Mr. Brewer said.

Fantastic idea. "I would like that. I owe Mr. Brewer an assignment. I could use your help."

Mr. Brewer cocked his head. "You do owe me."

Zach pulled a business card from his suit jacket pocket. "Here." He extended the card. "Call me tomorrow, and we'll set a time for next week. As for my masterpiece, it's a portrait of Kelton Maxwell that should be around here somewhere. If you were in class today, then you know what he looks like. I need to talk to Brew."

I gripped his business card as my insides waged a small fight between irritation over his dismissal of me and nervousness that everything today seemed to revolve around Kelton. "It was nice meeting you. I'll give you a shout midafternoon."

I quickly searched the room for Zach's masterpiece and Kelton. Satisfied that I didn't need to hide from Kelton, and disappointed that I was coming up empty on Zach's masterpiece, I continued to work the room. It was probably best I didn't spot the painting. If Kelton was posing in nothing but a cowboy hat, I had no doubt my tray of drinks would be splattered on the floor— along with me.

I weaved through the throng of people, passing those who had full glasses. As I passed a man dressed in a sharp, tailored suit standing next to a redheaded woman, I paused when I heard Kelton's name.

"Daddy, when are you interviewing Kelton Maxwell?" the redhead asked.

Their backs were to me as they faced an art piece on a stand, which I couldn't quite see. Regardless, her mousy voice was hard to forget from class today.

"Trudy, pumpkin, stop asking about the boy. I have his résumé and application. I haven't had time to read through it." He shifted on his feet. "Although I'm not sure posing half naked for an art class looks good on a résumé. He'll have to convince me he wants a job at my law firm."

So Kelton was sticking to his dream of becoming a lawyer. I was so proud of him.

"Daddy. You're so old-fashioned. So what if he models? Do you know how hard it is for someone to stay still long enough for us to sketch?" Trudy hooked her arm through his.

They stepped to the next piece of artwork. When they moved away and revealed the painting they'd been looking at, my jaw dropped. Piercing blue eyes stared back at me. I bit my tongue when all I wanted to do was moan at the beautiful, perfect man on the canvas. Kelton was casually leaning against a large oak tree with his hands tucked into his jeans pockets, bare chested and barefooted, hair tousled, and a half smirk on his chiseled face. Memories flooded my vision of Kelton and me playing in his tree house when we were ten years old. He loved trees and how the branches swayed in the wind.

He'd once told me that when the leaves rustled they were talking to each other. We would sit in his tree house listening to the trees on very windy days.

"It's a great piece. Zach, one of Brew's students, painted this," Kelton said as he came up next to me, the smoothness of his voice washing over me like a shower of melted chocolate. "Like it?" He gently placed a hand on my lower back.

"Not in the least," I said confidently, even though my knees were about to give out. I thought I'd forgotten what his touch was like, but the heat of his hand brought back more memories of when we used to tackle each other playing football. I had to drop that art class. I couldn't afford to let Kelton distract me from my goal.

He pulled on the bowtie of his tux with his free hand, stretching his neck. "Do you lie a lot?"

I do since this morning. "I'm not lying. You have several flaws, you know."

He snorted as he flexed his fingers where they were splayed on my back. "I'd like to hear them."

"Sorry." With my head down, I started for the kitchen and got a whiff of his fresh rain cologne. At that moment it took every bit of willpower not to whimper.

He grabbed my arm. "Wait. Why do you keep running from me?"

My pulse began beating like a jumping bean. "Why do you keep chasing me?"

"I'm not chasing you. I've been trying to apologize. Brew said you seemed spooked about something when you left class. He thought I scared you." His handsome gaze drank me in.

You did scare me. You still do. "Sorry, dude. You can be a creeper."

He raised his hand to his mouth as one side turned upward. Damn sexy grin had only gotten sexier with age.

"I have to work. I shouldn't have said anything." I gawked at him instead of doing my job.

"People are mingling and talking with drinks in their hands. So, talk to the creeper. You might find that I can purr like a kitten if you pet the right spot," he said in a serious tone.

I was so doomed to fail if I stayed this close to him. I was ready to tear off the wig and my contacts and throw myself at him. But for some reason, my legs wouldn't move.

He cocked his head to one side. "I can't help but ask. Do I know you?" He studied me like I was his lab experiment.

Get out now! a voice in my head screamed as I glanced past him.

A beautiful blond girl dressed like a runway model in a formfitting white strapless cocktail dress glided toward us with a smile etched on her face and her gaze fixed on either Kelton or me. Whoever she was after, her arrival was my cue to leave. My legs still wouldn't move. Damn curiosity.

"Kelton, there you are." She reached up with her delicate fingers and touched his face.

My guess? She was none other than Chloe.

Kelton scowled, clearly not liking that the girl was trying to direct his attention away from me. Either that or he was irritated that someone would try and tell him what to do. Which didn't surprise me. Kelton had never liked to be told what to do. Even when my father told him he wasn't allowed to see me anymore, Kelton didn't listen. The boy had a mind of his own. All his brothers were like that. Even at a young age the Maxwell boys had been brazen, not taking crap from anyone, at least not at school.

Dropping her hand, she said, "At least introduce me to your new friend."

"Pardon me," I said. "I need to work." I bolted. Once inside the kitchen, I let out a loud sigh.

"Animals out there?" Wendy asked.

I laughed when I should be fleeing. As I set down the serving tray, the girl in the white dress bounced in.

"Did I say something to make you run?" She placed a strand of hair behind her ear, exposing a large solitaire diamond earring. She definitely came from wealth. "I didn't mean to interrupt. Kelton can be an ass, and I just want to make sure he didn't upset you."

What! I wanted to hate this girl. I wanted to tear her big brown eyes out of their sockets and wiggle my nose, hoping she would turn into a toad. But I couldn't. Her voice was soft. She had a pretty smile, and she seemed genuine. Kelton would be the luckiest man alive to snag a beautiful and nice girl like Chloe.

"I'm sorry. I was the one who was rude." That was the first true statement I'd said in the last hour.

"Hi, I'm Chloe." She held out a dainty hand.

"I'm Emma." We shook.

"Chloe, have you been here the whole time?" Wendy wiped her forehead with a dishtowel.

Chloe placed a hand on her flat stomach. "I have, but I've been in the ladies' room. I think I ate something last night that didn't agree with me."

Wendy went over to her purse and returned with a Pepto-Bismol tablet. "Take this."

After Chloe chewed the tablet, the two began talking about Chloe's graduation party. I closed my eyes and counted to ten to get my heart to stop racing. As I did, I slipped my hands into the pockets of my apron. My hand closed around a business card—the key to finding Terrance Malden.

CHAPTER 4
KELTON

A booming bass pulsed as I strutted into the back entrance of Rumors, shrugging out of my tux jacket. The damn bowtie was enough to strangle me, especially when I stood beside Emma. Her jasmine scent about choked me with memories of Lizzie. The more I talked to her, the more I swore I knew her.

I pushed past a long line of girls waiting for the restrooms. They were all ages, shapes, and sizes for a Friday night. A handful smiled at me suggestively. I'd picked up one or two on occasion after Chloe and I had broken up. But I wasn't trolling tonight. I was here to listen to my brother, Kody, perform. He'd written a new song he was trying out.

When I passed the last two girls in line, one of them flipped her dark hair over her shoulder. "Did you see? Dillon Hart is here. I can't believe he's in a trendy club like this. I'm going to try and talk to him," she said to her friend. "I would love to get my hands on him. He's hot."

Her friend choked. "The only way you're talking to him is if you're a homeless girl under the age of twenty," the other girl said in a high-pitched voice. "And how do you know he's here? No one really knows what he looks like. My brother tells me he's a ghost in this city."

Dillon Hart's name had been mentioned once or twice in conversations among the locals who frequented the club on occasion. Word on the street was no one could pick him out of a lineup. But he did offer

S.B. ALEXANDER

food and a warm bed to runaway girls who wanted to get off the streets and away from their pimps. I wasn't one to eavesdrop, but I was curious. If Dillon Hart was in the club, then I'd like to meet him so I could shake his hand for helping keep girls safe. I slowed my pace.

"I caught a glimpse of him when I overheard the bald guy I bumped into call his name," the girl with the dark hair said.

I ducked into the manager's office not too far beyond the girls.

Kade whistled from behind his metal desk. His copper eyes grew wide. "My baby brother in a tuxedo." He sat back in the chair.

"Bite me. I didn't have time to stop at my condo to change. Got any spare clothes here?" I knew he did. With Lacey away at college and the club a good distance away from where we lived in Ashford, Kade spent at least three nights a week in Boston.

He flicked his head toward the private bathroom. Mr. Robinson had it built just for Kade when he handed over the management of Rumors to him after we graduated high school. I beelined it into the spacious room. He was older than Kross, Kody, and me by a year, but we were all over six feet tall and fit into the same size clothes, more or less. I opened a cabinet adjacent to the sink and snagged a pair of jeans and a Hinder Band T-shirt. I changed quickly and stuffed the tuxedo into the cabinet. Since Chloe and I were no longer dating, I hoped I would never have to wear that monkey suit again. For a second, I thought to throw the tux into the trash but decided against it.

I went back into the office. "I left the tux for you, bro. You can make use of it when you marry that beautiful girl of yours." Parking my butt in a chair, I propped my feet up on top of the desk.

"Where is she, by the way?" Kade glanced at his watch. When Lacey was home from college, Kade hardly let her out of his sight.

"No idea. Chloe spent the majority of time at the fartsy gala in the bathroom, and Lacey was with her. My guess would be they're still in the bathroom."

"What's wrong? Chloe okay?" Kade pinned me with a glare. "Did you upset her again? You know her old man will have your balls on a skewer."

"For three years you've been worried about her father killing me. I can handle Pitt. Besides, you know Chloe and I aren't an item anymore. And her old man was pleased, if you ask me." I couldn't say for sure, but Kade's best friend, Hunt, who worked for Pitt, mentioned Pitt had been in a good mood since Chloe and I had broken up.

"You're not using her for sex, are you?"

"Those days are done, bro." I wasn't about to stay with a girl who wanted more than I could give. I saw my future with me and only me, although I couldn't help but think of the girl who'd left me standing on the scorching tar street seven years ago. I dropped my feet to the floor. "Kade, have you ever thought about the Reardons? I mean, whatever happened to Lizzie and her family?"

He pinched his eyebrows together. "Where did that come from?"

I rubbed my chin. "For some reason, I've been thinking about Lizzie." Her scent. Her dark hair. Her blue-gray eyes. Her long neck. Her plump lips—the ones I kissed and would give anything to kiss again. I'd bet at the age of twenty she was more beautiful than I remembered.

"Are you thinking of Karen? The anniversary of her death is coming up. It'll be seven years since she died. And you always go weird on us around that time."

I leaned on my knees. "So? I miss her." Every one of us in the family missed Karen. She had been Daddy's little girl, Mom's princess, and to us boys she had been the most precious girl in the world. She had been happy, beautiful, and intelligent—sometimes too smart for her own good.

"Kel, we all miss Karen. But you hide for days around the anniversary of her death. I get that you have to work out your own shit. I get you loved her. We all handle emotions differently. Yet after seven years I'd have expected you to have come to terms with her death."

Easy for you to say. You aren't the one who can't remember if you left the gun cabinet unlocked. You aren't the one who was distracted by a beautiful girl who had walked into the garage that day as I was putting away ammo. My old man had told us that Karen found the combination to the gun safe. I wasn't sure I believed him. He always had a way of trying to protect us, even our feelings. Somewhere in the back of my mind I suspected he wanted to shoulder the blame so my mom wouldn't think that any of her sons were responsible for Karen's death. I couldn't bring myself to broach the subject with any of my siblings or my father, and I wasn't about to now. If my mom found out I might've been the one to leave the gun cabinet unlocked, she could relapse and have to return to the mental health facility where she'd lived for years after Karen's death. I couldn't handle that. I couldn't handle the screams that came from her room at night. I couldn't handle her depressed and crying all the time.

Most of all, I would die knowing that I was the one to send her back to the mental health facility. I would take my secret to the grave. Hell, I'd lived with it all these years. I could live with it many more if that meant my family was happy.

"No one gets over death. It's just not that easy." I pulled on my hair. "I often think about Gracie Reardon, too. How she must've been devastated. How could anyone handle killing their best friend, and at the age of twelve no less?"

"Kel, you need to talk to someone. Why don't you go see Dr. Davis? He helped Kody when Mandy died. And he's helped Lacey with her PTSD." Kade's voice held concern.

"I'm not going to a psychiatrist." I narrowed my eyes. "I'll deal."

"Then talk to Dad. He counsels military veterans every day. Plus he understands what we went through."

I snarled. "I said I'll deal." I was afraid that the minute I opened myself up, the guilt that had taken up a large space inside me would be real. Which would mean I was responsible for my sister's death.

He raised his hands. "Okay. I'll back off. So, have you heard from Davenport? Do you have an interview set up yet?"

I blew out a breath. "No. I called yesterday, and the receptionist said Mr. Davenport would be in touch. He was at the shindig with his daughter. I spoke to her briefly. But when I went to talk to him, he was gone."

"You haven't slept with her?"

I arched a brow. "Fuck no." I pushed to my feet. "I may crave sex, but I wouldn't stoop low enough to sleep with someone to get a job. I have morals, you know."

He circled the desk. "Bro, I'm sorry." He squeezed my shoulder.

The door opened. The *thump, thump* of the bass blasted in.

Lacey breezed in with her brown hair flowing behind her and her breasts poking out of her low-cut green dress. "It's crazy out there."

Sliding his gaze over the love of his life, Kade groaned.

"I'm out of here." I stalked to the door. Lacey was only home for the weekend, and when she was, she and Kade sucked face the entire time. I didn't blame him, but I didn't want to witness their escapades.

"Wait, Kel," Lacey said as she tried to wrap her small hand around my bicep. "Why didn't you wait for Chloe after the art gala?" She peered up at me with those green eyes of hers, reminding me of Emma.

"We're not together anymore, remember?" Then I got the hell out of there before she could give me the third degree about love and shit. Besides, I had another girl—with red hair and a light scent of jasmine —who drew my interest.

CHAPTER 5
LIZZIE

I jumped on the subway, or as Bostonians called it, "the T." A middle-aged lady sat across from me, holding onto her purse for dear life. Several other people from all walks of life occupied the other seats, reading, chatting, or sleeping.

My phone vibrated as the train sped down the tracks. I checked the screen. A text from Peyton. *How come you ran out after you thanked my mom? I wanted to invite you to a frat party at BU. Call me. We can change wig styles and give the frat boys a run for their money.*

I chewed my lip. Her invitation sounded like fun. But I didn't know how long I'd be with Dillon.

Sorry. I'm tired. Let's do something soon. In part, I lied again. I ran out because I was afraid she'd want to tag along, and bringing her with me would only get complicated. Plus, for the brief time I'd met Dillon, he didn't seem like the type of guy who would welcome Peyton. Not when he was selling me a gun.

Let's meet for lunch at BU next week.

Deal, I replied. Peyton and I had had loads of fun when we were at the University of Miami. The train braked, announcing my stop. I filed out of the train car with a handful of people. Climbing up the stairs, I pocketed my phone. Once outside, the cold wind hit me. I shivered as I got my bearings. I'd checked out the map before I boarded the train. I had to walk four blocks. Sweeping my long, dark hair around me, I tucked it inside my coat then began my trek to Rumors. I found my hair was a great neck warmer.

Speaking of hair, I was giving Dillon what he'd asked for—the real me. When I'd gotten back to my hotel room, I'd stared at myself in the mirror, debating for several minutes whether to show Dillon the real me or stay in disguise. If I showed up at the club as Emma with my red wig and green contacts, he might make a scene or cancel our business arrangement. I didn't want to bring any attention to myself. Plus, I couldn't afford to have him back out. I had no doubt that I could find another gun dealer in a vast city like Boston, but I wouldn't even know where to begin. I also didn't want to answer any questions that another stranger might have. Or do business with someone I didn't know. Not that I knew Dillon all that well. But he came highly recommended from his cousin, who I'd partied with in Miami. Besides, I was one person among a population of over six hundred thousand in this city. I had nothing to worry about, not with Terrance Malden out of town. I could be me for one night.

My eyes watered as I passed others heading in the same direction, crossed over streets, and turned a corner onto Massachusetts Avenue. The lighted sign for Rumors jutted out from the building. I sniffled as I entered a dim hallway. A burly bouncer sat on a stool at the entrance to the club, checking IDs. According to the club's website, a person had to be eighteen or older to enter.

I unzipped my jacket, flipped my hair over my shoulder, dug into my jeans pocket, and removed my ID and money. I had two IDs. My driver's license for Miami had all my real information. I'd also had a fake one made with a picture of me in the red wig and green contacts just in case. Tonight though, I carried my real ID. I handed it to the bouncer.

He pointed a small flashlight at my license. "Ten dollars."

After I paid and he slapped a band around my wrist, I went in. The beat of the music grew louder. One of the things I despised about nightclubs was the noise level when I wanted to carry on a conversation. I was more than curious how Dillon and I would chat or do business in a nightclub. Although, when I thought about it, a dark, loud, and crowded room was the best place for us to do the exchange. The majority of people at the club were there to party and dance. They wouldn't be paying attention to Dillon and me.

I held out my wrist to another bouncer who had a double chin, standing guard at the arched doorway. Strobe lights of red, green, and yellow whipped around the packed club. He sized me up, his gaze lingering on my cleavage. I'd worn a simple white V-neck T-shirt over a pair of skinny jeans with army boots laced up over them. I didn't mind when guys swept their gazes over me. But when they lingered too long on one spot, mainly my boobs, I wanted to tell them to screw off. Instead I scowled.

"You can check your coat right over there." He stabbed a finger behind me.

"No thanks. I'm a bit chilled." My body was still cold from the trek there.

I entered the club, merging into the crowd of gyrating people. The beat of the music pounded in my ears while people bumped into me. As I skirted around couples feeling each other up, I scanned the room for Dillon. He'd texted me earlier to let me know he would be in one of the booths. So I slipped through an opening to the perimeter where booths lined the back wall. I passed each one, quickly checking faces. Fortunately, each table sported a lit candle, making it somewhat easy to discern features.

As I approached the last booth nestled in the far corner, Kelton's voice floated by, extremely close. My heart stopped. I froze with my eyes fixated on a bald guy in the corner booth. His lips moved as he talked to someone I couldn't see sitting across from him.

Shoot! Would Kelton recognize me after all these years? I wanted to think that he wouldn't. However, knowing Kelton, he didn't forget anything. I swore if he examined me up close he would see the gold speck in my left eye. *It's a dark room. He won't see it. Besides, he's probably here with his girlfriend, so he won't give me a second glance.* I couldn't take that chance. Dillon had already questioned if I knew Kelton. If I gave Dillon any hint of knowing the sexy Maxwell, the deal would be off.

Kelton's voice was practically on top of me. "I'm looking for Dillon Hart. Is anyone in this booth Dillon?" he asked.

I quickly peeked over my shoulder. Kelton had exchanged the tuxedo for a tight-fitting Hinder Band T-shirt showcasing his bulging biceps and frayed jeans that hung low on his hips.

"Thanks," he said. When he moved to the next table, his eyes met mine.

Shit! Shit! I stood like a zombie in between the table Kelton was about to approach and the corner booth. He held my gaze for the briefest of seconds, cocking his head to one side until a girl skirted between us. I started to duck into the melee of dancing fools when a strong hand settled on my shoulder.

"I've been waiting for you," a male voice said, his breath tickling my neck.

I tensed, ready to kick and punch, only to turn and find Dillon, smirking. His skull nose ring glinted from a strobe light.

Before I could say a word, his hands were in my hair and his mouth was on mine, hot and urgent. I mashed my lips together, about to push him away, as Kelton continued his search for Dillon. "Are any of you Dillon Hart?"

I sucked in a sharp breath. Dillon took that as his cue to push his tongue into my mouth. He pulled me closer to his hard body as he continued to kiss me. If it weren't for his strength—and my reluctance to make a scene—I would've kneed him in the balls. Fortunately, he was keeping Kelton from noticing me.

He explored my mouth as he held my face in his hands. Suddenly, Kelton's voice dulled as I got lost in Dillon's sensual web. I began kissing him back, tasting spearmint as my tongue touched his.

He groaned, abandoning my mouth for my ear. "You're much more beautiful with dark hair." His voice was husky. "I know you want to crush my balls, but I didn't plan this. I saw you panic. You said that dude was a creeper."

"So you're saving me?" Each word came out on a breath. "Kelton is looking for you. Not me. And news flash. I can handle myself."

He chuckled. "I don't doubt that."

I was about to ask him how he even recognized me without the red wig when Kelton asked, "Dillon Hart?"

I held my breath, keeping my eyes on Dillon.

Dillon turned his head. Kelton stood with his back to the dancers. "What, man? Can't you see I'm a little busy with my girl?" he asked like a snapping turtle—if turtles could talk.

"You're Dillon Hart? I saw you outside BU with the redhead. Fuck, man. Two girls in one day?" He sounded jealous.

"I said I was busy." Dillon's jaw was moving rapidly.

"Chill. I came up to shake your hand. If you want to be a fucking rude asshole then I'll have you removed from the club."

Dillon's hands tightened on my arms.

My pulse went from a lazy cadence to a full-out sprint. *So much for not making a scene.* Out of my peripheral vision, I glimpsed Kelton flaring his nostrils. Suddenly, I became worried for another reason. If Dillon had a gun on him, things could go haywire quickly.

"Be nice, baby," I said as I pressed my body into Dillon's. "The man only wants to meet you, not shoot you."

"Who's your girl?" Kelton asked as he touched my shoulder. "Your voice sounds familiar."

I could change the color of my hair and eyes, but not my voice, and Kelton and red-haired Emma had already met. Since I wasn't in disguise, I wasn't prepared for him to know I was his childhood sweetheart.

Dillon growled. "Get your fucking hand off my girl."

I kept my side profile exposed to Kelton. As long as he didn't look straight into my eyes, I should be fine. I also was banking on the dim light to keep me shielded. The bald guy in the corner booth had a sharp focus on us, probably waiting for all hell to break loose. I didn't know for sure, but I'd bet he was here with Dillon.

Kelton removed his hand from me as he growled.

All of sudden, I had to pee and maybe puke. "I have to go to the ladies' room," I said to Dillon.

"Don't take too long." He flicked his head to the bald guy in the corner booth.

The bald guy got up.

I peeled myself away from Dillon's hard body then got lost in the crowd. As I weaved through the dancers, I decided to get the hell out of that place after my pit stop. *You're paranoid. He's not going to recognize you.* I silently screamed back at my subconscious, *Hell if he doesn't!*

My appearance hadn't changed that much since the age of thirteen, except that I was older. I had bigger boobs, and I'd lost most of my southern accent. But my voice hadn't changed from when we'd spoken at the art gallery. If Kelton put two and two together, he would figure out I was the redhead from art class, and then he would have questions. Ones I wasn't prepared to answer, especially since he could derail my deal with Dillon to get the gun.

I found the bathroom down a darkened hallway at the back of the club. I also found a long line. I settled behind a girl with long brown hair who was talking on the phone.

"Chloe, Kelton is here. And Kody is performing tonight. I need you to keep me company. Kade is busy sifting through résumés for a waitress. I don't know where Kross is. Don't worry about Kelton's brothers."

Great! I was standing behind the baseball star Peyton mentioned at the art gala. She was dating Kade. I cursed under my breath. The entire Maxwell family was here? Out of all the clubs in Boston, Dillon had to pick the one with the Maxwells in it. I spied an exit sign up ahead. I checked the hallway up and down. From the doorway to the club, the bald guy who'd exchanged a silent gesture with Dillon eyed me with his arms crossed over his massive chest. He shook his head.

I scrunched up my face at him. If he was going to chase me, then let the games begin. I wasn't staying in this club another minute, even though I had to pee. I'd find a bathroom somewhere else. Sure, Dillon would have questions about why I left. Or he would back out of our deal. Either way, I had a question for him. How did he know the real me? His cousin, the one I partied with in Miami, didn't know the real me. I'd been dressed in my red wig at the frat party where I'd met him.

More ladies filed behind me.

I slid out of line and went up to the bald guy. "Why are you watching me?"

"Dillon wants me to," he said as he narrowed his brown eyes.

"Tell Dillon I'll call him tomorrow."

For some reason the stars were aligned for me to run into Kelton not once, but three times in one day. I smiled. My mom had told me the day we drove away from Kelton seven years ago that if we were meant for each other, the universe would bring us together. I lost my smile, and her words of wisdom. My gut told me I wouldn't be so lucky to flee him a fourth time if I didn't get out while I had the chance.

I threaded through the throng of dancers, occasionally getting bumped or knocked in the head. Once I finally made it out of the club and into the hall by the coat check, I sighed heavily. The bouncer, the same one who'd sized me up earlier, raised an eyebrow.

"Rough night," I said, zipping up my jacket.

I'd gotten halfway to the main entrance when Dillon's voice echoed in the narrow hall. "Elizabeth!"

I cringed. The only person who'd called me Elizabeth had been my mother, and only when I was in trouble. Otherwise, my family called me Lizzie.

I took another step forward. Right now, I didn't want to deal with how he knew who I was. I was tired, cranky, hungry, and needed a bathroom.

"Elizabeth Reardon," Dillon said, his voice demanding.

I whirled around. The blood drained from me. Kelton was standing alongside Dillon, his mouth agape. At that moment, I wanted to run as fast as my legs could carry me, but I wouldn't get far with my knees trembling.

Dillon marched toward me, grinning as though he'd just caught the biggest fish on the boat. I clenched my fists, considering my next move. If I ran, Kelton and Dillon would hunt me down. I wasn't sure why Dillon would. I was the one who'd sought him out. But now it seemed he was chasing me. I never should have kissed him back. That had to be the only reason he wasn't letting me go. On the other hand, I was one hundred fifty percent certain Kelton would not let me leave. He was the most persistent person I knew. He'd claw and fight until he got his way.

Dillon drew close. The blood in my veins gelled as I mentally shouted every swear word that came to mind.

"Lizzie?" Kelton asked. "Lizzie Reardon. Is that you?" Kelton's long legs ate up the distance between us until he was closer to me than Dillon. His gaze desperately searched for an answer.

Dillon angled his head, glaring at me. I guessed I wouldn't be doing business with him.

Kelton was breathing heavily, as though he was trying not to pass out.

I debated whether to speak or just walk away. If I did speak, I ran the risk of Kelton connecting the dots between redheaded Emma and the real me. If I ran, Kelton would pursue me like a hunted dog. I was screwed. *You're screwed anyway. Your voice will give you away.*

I set my attention on Dillon. "I need a ride," I said in a high-pitched tone as if I'd just eaten a mouse.

"The car is waiting." Dillon waved his hand to urge me forward.

"Wait one fucking second." Kelton swung out his arm to stop Dillon.

Dillon did a double take at Kelton. "Dude, if you value your life, you'll get out of my way. You don't know who you're messing with."

"Fuck off." Kelton crowded my personal space. "You're lying." He zoned in on my eyes as though he was my optometrist, his breath hot on my face. "You are Lizzie. The girl I used to climb trees with." He continued to scrutinize me, his nostrils flaring. "I know it's you."

He was so close, yet so far. He smelled like rain and nature, enticing and fresh. He reminded me of the good times we'd had. The times when we'd lain on the grass in my backyard in the pouring rain, letting the cool droplets drench us in the heat of summer. My heart raced, and my chest expanded, my breasts coming infinitely closer to his body. I had no doubt he'd pinpointed the square gold speck. It was hard to miss. The guys I'd dated always noticed it too.

I stalked away, water filling my eyes. I couldn't allow myself to feel for him again or get him involved in my plan. I was in this world alone, and being alone was best for everyone. People I loved had a way of dying. Besides, I was leaving once I got all of my inheritance back. I left him once. I couldn't bear to see his heart break again. I shook off those thoughts. I was getting way ahead of myself. He had a girlfriend —a sweet mafia princess who loved him.

He grabbed my arm and spun me around. "Say something." His blue eyes pleaded.

Dillon pulled Kelton off me. Kelton threw the first punch, knocking Dillon to the ground. The bouncers ran up. The one with the double chin pried Kelton away, expertly securing his arms behind his back.

Kelton jerked his arms away. "I'm cool, George."

Dillon pushed to his feet, scowling as he felt his busted lip. Then he said to me, "Let's go."

Normally I wouldn't obey anyone who barked out orders, but walking away from Kelton was best for both him and me. I couldn't bear to reminisce about the past. A past I'd once loved—a past that encompassed my baby sister, my mom, my dad, and even my dog—a time of great memories, summer parties, Kelton and I hanging out in his tree house, Kelton and I playing baseball, football, and even roller hockey. I couldn't begin to think about our first kiss and the butterflies I'd felt when our lips touched. Or the one afternoon our lives had changed forever.

"Talk to me, Lizzie," Kelton said, keeping his distance, his hands visibly shaking.

I fidgeted with my stud earring, twirling it one way then the other. "I'm not the girl you think I am." None of what I said was a lie. I wasn't that girl he'd known back in Texas. Not anymore.

Dillon cupped my elbow.

"Funny." Kelton combed his large fingers through his thick black hair. "The girl I knew always played with the earring in her ear when she was nervous."

My stomach hurt, and tears pricked the corners of my eyes. I brought my hand to my chest, feeling under my jacket for the half-heart charm he'd given me. I rarely took it off. The piece of jewelry was a reminder of what had been good in my life and of what we'd shared as kids and friends.

Leave and don't look back.

I was about to pivot on my heel when Kelton started for me, but George grabbed him.

"Fuck!" Kelton shouted.

I flinched before walking away when all I wanted to do was run back to him. He gave me the sense of family. Something I hadn't had in ages and desperately craved. But Kelton was a luxury, not a necessity like the Maldens.

CHAPTER 6
KELTON

Someone staggered past me, bumping into me as they left the club. I didn't move. A stampede of drunks could've trampled over me, and they wouldn't have been able to break me. When Dillon called her name, a weird feeling swirled in my stomach. The last time I'd gotten butterflies was the day I kissed Lizzie before she moved away.

"Kelton." George, the bouncer, waved his hand under my nose. It smelled of cigarettes, and the scent brought me back to the present, which suddenly I didn't want to be in. "Are you cool?"

Fuck no. My head spun like an out-of-control plane dropping from the sky. A breathtakingly stunning woman was mere inches from me, denying she was Lizzie Reardon. I didn't believe her for one second. Not when the square gold speck in her left eye gave her away. Or not when she played with her earring because she was nervous. Or the fact she was all grown up with curves, rounded breasts, long legs, and plump lips that I badly wanted to taste. My heart hadn't beat this hard with excitement since the first time I'd set eyes on her back in the fifth grade.

"I'm good," I lied. I was all twisted up inside.

A group of people came toward us as George went back to his bouncer's station. I tugged on my hair. I wanted to touch her, run, hide, and kiss her. I could run and hide, but feeling her body against mine, or tasting her sweet lips, wasn't going to happen, and not only because she didn't want anything to do with me. I couldn't risk my own heart. I couldn't risk getting hurt. I couldn't risk taking that chance of falling for someone, especially Lizzie. She was my forbidden fruit. One touch, one taste and I'd never be the same. I wouldn't dare allow myself to take the chance on love again. I had one problem though. I had questions that needed answers.

I blew out a long breath then punched the wall.

George glanced over his shoulder. "Do you want me to get Kade?"

Fuck, no. If he found out Lizzie was in town, he'd start preaching. *You can't get involved with her. You can't bring her home. And you can't let Mom and Dad know she's in Boston. It would tear Mom up if we brought up the subject of the Reardons, and if she saw Lizzie she could fall back into a deep depression.*

It didn't matter what he said. My fears aside, I had to talk to her. I had so many questions about the past and present. *She doesn't want anything to do with you. She's with Dillon.* Yeah, maybe it was for the best. Talking to her without being able to touch her would be near impossible. It would be like the time my parents took me to the zoo. "Okay, son," my father had said. "You can see the giraffes, but you can't touch them. They could bite you." Well fuck me now. I'd love for Lizzie to bite me. The problem with that reasoning was her bite would hurt and feel fantastic all at the same time.

Confusion made me dizzy. I needed to drown in liquor or bury myself in a woman.

I trudged back into the club, barely registering the music. I plowed through the crazy hip- swinging, arm-flailing people. I would settle for a quick lay since getting a drink would be near impossible if Kade was working the bar. HHHe was a stickler for the drinking age, and I wasn't twenty-one yet. Now I just had to snag a willing lady who I could take into the bathroom for a quickie. When I finally made it through the sweaty dancers, the bar came into view. Leo was working tonight. *Pay dirt!* He always let me down a beer or two when Kade wasn't watching. A drink first, then I'd find a lady.

I came up alongside Lynn, one of the waitresses at the drink station on one side of the bar.

"Christ, what happened to you?" she asked, her frown full of concern. "Please tell me you didn't just have sex in the bathroom."

I smirked. "Not yet."

She punched me lightly in the shoulder. "Kelton, I have to clean those bathrooms. I'm closing tonight."

"Don't freak. I always clean up after myself." I acknowledged Leo, the tattoo-laden bartender, with a flick of my head.

She punched me again. "If you're looking for Chloe, she's in the office with Lacey and Kade."

Chloe was the last person I wanted to see. I wasn't in the mood for her sweet attitude or her ability to coax me into a quickie, which she usually did when I was frustrated. She was all about feelings, and I wanted raw and rough with someone who didn't want anything from me except a good time. Not to mention, I'd promised myself I wouldn't lead her on.

Lynn checked her notepad. I snatched a shot of tequila from her collection of drinks. As I knocked back the alcohol, she lifted her head and immediately slapped my hand.

"For fuck's sake, Kelton. Are you trying to get me fired?"

"What's he doing?" Kade appeared out of nowhere.

"I took one of her tequila shots." I didn't want to get Lynn in trouble. She was a single mom and needed this job to support her two kids.

Kade popped me in the back of my head. "I'll throw your ass in jail if you take another drink. Now, what the fuck happened to you? And don't tell me you got into a fight again."

I shrugged. "I won't tell you I got into a fight again."

"George filled me in. My office. Now!" Rage was stamped all over his face.

Fucking great!

Lynn gathered her tray of drinks and left. Kade glowered at me, crossing his arms over his chest. The music changed from head-bobbing to slow and moody. Which was just the right speed to set up Kody, who sang depressing songs. I checked the stage opposite the bar. Kody was hooking up his guitar. Several girls gathered around him to watch. My brother was doing something right. He always had girls at his feet.

"I think I'll hang here and wait for Kody to start his set." I wasn't in the mood for big brother to yell or tell me what my flaws were and that I should work on fixing them.

"Fuck you will. If you don't get in my office, I'll drag you."

I laughed. "Go ahead. I dare you." I was itching for a fight. I'd only gotten one punch in with Dillon. I could've used several more to release the tension.

"Stop being a dick." He grabbed my triceps, his strength stopping the blood from flowing.

Normally, I obeyed my big brother—or had up until I started college. I loved him and would die for him, but I was on my own, living in a condo with a roommate, and having the time of my life. For the past three years, I didn't have to hear him being the parent, which he had been for most of my childhood with our mom's mental illness and our old man deployed on military missions. Out of Kody, Kross, and me, I was the triplet who'd given Kade the most grief.

He let go. "Five minutes." His tone was less irascible.

"You can reprimand me here." I glowered at him. I wasn't about to hear him chastise me in front of Lacey and Chloe.

"Lacey took Chloe home." He gave me a half smirk. "Lacey coaxed her to come down here. Then as soon as Chloe got here, she was throwing up."

"Is she okay?" I didn't want to marry Chloe, but I wasn't a complete dickhead.

He nodded at someone.

I tracked Kade's line of sight to find George ambling down to the other end of the bar.

I shouldn't be surprised since Kade wrote their paychecks when Mr. Robinson wasn't around. He'd opened up another club not too far from Rumors.

"She said she ate something that didn't agree with her." He began walking away. "Let's go."

The faster I got this over with, the faster I could find a sexual partner for the night. I followed like a good brother. When I rounded the corner into the hallway, I ran right into Trudy Davenport. She smelled like an enticing plate of sex, sex, and more sex with her straw-berry fragrance. I sized her up while she giggled. She wore a tight-fitting miniskirt, showing her long-ass legs, with a top that made her tits scream, *Touch me.*

She mashed those dick-hardening tits right into my chest. "I was hoping to find you here."

"Mmm." I stared at her breasts like a complete dick.

"I talked to my dad about your résumé. He said he'd look it over and call you Monday."

"Sweetheart." I bit my lip. "I don't need your help. But I wouldn't mind—"

A hand landed on my neck. "Kel, office. Now," Kade's hardened tone zapped the lust that was making my dick swell to huge proportions.

She ran her soft hands up under my T-shirt. "If you need a friend later, I'll be listening to your brother." She winked and sashayed away.

I watched her hips sway then shook off the thoughts of tapping her ass as I met Kade in the office.

Once the door was closed, Kade said, "Sit." He tipped his head to the red couch underneath the small window.

I rubbed my bruised knuckles as I went to the fridge and removed a can of Coke and chugged half of it. After I let out a burp, I straddled the arm of the couch.

Kade scrutinized me with one of his blank expressions that Lacey hated. He was either picking his words or deciding where to begin his dissertation. "George tells me you punched Dillon Hart. Why?"

"Just come out and ask me what's really on your mind." Kade was immune to fights. They happened in the club at least on a weekly basis, according to him. Besides, the bouncers took care of removing anyone causing any disruption. No, Kade had something else on the tip of his tongue. I gulped down the rest of the Coke.

"George said it was about a girl named Elizabeth Reardon. You want to tell me more?"

I burped loudly then tossed the can into the metal trashcan adjacent to Kade. It clanged for two points. I sauntered to the door. "There's not much to say." I wasn't ready to discuss the girl from my past. I wasn't even ready to believe she was here in Boston.

Kade pinned me up against the door with his hand on my chest. "Is it Lizzie?" His face reddened.

"Chill, bro. It's not." I never lied to Kade—or any of my brothers. We were all tight. We told each other everything. At that moment, I couldn't tell him the truth. I was having a hard time believing the dark-haired beauty was Lizzie Reardon. The Lizzie I knew was tough but sweet. The girl tonight was different—cocky, badass, and she seemed to have a chip on her shoulder.

"Seriously, Kel. Tell me the truth. I know how fucked up you got when she left Texas. And you know you can't get involved with her. Any mention of the Reardons in our house—"

I pushed him. "It's not her. Okay?"

Kade stumbled, running both hands through his hair. "I swear, Kel." He sneered.

"I'm twenty years old, not thirteen. Give me a fucking break." I stormed out. As soon as I did, a wrecking ball hit the pit of my stomach. I hated to lie to my brother, but before I could come clean, I had to talk to Lizzie. First, I had to find out where she was staying.

CHAPTER 7
LIZZIE

After thirty minutes of stoplights and side streets, we drove up to a three-tenement house in a suburb of Boston. The bald guy who had followed me to the restroom sat shotgun while his buzz-cut crony drove. I sat in the back seat with Dillon. The tension between us was as thick as the ocean fog on a dark night. Dillon and I had argued when we'd gotten into the SUV. I'd wanted him to take me back to the hostel. When I said *hostel* he'd done a double take. Then he'd instructed the driver, who I learned was Rafe, to proceed back to the compound. Yep, *compound*. Whatever that meant.

I almost jumped out of the SUV at one of the stoplights, but I needed Dillon for more than a weapon. He'd proved to me that he had my back. He'd had Baldy watch over me, though I still wasn't sure why. Dillon had distracted me from a person I'd called a creeper. He also had a soft side that told me he could be a good friend. He certainly was a good kisser. Most of all, my curiosity was piqued about who exactly Dillon was and what he did other than sell guns.

Rafe pulled into a skinny driveway between two houses. Once he cut the engine, he and Baldy jumped out as if they had to put out a fire.

"So, are we having a sleepover?" I asked, arching an eyebrow.

"Do you want to sleep with me?" Dillon asked, searching me with his gaze much as Kelton had.

I let out a nervous laugh. Maybe if my heart wasn't for someone else. Although the last time I had been intimate with anyone was over a year ago with some guy I'd hung out with at a party. I remembered two things from that rendezvous. One, we'd agreed no names, and two, the sex had been surprisingly slow and sensual. The hunky guy wanted to take care of my needs first, which I thought was sweet considering we didn't know each other. Usually, one-night stands were fast and furious.

"Why am I here? I have a place to stay." I glanced out at the two-car garage. "And you probably don't want to do business with me anyway."

Leaning on the armrest that separated us, he rested his chin on the backs of his fingers. "A hostel. Are you broke?"

Yep. "None of your business. And there's nothing wrong with hostels." The place was a hotel, just on the cheap side.

"Tell me about Kelton Maxwell." His gaze dropped to my lips.

"You seem to know a lot about him. And me. Care to share?"

He laughed. "I do my homework on people I'm about to do business with. And don't forget—"

"Yeah, Russian mob and all that. I get it. How did you get intel on me?"

"Tell me how you know Kelton."

"For fuck's sake. I'm not going to the Russian mob. I'm not marrying Kelton." Although I always thought I would. "And, like you, my business is my own." I jumped out of the car, slammed the door, and started for the street. I didn't have time to discuss my life, and I didn't care to. Plus my bladder was screaming at me now. Before we turned onto this street, I'd spotted a gas station at the corner. I headed in that direction.

Three-tenement houses dotted the neighborhood, and cars were parked along the curbs. I had no idea where I was or how to get back to the hostel. I shoved my hands inside my jacket, tucked my chin to my chest, and set my sights on the Chevron station. Not surprisingly, the area was quiet at one in the morning. The bright lights of the main thoroughfare shone in the distance. Maybe I could get a cab back into the city or find the "T" after I used the ladies' room. As I walked, I blew out all the anxiety that had built up inside me, and with it a lone tear escaped. I brushed it away, but all I wanted to do was curl up in my bed and have a good cry. But wallowing in my sorrows wasn't going to get me my money back. Maybe I could seduce Terrance Malden into giving me what was mine. I scratched that idea. He'd probably use me and still take off with my million dollars. I could use a knife to threaten him instead of a gun. I could also take his son as a hostage. Now I was getting somewhere, although it would be easier to threaten Zach with a gun.

I smiled at my newfound plan. I'd cozy up to Zach, get him into a place I could hold him hostage, then call his father and demand my money. If I did that, the cops would be involved. I would get arrested. On the other hand, if Terrance stole my money, he was breaking the law, too. So he wouldn't involve the cops. Either plan involved a weapon. I had to turn around and make nice with Dillon. Well, after the gas station.

I was a block from the bright Chevron sign when a car's engine rumbled. I squinted at the headlights as the car wheeled slowly down the street toward me as though the driver was searching for a particular house. I was crossing over a driveway when the car braked in the middle of the street.

"Hey, darling, do you know where I can find Dober Street?" a deep male voice asked.

I kept my sights on the lighted sign, increasing my pace as the hackles on my neck rose. Maybe walking alone at the wee hours of the morning in an unknown town wasn't such a great idea.

You think? I silently screamed at my inner voice just as someone wolf-whistled.

Taking longer strides, I peeked over my shoulder. A guy wearing a knit cap was hanging out of the car window, watching me. Beyond his car, I spied another vehicle coming toward us. With the bright lights in my face, I couldn't make out if it was Dillon's car or not, and I wasn't hanging around to find out. When I turned back, I noticed a ring of rocks around a tree in the yard I was passing. I hastily grabbed one before continuing in the direction of the gas station.

A car door shut, and two men argued while footsteps pounded the pavement. My adrenaline spiked, flooding my body. A male figure got closer. Instinct told me to run, but my screwed-up stubbornness wanted to throw the rock that was securely in my hand. In one beat, I whirled around and threw.

The man ducked, shouting, "Fuck, Elizabeth!"

"Dillon?" Dillon's body came into view.

"Girl, if you had a gun, I'd be dead." He bit his lip, his wavy brown hair blowing in the wind.

I snarled then spun on my heel for the gas station.

"Wait. Where are you going?" He ran up to me.

"I have to pee." And puke. Then down a bottle of moonshine to coat my nerves.

He laughed. "You can pee at my house."

Crossing the street and into the lot of the gas station, I snorted. Hearing Dillon say the word *pee* was funny. He came off as a pierced, long-haired badass. "Your house isn't this close." I pointed to the store. "Who were those guys in that car back there?"

"Two morons trying to cause trouble. Rafe took care of them. Don't worry. You're safe," he said as he nodded to a man filling up his gas tank.

He'd rescued me again. It was odd for me to have a guy I barely knew and who wasn't the law protect me. The last time anyone saved me was an off-duty cop. I'd been out with girlfriends at a club in Miami when I got separated from them. I was about to take a cab home when two men jumped out of a car and grabbed me. If it weren't for that off-duty cop, I wasn't sure I'd be alive. My heart warmed at how Dillon cared.

I darted into the store and hurried down a short hall in the back. Once in the bathroom, I quickly emptied the contents of my bladder. After I washed my hands, I splashed water on my face then glanced at myself in the mirror. Christ, I was losing my tan after just a week of being in the freaking cold. Either that, or the week had caught up with me, making me as white as the sink. The paleness of my skin made the dark circles beneath my grayish-blue eyes stand out like a raccoon's. I needed to sleep for a month. Yeah, that wasn't happening. Not when I had work to do. I grabbed a paper towel, patted my face, then wiped my hands.

Once outside, I found Dillon with one foot pressed to the building, reading something on his phone. Snow started to fall.

"Can you call me a cab or show me where the 'T' is?"

He straightened. "No. You'll stay with me tonight. It's late."

I opened my mouth to protest.

He held up his hand. "Hear me out. No strings. You'll have your own bed. In the morning we'll talk business."

I licked my chapped lips. "You mean you're still doing business with me even though I know Kelton?"

"I haven't decided yet." He waved his hand in the direction of his house. "Shall we?"

"Do you have a girlfriend that's going to show up?"

He chuckled. "No girlfriends. Come on. It's freezing out here."

I was cold, tired, and could use a place where I didn't have to hear anyone yelling, playing loud music, or having sex. My intuition was telling me I could trust Dillon. "One condition. Tell me how you knew it was me in the club?"

"Quid pro quo. Fair?" He chewed on his busted lip as he peered down at me.

I nodded.

"Let's walk," he said. "I told Rafe to take the car back."

As we trekked back down the quiet street, large snowflakes fell, coating the parked vehicles. There was no sign of the thugs in the car.

"Rafe hacked into BU's computer system. Once he found your full name, he did more research and found a picture of you in the Miami Herald. I'm sorry about your parents." His tone was even, yet a hint of sadness edged the last of his words.

The Miami Herald had posted a write-up of the accident along with a picture of my mom, dad, and me. The Coast Guard had found my father's forty-foot yacht overturned, but no bodies. I'd been sched-uled to go with them that weekend to the Bahamas. But I'd gotten the flu. According to the Coast Guard, my parents encountered a storm with twenty-foot waves off the coast of the Bahamas.

A snowflake flake melted on my nose. "Thanks. So I guess it's my turn." We crossed over a side street. "Kelton and I grew up together. Or at least until I was thirteen. Then my father took a position with his company in England. I never kept in touch with Kelton. The first time I saw him since I left Texas was in the damn art class."

"Why don't you want anything to do with him?"

Because I was still in love with him, and I knew we could never be a couple. Because people I love die. Because my sister killed his sister. Because his family would never welcome me. Because I couldn't afford the distraction. "Bad history."

We walked the last two blocks in silence. I was thankful he didn't pry any further. I wasn't ready to spill the details of my past with Kelton, not without breaking down.

As we climbed the steps up onto his porch, I prayed tomorrow would be a better day. I certainly had a new plan to get what was mine, albeit a loose one.

CHAPTER 8
LIZZIE

I flipped onto my stomach in the most comfortable bed I'd slept in in ages. A stream of morning light weaved through the blinds—or at least I thought it was morning. I didn't care to check either. Since it was Saturday, I didn't have any pressing appointments or a job I had to be at. The only item on my list was to give Zach Malden a ring that afternoon. Burying my face into the goose-down pillow, I inhaled its crisp lavender scent as I stretched my body in all directions. When I did, I kicked something at the bottom of the bed. Then someone giggled.

I jackknifed into a sitting position, blinking rapidly. My gaze landed on not one, but two girls who had to be about seventeen or eighteen. Oh my God. Dillon said he didn't have a girlfriend. Or maybe they were his sisters. Both were sitting on my bed staring at me with beautiful smiles and big brown eyes.

The one closest to me was braiding the ends of her long brown hair. "Good morning. I'm Bee."

The other, who had shiny black hair styled into a pixie cut, waved. "I'm Allie."

"So, did Dillon find you on the streets?" Bee asked, securing the ends of her braid with a scrunchie.

My jaw fell to the mattress. "I'm sorry?"

"Who's your pimp?" Allie asked, inching farther onto the bed before lying on her side, propping her head in her hand.

My jaw locked. I'd made a grave mistake falling for Dillon's charm. Suddenly, it all made sense. He didn't want me to sell guns for him. He wanted me on his crew to sell my body. He kissed me last night as a test. I'd bet he wanted to make sure I could kiss well for the clients. I swept my gaze over the two girls, who were dressed in flannel pajamas. Bee's was printed with bears and Allie's with Hello Kitty. Allie seemed to have a hard edge to her by the way she was studying me. Maybe it was the hollowness of her eyes. On the other hand, Bee gave me the impression she was naïve and less tomboyish than Allie.

"I think I need to go." I eased back the covers.

"Please don't," Bee said. "We'd like for you to go to the movies with us. Dillon says you're going to be staying with us for a while."

My eyebrows disappeared into my hairline. "He did?" The man was way too confident. Either that or he was planning on locking me in this room. I diverted my gaze to the two windows, hoping a fire escape sat outside one of them since I was on the third floor.

Bee nodded, beaming from ear to ear as she took my hand. "You need a manicure. Oooh, Allie. Let's give Elizabeth a makeover."

Dillon hadn't wasted any time in sharing my name. I was curious what else he had told them.

Allie's gaze roamed over me, no doubt trying to figure out who the new girl was.

Bee flipped my hand so my palm was facing upward. "Why do you have calluses?"

"Lifting weights. Is Dillon home?"

"Yeah, he's in the kitchen making breakfast." Allie sat up. "The bathroom is down the hall on the left. We'll meet you on the first floor. Come on, Bee. Let's eat." Her voice was firm, leading me to believe she was the more adult of the two.

Bee pouted as she traipsed out with Allie. I flopped back onto the pillow. I couldn't imagine Dillon as a pimp. He was a gentleman last night. He wanted me safe. When we got back to his house, he didn't try to coax me to his bed or try to kiss me. He escorted me to this room and said good night. I stared up at the popcorn ceiling, debating what to do. No weapon was worth selling my body for. I had a small amount of cash in the bank, though I had to use it sparingly. The best course of action was to contact Peyton to see if her mom needed help with upcoming catering jobs. After the art gala, Wendy had paid me in cash. For two hours of my time she'd given me one hundred and fifty dollars. At first I'd given half of it back to her. It seemed like a lot, considering it far exceeded minimum wage. She'd insisted, saying I'd done a great job. Part of me thought Peyton had told her mom about my family and that Wendy felt sorry for me. Either way, I pocketed the cash after she argued with me.

The smell of bacon floated in the air, and my stomach grumbled. I climbed out of bed, dressed, and combed my fingers through my hair then set out for the kitchen, thinking about how to approach Dillon. The best way was to keep it simple. Tell him straight up I wasn't working the streets for him, and that he could sell me the gun and I'd be out of his hair.

I followed the bacon scent down to the first floor, swung around the staircase, then crossed a wide hall and into the open spacious kitchen. Allie and Bee sat opposite each other at a picnic-style table. Beyond them, through the window, three inches of snow piled neatly atop the wooden fence.

Bee beamed with excitement when she saw me. Allie kept eating, only eyeing me for a brief moment. Dillon stood at the stove, plucking bacon from a pan onto a plate.

"Sleep well?" he asked. His brown, shoulder-length hair had that bedhead look, and his jaw was scruffy. He was wearing a wife-beater, showcasing a tattoo sleeve of crosses, quotes, a Chinese symbol, and a woman's name, along his right arm.

My short-term memory vaporized as my limbs locked into place. I stared at the name, Grace, which was woven into the Chinese symbol on his bicep. My lungs burned as though Dillon had poured hot grease down my throat.

"Bee, help Elizabeth into a chair," Dillon said.

At the sound of my name, I snapped back to reality, switching my gaze from his arm to Bee, who had bounced over to me.

"I'm cool," I said weakly.

Bee went back to her seat. She and Allie began whispering—about me, I imagined. I had to look like a deer in the headlights.

I shuffled closer to Dillon, trying to recall my Chinese. My father had taken an assignment with his tech company in China for two months when we lived in Texas. My mom, Gracie, and I had visited him for a month. I'd been fascinated with the language and picked up several words. When we returned to the States, I kept up with learning the language until Gracie died. Then I lost all desire to do anything.

"You've seen a ghost," Dillon said as he touched my arm.

I'd seen more than a ghost. I was beginning to think Dillon and I were meant to meet. For what reason, I wasn't sure.

He carried a plate of bacon to the table. "Let's eat and talk." He set the plate next to a bowl of scrambled eggs, fruit, toast, and a stack of pancakes.

I moved over to the bench-style seating, my mind swimming with what question to ask him first.

"Girls, if you're finished, head upstairs and get ready," Dillon said. "I have a few things to do before we leave for the movie."

Bee and Allie kissed him on the cheek. Allie snagged a piece of bacon. Bee waved at me with a glowing smile. I couldn't help but return the gesture. Bee had an infectious way about her to the point where I wanted to hug her and let her paint my nails.

"I would like to know why they asked who my pimp was. If you're a pimp, I'm out of here." And I'd be taking the girls with me.

He filled his plate with eggs, the spoon dinging against the bowl as he scooped. "After all my help last night, is that what you think?" He mashed his lips into a thin line as he salted his eggs.

I ground my teeth together. "I don't know. What're two teenaged girls doing with you? Are they your sisters?" Dillon didn't give me the impression he was a guy who took advantage of girls.

He grabbed a fork and shoveled a pile of eggs into his mouth. He watched me while he chewed. "They're two girls who needed help. They were living on the streets with no chance of surviving."

"Where are their parents?"

"Allie ran away from a foster home. I found her pimp beating her. Bee is also a runaway, but not from a foster home. Her mother died when she was young, and she was left with a father who's a drunk. She couldn't take his shit anymore. I found her among the homeless crowd one night. They're both eighteen and make their own decisions. I've offered to help them reconnect with family, but they're not ready."

"Do you troll for girls or something?" I thought it was admirable that he rescued girls, but a part of me found it odd that he would.

He set his fork down with a smirk. "Elizabeth."

"It's Lizzie." *Elizabeth* reminded me too much of my parents.

"Lizzie, I try to help girls in bad situations. I don't expect you to believe me, and I'm glad you don't. That tells me you're cautious. Women should be more cautious and question things. I've been trying to teach Allie and Bee that very thing."

"Do you kiss all the girls you help?" A large part of me knew he was a good guy, but doubt niggled in the back of my mind.

"I told you I didn't plan that."

Yeah, but the effort he'd put behind the kiss and the way his body had responded told me he'd liked it. I couldn't blame him. I enjoyed his kiss. As badass and sexy as Dillon was, I was there on business. Although seeing Kelton again had kick-started my emotions for him.

"I'm not in Boston to get involved with anyone. Can we agree to get to know each other as just friends? Or business partners?" I wanted to complete our deal.

"You like that Maxwell guy?" His gaze roamed over my face.

I shrugged. "Does it matter? Don't answer that. Look, are you going to sell me a gun or not?" My stomach growled.

"Eat, then we'll talk." He started spreading jelly on his toast.

I dove in and filled my plate with eggs, pancakes, and bacon. I had a feeling my body and my brain were going to need all the fuel they could get.

⚜

AFTER BREAKFAST and a trip to the bathroom, I went in search of Dillon. I was on the second floor landing when Baldy's and Dillon's voices carried upward. I stopped.

"That Maxwell dude is here," Baldy said. "You want me to get rid of him?"

Kelton sure hadn't changed. He was as persistent as ever.

"No, Josh. The guy won't let up until he gets answers, and I don't want any trouble. We can't afford to have the cops sniffing around here."

Considering he sold guns, I didn't doubt the cops could be trouble. But the law wasn't an issue at the moment. I thought about telling Dillon I'd handle Kelton, but I wasn't prepared to face Kelton. Maybe after my mission was completed, I'd talk to him. That way my head would be clear, and he wouldn't distract me from my goal.

Josh's and Dillon's voices died when the door closed with a resounding thud. I flinched then sprinted down one flight before ducking into a living room at the bottom of the stairs. I had to at least hear what Kelton wanted.

Two tall windows anchored the sides of the wide window in the middle. Luckily the curtains were drawn, but the men had to be on the porch because their voices were loud but not exactly clear.

Footsteps and giggles broke me away from dialing in on Kelton and Dillon's conversation.

"What are you doing?" Allie asked.

I put my finger to my mouth.

"Oooh, you're eavesdropping," Bee said excitedly as she bounced in, her ponytail swaying back and forth. "Over here." She pointed to a door adjacent to the stairs.

I followed her and Allie into a room that had a pool table and stank of cigarettes.

Allie hopped up and sat on the pool table, watching me. I went to the window. This room had the same style windows as the living room, and the curtains were drawn.

Bee touched her lips with her forefinger. "Dillon sometimes leaves the window cracked in this room when they're playing pool," she whispered. "And the guys were in here after dinner last night."

I swiped my hand down one end of the curtains, feeling for a draft. Sure enough, cold air seeped in. I squatted and angled my ear at the opening in the window.

"I want to talk to Lizzie," Kelton said. His voice was clear and crisp. "Is she here?"

"How did you find out where I lived?" Dillon asked.

"I have mob connections. Now where is she?" Kelton's voice was unyielding.

I cringed at the word *mob*. The organization Dillon wanted to stay away from.

"Man, you don't give up. Have you asked yourself why she walked away from you last night?" Dillon asked.

I wanted to peek through the curtains. Body language was always a better way to discern a person's emotions. Truth be told, I wanted a glimpse of Kelton too.

"You know, Hart? Last night I had every intention of shaking your hand for helping girls get off the streets. But now? Now I want to ram my fist in your face again. I'll find Lizzie, and she'll talk to me."

Dillon harrumphed. "What makes you think she'll talk to you?"

"Obviously she hasn't shared her past with you. Such a shame if you two are intimate, but she owes me."

His last sentence gave me whiplash. He had been the one to declare that he'd find me one day. That didn't mean we owed each other anything. The pain in my heart warred with the angry heat pinching my cheeks as I thought back to the day Gracie accidentally killed Karen. Blood had covered Gracie's face as tears streamed down it, her breathing had been labored, her hands shaking. I couldn't imagine being in the Maxwells' shoes when they lost Karen. That aside, not one person among the Maxwells had tried to find out how Gracie was or said that they were sorry for what happened. My sister hadn't died that day, but she might as well have.

A cold hand touched my face. "Lizzie." Bee's flowery voice brought me out of my trance. "Allie and I are here for you. Don't cry."

A salty tear slid down my cheek, finding its way into my mouth. I blinked to find Allie and Bee at my side, rubbing my arms. I was beginning to believe the three of us had many things in common, but one that stood out—we were standing in Dillon's home, brought together by fate.

"Is that your pimp outside?" Allie whispered.

I busted out laughing. They both joined in.

"No. But I should talk to him." Kelton wasn't going to stop until he got what he wanted. I couldn't let Dillon deal with my problem. Besides, the cops would be here if they beat each other. I didn't want trouble.

I shook off the tears, the nerves, even the pain poking at my heart, as best I could. I stuck out my chin and made my way out of the house and onto the porch. Allie and Bee were on my heels. I wanted to laugh, cry again, and hug them for sticking by my side. I mean, we didn't even know each other.

Dillon and Kelton stopped talking. Kelton's Adam's apple bobbed.

"He's hot," Bee said close to my ear.

I was beginning to love this girl. She was so right. The dark-blue Henley underneath his leather jacket ignited his midnight-blue eyes.

"It's okay, Dillon. We do need to talk," I said as Allie grabbed onto my hand as though she wanted to protect me. I swear. I was a second from bawling like a starving baby.

"Girls," Dillon said. "Let's go inside."

For a second, Allie and Bee didn't move. Then Dillon raised his brow. The girls huffed at the same time before going back into the house.

Dillon came up to me. "If he gets out of line, knee him in the balls," he whispered in my ear. "And I'm just inside if you need me."

My heart swelled with so much emotion at my overnight family. I would've said thank you, but I didn't think I could speak.

Once Kelton and I were alone, we didn't say anything until a hard wind blew, rustling the branches on the oak tree in the front yard. Snow fluttered to the ground.

"Remember the tree house?" Kelton asked as he relaxed on the edge of the porch railing.

Lord, please help me through this conversation. I don't want to cry. I don't want to be rude. I don't want to touch him. You cannot let me touch him. If I did, I'd be a goner. I was so screwed up. I wanted to disappear and never see him again. At the same time, I longed for him to hold me, kiss me, and tell me he still loved me.

"What..." I cleared my throat. "What do you want? I don't owe you anything," I said evenly.

He rubbed his neck. "Is one of those girls Gracie?"

I shook my head as I pressed my hands on the wood slats, willing the tears not to surface.

"How's she doing?" he asked, his tone repentant.

"After seven years you want to know how she's doing?" I mashed my hand into the siding hard, hoping it would swallow me up.

"What's that supposed to mean?" He knitted his eyebrows. "You moved away like we had the plague."

I inhaled sharply, the cold morning air prickling on the way down. "Your family didn't bother to check on her. My father contacted yours to see how your family was doing. He left all our information with your dad. After that we never heard from him."

He straightened to his full six-foot height. "I didn't know that. But why didn't you return my emails or phone calls after you moved?"

"Is that what you think I owe you?" I squinted so hard it hurt.

"We loved each other, Lizzie." He took one confident step toward me and stopped.

"That was a lifetime ago. We were thirteen, Kel. Then someone died, and life changed."

Bee squeaked. I had no doubt Dillon, Allie, and Bee were listening. Honestly, I didn't mind. I was certain Dillon was there just to be sure I didn't need his help. If Dillon and I were building trust, then here was his chance to get to know a little more about Elizabeth Reardon.

Kelton shoved his hands in his jeans pockets. "That didn't mean we couldn't talk."

"So, are you saying you would've still loved me, even though my sister was the one who pulled the trigger?"

Another squeal filtered out from inside, followed by Dillon shushing them.

"You wouldn't have looked at me any differently? Your parents wouldn't either? Your brothers?" I wasn't sure I could face his family. Something as tragic as what had happened changed people.

His gaze dropped to his booted feet.

I went to the other side of the porch. Five feet was way too close to Kelton. "Yeah, I thought so. Your family will always blame mine. My presence in your life would always remind them of that day. It was best to cut all ties with you."

He inched closer, maintaining the distance between us. "It wasn't your fault. It wasn't even Gracie's fault."

I used the porch rail to support me. "In part, I agree." My dad had always taught us not to touch a gun, especially when he'd learned that Mr. Maxwell had been schooling the boys in how to shoot. "I saw how determined Karen was to be like you and your brothers. She wanted to do everything you boys did, including shooting and hunting. When I think back, part of me gets angry with your dad. He didn't bother to teach Karen gun safety. If I recall, his reasoning was that girls shouldn't handle guns. The other part of me gets mad at my sister. She knew not to go anywhere near one." I gripped the rails on either side of me, feeling as though I'd just discarded seven years of anger, hurt, and sadness that had been targeted at the Maxwells.

He swung his pensive gaze out toward the street. A lady bundled up in a heavy coat, hat, and scarf cleaned the snow off her car.

He threaded his fingers through his hair. "Why are you in Boston? Have you been living here long?"

The past week had felt like a lifetime, especially the last twenty-four hours. "Where are you going with this?" I wasn't sure where or how I wanted this conversation to go.

He stalked over to me.

I dug my palms into the railing, tensing every muscle in my body. My pulse beat in my ears, growing louder the closer he got. The tips of his boots touched mine. I dropped my gaze, afraid to meet those damn blue eyes that caused my insides to do funky, sexy things.

His military-style boots were unlaced at the top, his jeans were ripped at the knees, and his red briefs peeked through a hole just under his right pocket.

Lord, you're not helping me.

His cold fingers landed underneath my chin. "Look at me, Lizzie."

Oh, hell no.

Steam blew out of my nose.

"I've missed you," he said softly, his thumb moving back and forth on my chin as his chest rose and fell rapidly.

My brain became fuzzy as he continued to hold my chin between his fingers. Every emotion I had for Kelton was locked in a box and stored away. Yet, at that moment, the way he continued to rub my chin, light and soothing, the closeness of his body, his warm breath breezing over me, and his hands on my face, was too freaking much.

I pried my hand from the rail and pushed against his hard abs. He didn't move. I tried again.

"I'm not leaving yet," he said in a husky voice that sent an electrical charge to the center of my heart.

He grasped my wrist before dragging my hand over his heart. I was catapulted back in time to when we'd stood on my front lawn the day we'd moved. He'd given me my half-heart necklace. Then I'd asked him where the other half was. He'd taken my hand, pressed my palm to his heart, and said, "Right here."

His cinnamon breath shattered the memory. I quickly checked to ensure the charm I'd never taken off was still hidden beneath my shirt. When I lifted my gaze, time stopped. He was looking at me the same way he had when we were thirteen—with love stamped in his eyes.

I swallowed several times to try and get the lump in my throat to go down.

Then he slowly dragged his thumb over my lips. "They're still as pink as ever," he said, his gaze on my mouth.

I touched the scar on his chin, smiling, remembering the time his foot had slipped on the rungs of the ladder to the tree house. He brought my fingers up to his mouth and kissed them lightly. Goosebumps fired along my arms. I knew I should create some distance between us, but the spell he had me under was strong. We stared at one another, trying to figure out words, life, what was going through each other's minds in that moment. At least I was. Until his lips brushed mine.

I held my breath. If he full-on kissed me I'd want more, and more wasn't possible. Not with our past.

A car door slammed in the distance. Kelton edged back, releasing me. One of Dillon's neighbors was starting her car.

"Kel, what do you want?"

He ran a hand through his hair. "Don't worry. I'm not here to disrupt your life. I just needed to confirm you were really Lizzie. You didn't give me a chance last night."

My heart fluttered and sputtered. He sounded sad and happy at the same time.

"Okay. You've seen me. Now what?"

"Now I leave you to your life," Kelton said. "It was good to see you." He swept his gaze over me as if he was taking pictures with every blink of his eyes. Then he gave me a half smile before dashing off the porch as though I was contagious. He jumped in his Jeep and sped away.

I pushed out all the air in my lungs as I touched my lips. I wanted him to kiss me. I wanted to feel thirteen again. I wanted to go back and erase the day my mom screamed at the top of her lungs when Gracie came into the house with blood splattered on her face and hands. But what I wanted I couldn't have or change. However, I could shape my future. Kelton and I would be better off staying away from each other.

The front door groaned before Dillon stepped out with a green army coat in his hand. "Is the coast clear?"

I bobbed my head.

"Here, put this on." He held out the coat. "You have to be freezing. I would've brought it out to you earlier, but I didn't want to interrupt."

Dillon continued to surprise me. He was definitely a sweet man. I took the coat from him, even though I wasn't cold. I had on my clothes from the night before, but I'd found a heavy sweater in the bedroom I'd slept in, since the house had a chill to it. "We can go inside."

"Let's talk first. It's a little more private out here." He sat on the bench underneath the window. "Come." He patted a spot next to him.

Easing down next to him, I draped the outer garment over my legs. "My conversation wasn't private," I said evenly.

"I'm sorry about that. I had to make sure he wasn't going to hurt you. And after their last squeal, I sent the girls up to get ready for the movies and closed the window. Are you okay?"

Kelton would never hurt me physically. Emotionally was another story. "I'm good." I was, and I wasn't. I'd gotten one thing off my chest, and it felt like a load of bricks had been lifted off me. On the other hand, I wanted someone I couldn't have. I couldn't build a relationship with Kelton. Our past would never allow it. His family would never allow it. Most of all, his girlfriend would never allow it. "So, you're not going to chastise me about the Russian mob and all?"

"He's not going to cause trouble. He wanted to shake my hand, not out me to his future father-in-law."

Sadly, the last part of that statement drove a stake through my heart.

We both watched his neighbor across the street shovel the sidewalk.

"I'd be lying if I said I didn't want to explore more of our kiss. But I can clearly see you still have feelings for Maxwell. I would like to be friends, and I do want to help you," Dillon said. "Tell me what the guy stole from you. And who he is. And if it's Kelton Maxwell, I'll make his life hell."

My heart warmed at his big-brother-like gesture. It was too bad he couldn't help get my heart back from Kelton. "Do you help every girl you meet?"

"Not every girl. I can't help those who don't want help." His voice trailed off as he bent forward, digging his elbows into his jeans-clad thighs.

"Why do you, by the way? I mean, help girls off the streets?" In my mind, Dillon was a walking contradiction. On the one hand, he sold guns, although I hadn't seen any. Yet he wanted to help girls in distress. My intuition told me the name *Grace* inked on his arm had something to do with his answer.

"I'd rather not talk about it right now." He sat up.

"Okay, but why me? I'm not homeless."

"You know my cousin, and to be honest, I don't want to see you get swallowed up by the streets of Boston. Again, I'd like to help you."

It would be so easy to have Dillon and his crew threaten Terrance into giving me my money back. But this wasn't Dillon's fight, and while I could use the help, I didn't want him risking himself. He'd said he didn't want any trouble. I imagined if the cops came poking around they'd have several questions regarding Bee and Allie since they were runaways, even though they were of legal age. I couldn't jeopardize their lives either.

"I have to handle this on my own."

His focus was somewhere out in the yard or on the street. The branches of the oak tree scraped together.

"Is a gun necessary to take care of your problem?"

"Let's just say I'd feel safer if I had one. And to put you at ease, I'm not planning on using it to kill anyone. And before you ask, I know how to handle a gun safely." I'd learned everything I could about them after Gracie had accidentally shot Kelton's sister. At first, I hadn't wanted to go near one, not after seeing my sister so distraught. Anytime she saw cop shows or guns on TV or someone was talking about them, she'd go into a deeper depression for days. More importantly, I didn't want to be afraid of them.

"Then you'd be fine with a Taser? It would protect you long enough for you to get away without putting a bullet into someone."

The last thing I wanted to do was put a bullet into anyone, but as angry as I was with Terrance Malden, I couldn't be sure what I would or wouldn't do. Although if I did take Zach hostage, then a gun would be more threatening. But maybe a hostage situation was not the way to go. I didn't want to get arrested. I had to come up with a plan without getting myself thrown in jail. In the meantime, maybe it was for the best that I arm myself with a Taser. At least a Taser would incapacitate Terrance until I could tie him up and get him to talk. I shrugged. "I guess you're right. A Taser would be fine."

The house door opened, and some heat drifted out along with Josh. "Boss, phone call on the landline."

"I'll be right in," Dillon said as he pushed to his feet.

Josh left the door cracked as he vanished.

"I'd ask you to stay with us while you're in Boston, but I have a feeling your answer would be no. I'd like you to consider it though. Bee and Allie would love for you to stay too."

"I'll think about it." The thought of not sleeping at the hostel appealed to me, especially since I was spoiled from the comfortable bed I'd slept in the night before, and I could save some money. Although the downside would be Kelton. If he showed up again, I wasn't sure Dillon would be so accommodating.

"Good. Why don't we go in?" He held out his hand.

"I need to make a phone call first."

He reached the door. "Lizzie, if you ever need an ear, I'll listen." Then he went inside.

Tilting back my head so that it rested against the house, I closed my eyes and yawned. It wasn't even noon, and I could snuggle in bed and sleep for a week. But I couldn't relax. After another deep yawn, I pulled out Zach's card and my phone then dialed his number. It was time to set the wheels in motion.

CHAPTER 9

KELTON

I danced on the balls of my feet in the boxing ring in our garage. I cracked my neck, waiting for Kross. The entire family was home. We usually tried to get together on Sundays, especially when Lacey was down from college. My mom adored her and couldn't wait for Lacey and Kade to marry.

"Come on, Kross." I was itching to punch someone. Preferably Dillon Hart.

"Chill," he said as he hopped into the ring. "Dinner's not for another hour. What's bugging you anyway? You've been a dick since you walked in. What? You only get laid four times this week instead of seven?"

Zero. I even abstained from Trudy Davenport's advances again. "Are you going to talk or punch?" After I'd left Lizzie standing on Dillon's porch the morning before, I hadn't been able to concentrate. Hell, I hadn't been able to focus since I'd first seen her Friday night. I'd planned on drinking or getting laid. Neither had happened. Sleep was impossible. Food didn't smell good. Not when her jasmine scent was part of me. I wanted to taste her more than I wanted to scarf down my favorite meal of pizza and beer.

So, when Kross asked me to spar with him, I jumped at the chance —anything to relieve the tension that seized every muscle in my body.

We shuffled around each other as Kross smirked. That was never good. Kross had been boxing since he'd graduated high school and had been doing it professionally for the last year. One of his key moves was curling his lip on one side before he knocked out his opponent. He threw a left hook, hitting me square in the jaw, the pain blurring my vision for a second.

"Is that all you got?" I threw one of my own, connecting with his nose.

He didn't flinch. "Nice one. I see you've been practicing."

Yeah, with walls. I jabbed with my left.

Kross ducked. "How's that new place you're living in?" He came back with a right hook, knocking me into the ropes.

I opened my jaw then closed it before moving it from side to side. "It's big for just me and Zach."

The door to the garage creaked, and in strode a pissed-off Kade. Something told me he was about to unleash his anger on me. I couldn't imagine it was Kross, since he'd been out of town with his coach, scoping out future opponents.

He stalked closer, pounding his large feet against the cement floor. "You lied to me, Kel. Care to explain why?"

Kross glowered. "Since when do we lie to each other?"

Since Lizzie Reardon showed up at Rumors.

"Start talking." Kade settled against Lacey's Mustang with his arms crossed over his chest. "Or I'll get in that ring, and you'll be out for days."

Kade hated to be lied to. Which was ironic since Kade had lied to Lacey in the past. He had his reasons, and I certainly had mine.

Kross jumped out of the ring, took off his gloves, then wiped his face with a towel.

"Well?" Kade asked.

I cursed myself for lying as I followed Kross's lead. Once I got the sweat off me, I pulled on a T-shirt and sat on the edge of the ring. Kross joined Kade against the car. I swung my gaze between them, trying to think where to start. Both waited with equal expressions of you-better-start-talking-or-I'll-make-you-talk. I didn't have much to tell them. Kade was concerned, mostly about our mom. I couldn't blame him. The last thing I wanted was to bring up the past. My mom was home. She seemed happy, although she still had her moments. When it snowed, she got quiet. Since her time in the mental health facility, she'd come to associate snow with Karen and the angels. She'd always tell us boys that snow was an angel's blanket.

"Does this have anything to do with Chloe?" Kross asked.

"No," Kade barked. "Lizzie Reardon."

Kross gasped. "What the fuck? Lizzie, the girl Kelton sulked over for months after she moved away?" His jaw hung open.

"Yo, I'm right here." I gripped the base of the cushioned ring. "And I didn't sulk." I just lost my fucking heart and mind.

"Like hell you didn't," Kade said. "But that's not the problem. Is it now?" His face reddened.

No, the problem was me. I was still trying to get the image of me almost kissing her out of my head. I itched to taste her, kiss her, and run my hands through her long thick hair. But I wasn't ready to take the plunge. My heart wasn't ready. Although if I did those things, maybe I could get rid of the desire to feel her again. To feel what it would be like to kiss her one last time. I mean, to really kiss her.

You're an idiot. You know one kiss and you would drop to your knees and worship her.

I growled. My insides waged war with pain slicing through my gut. She was in Boston. So close, yet so far. I'd hoped she was in the city searching for me. But it was clear she didn't want me to recognize her. Even after our encounter on Dillon's porch she was pushing me away.

"Kel." Kade raised his voice. "Is it true? Is the girl really Lizzie Reardon?"

Kross hadn't closed his mouth.

I inhaled the sweaty air. "Yes. So fucking what?"

"Why did you lie, man?" Kade squinted as though the sun was blaring in his face.

Kross shook his head. "We're not going to castrate you yet."

"Come near my balls, and—"

"Enough." Kade scratched the back of his head. "Dillon Hart paid me a visit at the club last night. He doesn't want you anywhere near Lizzie. And how did you know where he lived?"

"I asked Hunt to find out." He worked at the Guardian, a company owned by Jeremy Pitt. They did all kinds of security checks when someone hired them as a bodyguard.

A muscle jumped in Kade's jaw. "I told Dillon you wouldn't be bothering him or Lizzie again. Right, Kel?"

"I'm sorry I lied." The pain in my gut eased slightly. "I didn't know for sure if she was Lizzie. The hall was dark, and she didn't exactly fess up. I had to see if my instincts were correct. I paid a visit to Dillon's house yesterday. Yeah, it's Lizzie Reardon. But don't worry. I won't ever bring her up in this house."

"And what about Dillon? I don't want to bail you out of jail or find that you're in a coma in some hospital."

Big brother was always trying to protect his family. I couldn't blame him. He'd been through enough when his high school nemesis had ambushed Kody and sent him to the hospital to get revenge against Kade.

"I don't mess around with other guys' girls." I wasn't completely sure if they were dating. However, they had been kissing when I interrupted them at the club. Regardless, I would hate if the tables were switched. Better yet, I'd kill any dude who came between a girl and me. At least I didn't have to worry about killing anyone since I didn't have a steady girl.

"You can't see her," Kross said. "We know how fucked up you were when she moved away. And Mom."

I stood. "You too? I was thirteen. Let's not forget how ornery you were when you had to leave your girl behind when we left the academy."

"Still, dude. My girl wasn't a reminder of what happened." Kross pushed off the Mustang. "If we have to see Mom return to the mental health facility, I'll—"

Kade caught his arm. "Easy."

Kross jerked out of Kade's hold. "I'm cool."

I snarled. "You think I'd do anything to hurt Mom?"

Kade rubbed his jaw. "It's your *dick* we're worried about."

I growled. "Bite me." I stormed out, passing Lacey.

"Kelton, I want to talk to you about Chloe," she said.

I waved my hand in the air. "Later." Like a lifetime later. With Lacey and Chloe as cousins, I was in the middle of a situation that was sure to blow up. More between Lacey and me. I adored my future sister-in-law, but I wasn't about to listen to her speech about why I should get back together with Chloe. I had bigger problems. I had to keep my distance from Lizzie. But I wasn't sure I could.

⚜

I SHOWERED QUICKLY, dressed, then opened my bedroom door to find Lacey with her knuckles raised, about to knock.

"I don't want to talk about Chloe. What's gone on between us is our business," I said nicely.

She splayed her fingers. "Five minutes. Then I'll leave you alone." She pushed past me and took a seat on my desk chair, sitting regally with one leg crossed over the other, hands in her lap. She'd taken after Chloe more and more. Actually, Chloe's mother was big on proper etiquette.

I leaned against the doorjamb. Might as well get this over with.

"Something is wrong with Chloe, and she won't tell me. And I don't think it has anything to do with the breakup, even though you know she's in love with you."

I was well aware of that fact. Suddenly, I wanted to bang my head against the wall until my brain shut down. "I've told you several times, I don't do love."

"Yeah, because you've seen how Kody still hurts over the loss of Mandy. Blah. Blah. Blah. You've got to open your heart someday."

Screaming, yelling, or even tearing out my hair wouldn't do any good. I wanted to tell Lacey to back off. But she was only looking out for her cousin. I got that. "You did warn Chloe about me when you first met your cousin. I've also been very clear with Chloe about my intentions. She deserves someone who is willing to give as much love as she gives in return. I'm just not that guy."

She popped out of the chair and glided over to me. "Will you ever be that guy?"

Maybe someday. "No."

"You will." She pointed a finger in my face. "And when you do find that special girl, you'll never be the same. Or maybe you'll be less of an ass."

I was never the same when Lizzie moved away. Hence one of the main reasons I couldn't or wouldn't fall in love. "But a lovable ass."

"Pfft."

"Lace?" Kade called. "Dinner is ready. Bring Kelton."

"Do you know what's wrong with Chloe or not?" she asked.

"I can't say I do." I tipped my head to the hall. "Go. I'll be out in a sec."

I wasn't exactly hungry. But my mom would be disappointed if I didn't make it to dinner. She'd also be worried if she thought I wasn't feeling good. I straightened, combed my hands through my wet hair, and wound my way down to the dining room.

Dad took the head of the table near the window. To his right was Mom, then Kody. To my dad's left were Kade, Lacey, and then Kross. They were passing around salad, rolls, and lasagna, filling their plates as they chatted.

I slid into the chair next to Kody, inhaling the spicy aroma of the lasagna.

"Lacey, when does baseball training start?" my dad asked as he poured dressing on his salad.

"Next week," Lacey said.

She was a big deal for Colby College. She'd perfected her fastball, curveball, and slider along with a change-up pitch she'd learned her freshman year on the team. The media whispered about her being scouted by one of the major-league organizations. One thing I admired about her was her dedication to the game. I didn't know if women would ever make it into the major leagues, but if any female could, it would be Lacey.

My dad beamed her way. He had a huge soft spot for her, as though she was his daughter. I wouldn't doubt he was thinking of Karen. My sister had wanted to play sports, mainly football. Mom reached out with her small hand and touched his unshaven jaw. He kissed her palm. They each seemed to know what the other was thinking.

"Kelton," Dad said. "Have you heard from Mr. Davenport about your summer job?"

Mom peeked around Kody. My heart warmed to see how proud she was of my intentions to become a lawyer. Sometimes I had to pinch myself that she was even home. My dad said her medication helped a great deal. I believed time was a better medicine. But if the past showed up at our door, all the healing could be gone in a second.

"Not yet. Probably tomorrow." Trudy had relayed that message to me when I'd seen her at Rumors. "If not, I'll call."

"You need that job for your résumé and law application to Harvard," Dad added.

"Martin," Mom said in a small voice. "He knows that already."

Dad had been asking me for the last two weeks about the application process. Normally he didn't ride any of us about what we had to do, but with only me in college, he seemed to be particularly interested in making sure I graduated and got into Harvard Law. He'd wanted all of us to get a degree, but Kody, Kross, and Kade had other interests, at least for now.

I took a bite of lasagna, the spices exploding on my tongue. After I finished chewing, I said, "I have the packet ready to submit this fall. The only thing missing is the summer job." I'd interned at a small law firm in Boston last summer. But my father and I figured a larger and more influential law firm, like Davenport, would seal my application.

"How's the club going?" Dad asked Kade.

"Busy," Kade said in between bites.

Lacey wiped her mouth. "Speaking of the club. I meant to ask you." She glanced at Kade. "I overheard some guy talking to you last night. Who's Lizzie Reardon?"

My mother dropped her fork, the sound booming louder than a detonated bomb against her plate. My dad all but choked. Kade froze with a dinner roll halfway to his mouth. Kross stopped chewing. Kody kicked me hard underneath the table.

Motherfucker.

My pulse went from fifty beats per minute to a thousand in Mach time. I tried to swallow the large chunk of cheese that was lodged in my throat, but it wouldn't move.

Lacey's face began to resemble my father's, whiter than the snow falling outside. Before I could move or say anything, my mom rose gracefully and left the room.

"Don't anyone move," Dad ordered in a lethal tone that I hadn't heard in years, before he chased after my mom. The last time he was this pissed was right after Kody and Kross had beaten Greg Sullivan, Kade's nemesis, into a coma.

"I'm sorry. Did I say something wrong?" Lacey set down her fork.

"You're still not sharing things with your girl?" I asked Kade through clenched teeth. Damn brother always seemed to keep things from Lacey. Which always got him into trouble.

"Until you walk in my shoes, shut the fuck up," Kade barked.

I hoped to never walk in his shoes. He worried constantly. He frequently got migraines. He was protective as hell. I swore he would develop an ulcer before he hit twenty-five.

Kody sat back in his chair. "Is Lizzie Reardon in Boston?" His voice hitched.

"Yes," I said. "You were practicing on your guitar when our brothers were about to cut off my nuts earlier."

"Would someone tell me what's going on?" Lacey demanded. She was worrying her bottom lip.

"Lizzie Reardon is the sister to the girl who shot Karen." Kross glared at me.

"And the girl who broke Kelton's heart at thirteen," Kody added.

"What!" Lacey slapped Kade on the arm. "Why didn't you tell me?" She covered her mouth with her hand. "Oh my God! Your mom? I should go apologize." Lacey started to stand.

Kade grabbed her wrist. "Let my father handle this." The color drained from his face.

Years of healing had probably just gone down the drain. But I prayed it hadn't. No sooner than we'd had a chance to process what was happening, my dad entered, scratching his chin, trying to hold in the anger that was evident by the hard look he nailed on all of us.

"Everyone out except Kelton. And Kade, please sit with your mother." His voice was taut. "She's in her bedroom."

They scrambled to their feet and left.

Silence filled every nook and cranny in the dining room as my old man began to pace across from me. I thought of many things to say but none that would ease the rage flowing through him. He had to calm down first before he would even listen.

"Is Mom okay?" I held my breath.

He heaved a loud sigh, sat down, put his face in his hands then ran them through his graying brown hair. As he lifted his head, his body slumped, and he blew out all the air in his lungs. "I don't know. But three years, and all could be lost with one question." His voice wobbled. "Now, tell me what the fuck is going on? Are you seeing Lizzie?"

"No, sir. I did, however, talk to her." No way was I lying to my old man.

"Do you plan on seeing her?" He stuck out his chin.

My father and I hardly talked about women, although he'd asked me recently if I was serious about Chloe. I told him I wasn't in love with her and she didn't do it for me. He'd said I would know when the right one came along. In the meantime, he counseled me to be honest with Chloe. I shared with him that I'd been upfront with her from the very beginning.

"Why does everyone think that I would fall for Lizzie again?"

"You're avoiding the question, son."

I chewed my lip. "It doesn't matter if I do or I don't. She has a boyfriend."

"Boyfriend or not. You two were inseparable as kids. I know how broken you were when she moved away. I would bet that you've thought about her many times over the years, and now that she's here in Boston, I'm sure you're curious. You probably have questions. And I'd suspect that your heart never really got over her."

Says the psychiatrist to his son. "I'm not going through the hurt and pain again. So don't worry about Lizzie showing up here."

"Don't live your life on the premise that all women will run from you. Remember it wasn't Lizzie's fault she moved away. Her father took another job."

I jerked my head back. "Are you saying you don't mind if I see her?"

"You're an adult. I'm not about to tell you who to date and who not to date. However, Lizzie's presence in our lives could be complicated, not only for your mother, but for all of us. Could you look at her and not be reminded of what happened to your sister?"

When I look at Lizzie, I only see her beauty. I only know when I lay eyes on her my stomach goes haywire. "It doesn't matter. I don't plan on getting serious with her or any woman."

My dad smiled, albeit sadly. "You will find that special woman one day. And when you do, you'll see the world in a whole new light." His voice trailed off as though he was thinking of my mom.

I was already beginning to see the world in a new light. One I wasn't sure I wanted to see. Ten seconds of silence ensued before I said, "Lizzie said her father contacted you to check on us. But he never heard from you. How come you didn't keep in contact with the Reardons?" Our family had had to heal, but so had the Reardons. Not to mention that the psychiatrist in my father would have wanted to know and help.

He twisted a cloth napkin at the corners. "Our life got busy with your mom and our move from Texas to Massachusetts. It was a tough time for all of us."

I interlaced my fingers and set my hands on the table. "Do you blame them for what happened?" Over the years, our family had been concentrating on taking care of Mom and trying to get on with our lives.

"Christ, no. If anything, I blame myself for not teaching Karen gun safety. Every day I kick myself for not allowing her to learn." He lowered his gaze. "I just wanted my little girl playing with dolls, not guns."

"And Mom?" I wasn't sure if he talked about that day with her, or if the topic was part of her therapy.

"I've tried to broach the subject. I've even suggested to her psychiatrist to try, but every time she either changes the subject or drops into a deep depression for days. I don't know how she'll react if she continues hearing Lizzie's name." He was knotting the napkin.

My dad was a strong individual. He was retired from the Special Forces, had fought in many military campaigns, and had led a team of soldiers. But when it came to Mom, the wall of strength he erected fell, and behind it was a man who worried about his family and the love of his life. Seeing him powerless and concerned only confirmed why I didn't want to do love.

"Dad?"

His head came up slowly, his warm gaze urging me to continue.

"I know you said Karen found the combination to the safe. I also know you try to protect us. But what if...?" I couldn't bring myself to even ask. Kade had said I needed to talk to someone. I locked my shaking hands underneath my legs. "What if... it was my fault?" I tensed.

He angled his head, his eyebrows bunching together. "What do you mean?"

My heart rammed against my ribs. I shuddered. "For the last seven years I've been trying to remember if I was the one who left the gun safe unlocked."

His gaze darted back and forth over me as he continued to play with the napkin that was turning into one big knot. "Is that what you think?"

I jumped out of the chair, my hands pulling my hair while my pulse pounded in my ears. "I don't know. Lizzie walked into the garage that day as I was putting away the ammo. I got distracted. You trusted us. I'm so sorry." I lowered my head, my eyes catching a glint off my butter knife. I was ready to use it on myself.

The longer we didn't speak, the quicker my heart sped up.

He cleared his throat, but his voice still broke when he spoke. "Look at me, Kelton."

I glanced at him. My pulse was erratic. Beads of sweat coated my forehead.

With soft eyes, he said, "You're right. I do protect you boys at all costs. But if you had left the safe open, I would've confronted you immediately. I always checked behind you boys. I did that day after you left the garage with Lizzie."

On shaky legs, I shuffled back to the wall, plastering myself against it. Then I covered my eyes with both my hands as I lost my shit. I hadn't cried that hard since the funeral. For seven years I'd been carrying around the thought that I might have been responsible for my sister's death, always afraid to broach the subject with anyone.

Hands were tugging at my wrists. "Son, I promise. You didn't leave the safe unlocked. I told you boys she'd found the combination in my office. You know she went to great lengths to get what she wanted."

That was true. We all did when we didn't get what we wanted. I dropped my arms. "I need air."

My father pulled me in for a tight hug. "Why didn't you tell me? All these years you kept this bottled up. Is this the reason you act weird around Karen's anniversary?"

I could only nod as he held me. Every year around the time of her death I became a recluse. I'd either lock myself in my room, disappear into the woods behind our house, or—once I was old enough to drive —head down to Cape Cod and sit on the beach.

"You need to talk about your feelings more," he said.

I gently pushed away, wiping my eyes. "I'm good." I was a fucking mess. Sure, I was relieved beyond belief that I hadn't left the safe unlocked, but my mom could relapse. I couldn't handle my family being broken again. And to put the cherry on top of my meltdown, I wanted a girl I couldn't have and one my heart couldn't handle. "I need to see Mom."

"Sure, but Kelton? Do me a favor? Try talking about what bothers you."

I'd rather punch walls or spar with Kross.

"I love you, son." Then he tapped my heart. "This should be reserved for the right woman," he said with conviction. "Now, see how your mom is doing. I'll be there in a minute."

I left with my head swimming in a sea of mixed emotions from worry over my mom, to relief that I hadn't left the safe open, to his words of wisdom. Right now the only woman in my heart was my mom. She was everything to this family, and if she relapsed, it would rip all of us to shreds, especially my father. I couldn't allow that to happen.

Slipping past the kitchen where Kross, Kody, and Lacey were whispering, I wound my way down through the house, not knowing what to say or how to rewind time and change the past—or even the past two days. I should've told Kade on Friday night. I should've told him yesterday. It wasn't Lacey's fault. This was on me. If I hadn't gone over to Dillon's, then he wouldn't have approached Kade.

My parents' bedroom was tucked away in its own wing. The door was cracked open. I poked my head in. Kade was sitting in one of the oversized chairs while my mom sat in a chaise longue. The seating area of the bedroom faced the French doors. It was pitch black outside, so it was hard to see anything.

"Hey," I said softly. "Can I come in?"

Mom turned her head, her black hair shining from the soft glow of the floor lamp next to her.

I padded in on the plush tan carpet and settled onto the edge of the chaise longue. Kade rose then kissed Mom on her forehead and left.

She reached out and grabbed my hand. "Do you ever think of Gracie and how she's doing?" she asked.

I placed my free hand over hers, soft and fragile. "I do." It was the truth. Of course, Lizzie had dominated my thoughts over the years, but I'd occasionally wondered about Gracie.

"You know it's supposed to snow again tonight. Maybe the angels will watch out for Gracie."

"I'm sure they will, Mom." I hoped they did.

"How is Elizabeth doing?" Sadness was stamped in her pretty blue eyes. "Have you seen her?" A lone tear escaped, trickling down her porcelain face.

I was officially going to hell. A son should never make his mother cry. "Briefly. I guess she's doing okay." I wasn't certain about that. The girl didn't want to see me or talk to me.

"I would like to see Gracie," she said. "Is the family in Boston?" She withdrew her hand from mine then snagged a tissue from the box on the side table.

My mind raced. My father had just mentioned Mom never wanted to talk about the Reardons. "I don't know." Lizzie was in town. But did that mean her family was too? "Let's talk with Dad first." This was a decision for my father to make, although if it helped for Mom to talk with Gracie, I was on board. Although that meant I would have to see Lizzie again, and that alone scared the fuck out of me.

I BOUNCED my knee as I sat in Mr. Davenport's office, waiting on him to finish reading my résumé. He was poised behind his desk, pen in hand, the sleeves of his crisp white shirt rolled three quarters of the way up his arm. Every now and then he traced a chunky finger over his bushy gray eyebrow.

I started to bounce my other knee as I fixated on Boston's cloudy skyline. My nerves had been doing a number on me since Sunday. I hadn't been able to think about much or focus, mainly because my old man had asked me to contact Lizzie. My mom had asked to see Gracie Reardon. My dad was elated. He'd been trying for years to bring up the Reardons with Mom. According to him, this was a huge step in the right direction for her, maybe for all of us. I wasn't so sure about me. The more I saw Lizzie, the more her presence would tug at my heart, pulling and reeling a little at a time as though she was wrestling with a king mackerel. I was afraid I'd flop in the boat and confess my undying love, only for her to disappear.

Mr. Davenport cleared his throat. "Why do you want to be a lawyer, Mr. Maxwell?" He sat back in his leather chair, pen still in hand.

I squeezed my kneecaps to steady them. "To defend the innocent." Ever since I'd begun watching the legal series *Perry Mason* with my mom, I'd wanted to be a lawyer.

He cocked an eyebrow. "And what if your client isn't innocent?"

"I don't plan on representing those who are not. If they're guilty, they can find another attorney. Here at your law firm, don't you choose who you represent?" The last sentence came out a little cockier than I wanted.

He harrumphed as he studied me over his reading glasses. "Sometimes clients lie."

I lifted a shoulder. "If they do, then I drop them. I believe in the law. It's there to protect people and to reprimand those who disobey it. Why would I want to defend someone who committed a murder? I'm not about making a name for myself like some attorneys who just want to be on television. I'm about protecting people, and since I don't want to be a cop, I can at least protect their rights." I didn't exactly need to get a job at this law firm. However, I did want to make my old man proud.

"I see you worked at Brady, Schlenk, and Schiel last summer, and you're now working as a model for an art class. Elaborate on the modeling job."

"It pays well." Mr. Brewer paid me a hundred dollars an hour to pose. He'd said I kept his classes full of students, which in turn was job security for him. "And it's only two hours a week, which gives me time to concentrate on school." My old man had said my modeling job might raise questions with Mr. Davenport.

"My daughter Trudy tells me you pose naked?" His dark eyes were appraising.

"With all due respect, Mr. Davenport, what does me posing naked have to do with a job in your law firm?" He probably didn't like his not-so-innocent daughter ogling naked men in a prestigious learning institution.

He sat forward, propping his elbows on the desk. "Mainly that I run a tight ship around here, and a clean one. I don't need naked pictures of the summer intern floating around the office. Neither myself nor Human Resources would be pleased when complaints started rolling in."

"I can assure you, I won't be passing them around." I didn't need the hassle—or women groping me. "And the pictures of me are taste-fully done paintings. Mr. Brewer is also very strict about his rules regarding no camera or cell phone use during class." Brew had caught one student snapping a picture with her cell phone, and he kicked her out, but not before he'd deleted the picture.

He fiddled with the expensive pen, the pressure building between us. "Have you ever been in trouble with the law? A police record?"

A background check had been part of the application process, and as I'd stated then, I said, "No, sir." Sure, I'd been in fights, but Kade had taken the blame. Or I'd gotten lucky. Like the time Kade, Hunt, and I had gotten into a brawl with Greg Sullivan and Aaron Seever. Thanks to Pitt's relationship with BPD, we hadn't been thrown in jail that night.

"Good. We don't hire anyone who's on the wrong side of the law."

He went on to explain what he expected out of me if I were selected. Thirty minutes later I left, undoing my tie. I'd answered the questions truthfully, and I'd been polite and professional. From there it was a waiting game. Three candidates sat in the reception area. One was whiter than the handkerchief poking out of his suit pocket. I did want the job, but at that moment, my mind was elsewhere. My future was important, but not as important as my family.

It was time to hunt down Lizzie, as my father had asked. I just had to restrain the feelings I had when I was around her.

CHAPTER 10
LIZZIE

I was surprised at how close the hostel was to Zach Malden's place. Apparently he was living in an affluent part of Boston known as Beacon Hill. I gaped at the richness of the neighborhood. Townhomes in Louisburg Square listed upward of eleven million dollars, and the area was one of the most expensive neighborhoods in the USA, according to the Internet.

I clenched my fists. If Zach Malden lived in one of those homes, his father had to be filthy rich. Hopefully my inheritance hadn't contributed to the purchase of an elegant piece of property. Snow crunched beneath my boots with every step I took down the brick sidewalk. Maybe I would get lucky and Terrance would be home. I let out a nervous laugh. I was ready to threaten him into giving me my money back. The Taser Dillon had given me was secured in the backpack I had draped over my shoulder. I'd never threatened or harmed another human in my life. But as the cliché said, desperate times called for desperate measures.

I checked Zach's business card. I was looking for number twelve. The number *fourteen* was tacked on the brick townhome on my right. The street was quiet for a Wednesday morning, the scenery reminding me of a postcard picture, with fluffy snow blanketing the park that split the street in half and old-fashioned streetlamps poking out every few feet.

As I approached my destination, I saw a girl sitting on the stairs bundled up in a parka and a light-blue, furry knitted hat. She was wiping tears away with her gloved hands when I stopped at the bottom of the stone steps.

"Chloe?" I rarely forgot a face.

Her eyes were red, mascara streaking down her cheeks. "Emma? Do you live around here?" She sniffled.

Seriously? Me, live around here? In a month I would have debt collectors on my butt, or at least a large-bellied landlord hunting me down. I wouldn't put it past the man to send out his search dogs. Dillon had said he didn't want the mafia on his ass. Well, I didn't want a raging Latino man on mine. His temper probably surpassed that of any mafia man.

I pressed a booted foot onto the bottom step, quickly glancing at the number *twelve* above the green door. "Did Kelton hurt you? I can kick his ass for you." I had once or twice when we were kids. I wouldn't mind tussling with him again, if only to touch him, to feel what it would be like to roll around on the ground with his hard body tangled with mine.

She smiled, but it never reached her brown eyes. "No."

Then it dawned on me: if Chloe was there, was Kelton? I had to think. I couldn't walk into Zach's house if Kelton was there. I wasn't sure if he would recognize me with the red wig on or not. *So what if he did? He already knows who you are.* That might be, but he would have questions, and if Kelton made a scene and I had to expose myself, I couldn't risk Zach seeing the real me. We'd met once years ago. I didn't know if he knew his father's friends. If he did, then he certainly would at least know the name Reardon. At the moment, he didn't know my full name. The other problem I had was that Kelton didn't know what I was up to. He definitely would try to stop me. Or if he and Zach were chummy, Kelton would more than likely protect his friend.

"So are you waiting on Kelton?" *Please say no.*

"Kelton and I aren't together anymore."

She was a sweet and beautiful girl. "I thought you two were getting married? You seemed happy at the art gala." Kelton hadn't, but she had.

She wiped her nose. "Are you kidding me?" Her voice rose. "There isn't a girl on this planet that could snag Kelton. He'll never settle down." She flicked another worried glance at the townhome.

My heart was doing a happy dance that they weren't an item. But in an instant, I squashed it. Single or not, I couldn't get involved with Kelton. "Does Kelton live here?"

The door to the townhome opened with a click, causing Chloe to jump to attention, blocking my view. I was reluctant to move to see who was coming out of the house.

"Chloe, why did you leave?" Zach asked in what sounded like a sleepy voice. "We need to talk more about—"

A mousy sound escaped me. She didn't waste any time finding another man. Then heat thawed my frozen cheeks. I liked Chloe and didn't know the whole story. Shame on me for judging her. Zach could be painting a portrait of her. Or they could be friends. But the tension between them was telling me differently.

"Zach, I have to go." Chloe moved to her right, exposing me.

Like an idiot, I waved as if I was the queen in a Fourth of July parade.

Zach's eyelids were droopy. He rubbed his hand over his bare chest then the curly hair matted to his head. He checked his watch.

"On the phone, you did say Wednesday at ten a.m. But I can come back."

Chloe stood on the stairs as if the cold had turned her into a statue. "I have class." She bolted like white lightning.

"Chloe!" Zach called as he stomped out in his bare feet. "Shit." Then he mumbled other words I couldn't make out.

Awkward was an understatement. I thought to say something snarky to him or even kick him in the balls for making her cry, but one, I had my own problems, and two, I couldn't piss him off.

"Seriously, I can come back." I didn't want to postpone my plan, but I needed his full attention. I had to befriend him before he would tell me the whereabouts of his father. Or maybe I had to revert to my other plan of kidnapping him. I wasn't ready for the latter. I had to find a place to hide him first. I could tie him up in my room at the hostel. No one would be the wiser. I hardly ever saw a cleaning lady, and the place was pretty loud most of the time. People would just think he was grunting from great sex. I held in a laugh.

"No, Brew wants me to help you." He waved his hand toward the open door. "Come on."

I trudged up the steps and into the warm foyer. My eyes bugged out. I was like one of those bobbleheads as I took in the palatial home.

A curved elegant staircase commanded the room, reminding me of a snippet out of *Cinderella*. Shiny wood floors ran throughout the first floor. A formal dining room sat to my right, a library to my left.

I twitched when the door closed. "Wow. Nice place." My voice was sweet as I envisioned beating his father until he gave me my money back. "Are your parents home?"

Zach came up beside me. "My mom lives in Chicago, and I haven't a clue where my father is, other than that he doesn't live here. Let me put a shirt on." He pointed to the library. "Have a seat in there. I'll be right back." He hesitated, apparently unsure of his next move. All of a sudden he took the stairs two at a time.

Calm down. Just get to know him. He'll cave. I wasn't so sure about that, at least not today. Zach's mind seemed preoccupied with Chloe.

I made my way into the library. Bookcases covered two walls from floor to ceiling, and a leather sectional sofa sat in front of a marble fireplace. On the opposite side of the room, a massive wooden desk stood proud in front of curved windows overlooking the park across the street. I set my backpack down on the floor near the sofa then perused the bookcases, checking out the rich leather-bound works of Poe, Thoreau, Shakespeare, and other greats in literature.

Zach's voice broke my attention. "Do you like reading?"

He'd donned a pair of jeans and a BU T-shirt and appeared to have splashed water on his head to tame the curls.

"Only when I have to for school." I'd rather use my free time to play paintball or work out at the gym. "Your parents sure have great taste in décor."

He strode over to the desk, his thick thighs eating up the space. "My parents don't own this place. A friend of my old man's is out of town for the winter. I'm just house-sitting it for him."

"Your father has some rich friends. Doesn't one of the Kennedys own a home on this street?" I'd read that on the Internet.

He snagged a sketchpad and a handful of colored pencils from the desk then plopped down on the sofa. "You're here so I can show you some technique, not to discuss my old man." The last three words were spoken with disgust. Maybe he would help me after all, since he didn't appear to be enamored with his father. Then again, family usually stood above all else.

"Sorry." I joined him on the couch. "I know how parents can get under your skin," I lied. Sure, my parents and I had argued, but I'd never spoken about them as though I hated them.

He spread out the pencils and opened the sketchpad on the wooden coffee table. "You don't know my father." He picked up a blue pencil.

Yes I do. Then a frightening thought occurred to me. If he didn't get along with his father, would Terrance pay the ransom for his son's safety? My plan was unraveling even before I had a chance to put the wheels in motion.

"He can't be that bad."

"Does *your* father gamble away your college fund?" The pencil in his hand split in two.

I choked. His father gambled. Which meant my money was gone. Alarms blared in my head. *Don't panic yet. You don't know that for sure.*

He patted me on the back. "Would you like some water?"

Tears stung my eyes as I swallowed and cleared my throat. "I need to go." I stood. "I'll tell Mr. Brewer it was my fault I had to reschedule." I could give two cents about my art teacher.

"Wait," Zach said.

I flew out of the library, into the foyer, and right into a hard chest. I craned my neck up and into my past. *Someone please, please kill me now.* I couldn't get away from Kelton. He shouldn't have been there. Sure, Zach and Kelton knew each other from art class, but I hadn't gotten the feeling they were friends.

His strong hands gripped my arms, but the heat of his palms did nothing to take away the cold inside me. "Whoa. Easy. Did Zach do something to hurt you, Emma?"

I shook my head, my nose brushing his rain-scented dress shirt. My gaze traveled up at a slow place, landing on his strong jawline. It sported a menacing shadow.

He dropped his hands, and I ran to the door.

"Emma," he called.

I turned the knob.

"Lizzie?"

I closed my eyes and almost lost all of the air in my lungs. Why was I surprised? It had only been a matter of time before Kelton connected Emma and me. I glanced at Kelton. He cocked an eyebrow. *Yeah, you figured me out.* And as much as I longed to stay and catch up on old times, I wasn't in any state of mind to answer questions. I flew out of the townhome as if I was the Flash. I kept running for four blocks before I stopped to catch my breath. Then tears poured out, turning into icicles along my cheeks. I wasn't one to give up, but I wasn't sure how many more hurdles I had to overcome to get back what was mine.

"Nothing is ever easy in life," my dad had once told me.

"Strength comes from within. You're strong," my mom had said. "Always fight for what is right and what is yours."

It was time to seek help. I went to grab my phone, and horror careened through me. My phone was in my backpack on Zach's floor.

CHAPTER 11
KELTON

I knew the moment I grabbed onto her. I was holding Lizzie. Very few women I've met over the years smelled of jasmine. Plus her hesitation gave her away when I called her Lizzie. Her red wig and green contacts were a decent disguise. Yet before I gave myself a high five, I wanted to see Lizzie, not Emma. I wanted her to come clean. I would've chased after her, but first I had to find out what the fuck was going on between her and Zach. Friend or no friend, I'd beat his head into the wall if he'd so much as laid hands on her.

I clenched my teeth as I walked into the library. Zach was just saying goodbye to someone on the phone. As soon as he hung up, I said, "What the hell, man? What did you do to the girl?" I stumbled over a backpack.

Zach relaxed against the couch as though he'd had a rough night. He was about to have a fucking rough day if he said he and Lizzie had tumbled in the sack.

"Hell if I know. We were talking about my loser of an old man and she lost it, choking like I said something that hit a nerve."

I snagged the backpack. "So you didn't screw her?" I fisted my free hand.

"Brew wanted me to help her since she started art class late. She's smoking hot, but no. You know I'm not into redheads."

Since Zach and I had been roommates at the BU dorms and now at this place, we knew each other's taste in women. Zach only dated blondes.

"Is this hers?" I held up the backpack.

"I think so." He kicked up his feet onto the coffee table. "Where have you been for three days?"

I set the pack at my feet then took off my suit jacket. I had an inkling Lizzie would return for it. "Family business, and I had that interview." I wasn't ready to tell him about Lizzie and her family and how we were connected. He had his own problems. His old man was a staunch gambler. The man frequented casinos and shady underground poker joints.

"Shit. And?" he asked.

"Won't know for a couple of weeks."

His phone chirped. He jumped up as if he'd just been caught jerking off. "I got to take this." He scurried out of the room.

I eased down onto the couch, staring at the canvas bag, debating if I should sift through it. I didn't have Lizzie's number. So I couldn't call her.

A Kenney Chesney song started playing from the bag, sounding muffled. Slipping my hand inside, I pulled out... a Taser? What the hell was Lizzie doing with a Taser? I didn't like what was unraveling. Lizzie running around Boston in a red wig carrying a Taser. The depressing song kept playing. I dipped my hand back in and found her phone. Dillon's name lit up the screen.

I probably shouldn't have answered it, but I wanted to screw with him. "Hello." With my free hand, I rummaged through the rest of the bag and found a wallet.

"Who the fuck is this?" Dillon's voice was full of grit. "Where's Lizzie?"

I didn't need any more confirmation than that. "What's your girl doing running around Boston in a red wig?" I opened the flap of the wallet. Staring back at me was a picture of Lizzie on her license.

"Maxwell? Is that you? If you so much as touched her—"

"What? Are you going to beat my head in?" I'd like to see the fucker try. I hadn't been in a good brawl since Aaron Seever and I had gone a few rounds in high school.

"Where is she? Is she okay?" He'd lost the attitude.

"I don't know. What's she doing with a Taser? Did you give it to her?" Something smelled rotten. My gut was telling me Lizzie was in trouble, although somewhere in my subconscious I'd known that since she hadn't wanted to show the real her, in an art class no less.

"Are you on my phone?" Lizzie asked, annoyance dripping from her tone.

I turned, not even having heard her walk in. "Trying to slink in unnoticed?"

"Is that her?" Dillon's irritated voice returned, blaring through the speaker. "Let me talk to her."

I hung up as he spewed swear words like a veteran sailor.

Lizzie ran over and started gathering her things. "Stay out of my personal stuff." She tried to get her voice deep and scary. All that came out was a high-pitched squeal. One that I used to pull out of her by taking Harry, my pet lizard, out of his aquarium whenever she was in my room.

Her hand reached for the Taser. I got it before she did. "Not so fast, Lizzie." I emphasized her name.

Her perfectly smooth skin pinched around her fake green eyes. "You think you're smart because you figured out who I am?"

"Baby doll, I am smart. I have a high IQ." I smirked.

She hiked the backpack onto her shoulder. "You're still a douche. Age hasn't changed you one bit."

Fuck, I hope not. "Why would I change? What you see is what you get. Unlike you. Who are you hiding from?"

She stuck out her hand, her hip, and her bottom lip. "Give me my Taser."

My gaze roamed over her slow and steady. High cheekbones, toned thighs that filled out her black jeans, ample breasts beneath a tight red sweater, and lips I salivated to bite, taste, and tease until she lost the attitude.

I pushed to my feet, tucking the Taser into the waist of my pants at my back. "You have to come and get it."

She rolled her eyes as she lost her pouty look. "Still playing games like you were six years old."

"Still pouting like a little girl who lost her Barbie doll." *Please pout some more.* I loved it when she stuck out her lips.

She growled instead. The woman actually growled, low, deep, and ball-squeezing as all get out. My dick twitched. *Do it again.* Or maybe not—I was a second away from being as hard as the marble fireplace.

"Seriously, if you don't give me back my property, I'll have to kick your tight ass."

I gave a half smirk, inching toward her. "You think my ass is tight? Have you been checking me out?"

"I don't waste my time on obnoxious guys, and you have one too many flaws." She held out her palm, shuffling backward. "Now hand me my Taser, and I'll be out of your life."

I pressed forward. I couldn't let her leave if she was in trouble. Yet the more she kept pushing me away, the more determined I was to understand why. I hadn't seen her in seven years. So I couldn't imagine what I'd ever done to make her hate me. I'd also promised my old man that I'd talk to Lizzie about Mom seeing Gracie.

She gave a quick glance over her shoulder, moving slowly around the couch.

"Flaws? There's not a flaw on my body. You should know that since you saw me with only a cowboy hat on in Brew's class."

She growled again.

Fuck me. I had a ton of control over my dick, but if she continued to growl, I was about to jack off without my hand.

"Conceited much?"

"Just pointing out a fact," I returned as we tangoed around the couch. "Let's make a deal." Let me kiss you. Nah, I couldn't. Not until she took off that wig and her contacts. I had to see the real her, feel her soft, dark hair flow through my fingers, and look into her blue-gray eyes.

She snarled. "I don't deal with the devil."

"Baby, I do. Tell me who you're hiding from, and I'll give you back the Taser."

Bumping into the table behind the couch, she stopped, seemingly thinking about my offer.

I settled in front of her, and we stared at each other. I thought back to Dillon's porch and how close I'd been to kissing her. I had a feeling if I even attempted to press my lips to hers, she'd haul off and punch me. She'd done that the first time I'd kissed her on the cheek in the seventh grade. That feistiness was one of the traits I loved about Lizzie. But we weren't in grade school anymore. My body hummed with the need to kiss her. My mind, on the other hand, was telling me to back off. One kiss, and I wouldn't stop. I'd be ruined. If she rejected me, I wouldn't be the same. My brothers were right. I'd be fucked up again. Apart from that, I couldn't kiss a woman who didn't want me to, and not one who had a boyfriend.

Her gaze roamed over my face, slow and sure.

I reached out and gently touched her fake hair. "You're prettier without this wig." My voice was hoarse.

The barrier between us dissolved as she exhaled. Then she lifted up on her toes, planted her hands on my chest, and brought her lips close to mine.

I let go of her hair as my heart flipped like an out-of-control gymnast doing back handsprings. Then she snaked her hands underneath my shirt to my back. The lust coursing through me receded when her hands crept lower to the Taser.

I sprang backward. "Nice move. I see you're still as cunning as ever."

She pursed her lips. "And I see you're not falling for my charm like you used to. Doesn't matter. I'll send Dillon over for his Taser. I'm out of here." Disappointment colored her tone as she marched out with her head held high.

I'd chased her like I had when we were kids, and she was mad at me. A warm feeling spread through my chest at the notion some things between us hadn't changed. Only now she was even more beautiful when she didn't get her way. "Lizzie?"

She stopped feet from the front door, not bothering to turn around.

"I really would like to help you. I know your boyfriend can, but I know important people in this city." I could ask Chloe's dad to help. He'd been instrumental in helping Lacey and her father when Lacey had been kidnapped, and he had connections within the BPD.

"I'm good." Her voice wavered.

All of a sudden, I felt like a schmuck. Okay, I was. I wasn't good at handling women who cried. I wasn't like Kade. He always had the right words to say or knew the right thing to do when Lacey cried or she was having one of her PTSD blackouts. I'd experienced her having one of them in high school when her house had been broken into. It had gutted me.

"You can have the Taser back." I removed it from my pants.

"I don't need it now. But thank you," she said sweetly, making her way to the door.

"Lizzie."

She spun around, a tear cascading down her cheek.

Daggers stabbed at my heart. When we were kids, I had beaten any boy who'd made her cry. "My mom would like to see Gracie."

Another tear trickled down. Then she ran out the door.

A slow burn of anger and frustration steamrollered through me as I ran after her. I was fuming at myself for being a dickwad, but I was also irritated that she hadn't answered me and angry she was always running away from me.

"Lizzie," I shouted as my feet hit the brick sidewalk. "I do want to help."

I stopped as she sprinted away. Well, if she didn't want my help, then maybe Dillon could shed some light on what the fuck was going on in Lizzie's life.

CHAPTER 12
LIZZIE

In the half-bath at Dillon's, I shoved my wig and contacts into my backpack then glanced in the mirror. Either the room was too small or I was developing a nasty case of claustrophobia as I tried to catch my breath. Mascara smudged the underside of my eyes. My nose could pass for Rudolph the red-nosed reindeer, and the whites around my blue-gray eyes were redder than a tomato. I was one hot mess. I'd been crying since Dillon had picked me up over an hour before. As soon as I'd gotten in the car he'd asked, "Did anyone physically hurt you?" When I'd said *no* he hadn't pried any further.

My mind skipped from one thing to the next and back, repeating like a broken record. My money was probably gone, Kelton's mom wanted to see Gracie, and I wanted Kelton to wrap his arms around me and tell me everything would be okay like he did when we were kids.

Anger, fear, sadness, despair, and pity all yanked at my heart, jabbed at my stomach, and caused my hands to tremble. "What are you afraid of?" I whispered into the mirror.

Everything. Life. Being alone. Love. Kelton. His family. Before I'd arrived in Boston my only fear had been not getting my money back. Now the list was growing at a rapid rate.

"Fear is good," my dad had said. "It gets the blood pumping. Rising above your deepest fears makes you a better person."

I wasn't so sure. "Stop feeling sorry for yourself, clear the blinders, go out and fight for what's yours." I laughed at my own words as a tear trickled down my cheek.

A knock sounded. "Lizzie, are you okay?" Dillon asked.

"Yeah. I'll be right out." I let the faucet run a second before I splashed cold water on my face. I ripped off two squares of toilet paper then cleared the black around my eyes. After I'd cleaned up, I fluffed my hair, pinched my cheeks for color, and met Dillon in the kitchen.

"Cool?" He poured tea into a mug that had *Best Friend* inscribed on the side.

I folded myself onto the bench with my back to the window. I didn't care to look out into the dreary day. He set the mug down along with a sugar bowl, his brown eyes assessing me. Then he sat opposite me, a few strands of his hair toppling forward.

"Thank you for picking me up." I didn't want to go back to the hostel. The place was depressing. I thought about calling Peyton, but I wasn't ready to involve her, and she couldn't help, not in the way I needed. The only thing she could do was console me. I didn't need any more pity. I'd been giving myself a good dose of it since I ran from Kelton. What would get me out of my funk was tough love, strength, and someone who had enough connections and muscle to help me. Kelton had both, but I couldn't bring myself to open up to him. I didn't know for sure if he was living with Zach, although him at Zach's place was a clear indication that they were at least friends.

"Is anyone here with you?" I scooped two sugars into my tea. I suspected the house was empty since if Allie and Bee were there they would have been bopping around, using me as a guinea pig for hair, nails, and makeup, which I didn't mind. I rather enjoyed all the attention. And Josh and Rafe, Dillon's sidekicks, would be lurking in the shadows.

"Just you and me. Everyone is working." He cracked his knuckles.

"And you don't work?" Maybe he made all his money selling guns.

He brought his fingers up to his lips. "Tell me what's going on. Is it Maxwell?"

"Not really." In part Kelton had something to do with why I was a walking disaster. "Are you still open to helping me?"

"I told you I would." He propped his elbows on the table. When he did, part of his Chinese symbol tat peeked out of from under the sleeve of his black T-shirt.

He followed my gaze to his arm then said, "It means hope." He lifted his sleeve, exposing the tat and the name *Grace*.

"Who's Grace?" I asked.

He closed his eyes briefly. "My sister." He pulled his sleeve down. "She disappeared when she was sixteen. I've been searching for her for the past two years."

"Did she run away?" I blew on the tea, a little freaked out that we both had sisters named Grace. I'd assumed the name would be of a former love interest.

"Supposedly. At least that's what my old man said." He tucked his hair behind his ear, his fingers dragging down the side of his neck. "I'd been working on a merchant ship and was gone months at a time. One day, when I got back, she was gone. She packed her things and took off. I imagine she was tired of his drinking." His jaw tightened.

I took a sip of tea. "And your mom?"

His Adam's apple bobbed. "Ran off with a loser when my sister was five. Cops have Grace's picture, but they don't exactly put all their efforts into searching for runaways."

"So you sweep the streets looking for her. Is that how you found Bee and Allie?"

"Something like that. It makes my blood boil to see young girls homeless or prostituting themselves. If I could help all of them I would."

To lose someone to the streets knowing she could be alive but couldn't be found had to be painful and frustrating. At least the chance existed that his sister was still out there. My heart hurt for him, and at the same time, I had a newfound respect for Dillon.

I deposited my mug on the table. "My sister's name was Grace too. Although we called her Gracie."

The doorbell rang.

"Hold that thought." Dillon's boots scuffed along the tiled floor then resonated in the hallway.

Tick tock. Tick tock. The sound from the clock above the stove was soothing.

Kelton's voice drifted in, and my nerves sparked to life. I couldn't get away from him. I shouldn't have been surprised. Actually, I'd thought he would've chased me down the street when I ran from the townhome. I was relieved he hadn't. I wanted to—no, needed to—get my thoughts together before I asked why his mom wanted to see

Gracie. I wasn't sure I was ready to confront the Maxwells. Part of me was still angry with Mr. Maxwell for not teaching Karen gun safety. Another part of me was afraid if I saw the family together I'd break down so hard I couldn't crawl back to life. Too many memories. Ones I didn't want to relive.

"I don't want any trouble. I'm here to talk to you," Kelton said. "And to return this."

The door clicked shut.

I threw my head back, holding in a frustrated groan.

Heavy footsteps padded closer before Kelton paraded into the kitchen. Gone was the stuffy business suit. In its place was a sexier Kelton wearing a baseball hat turned backward, a BU sweatshirt that clung to his upper body, ripped jeans that hung low enough on his hips to expose yellow boxer briefs, and untied army boots. My body temperature shot up the charts.

"You're like a cockroach that can't be killed," I said.

"A lovable cockroach. That bites." He went over to the small butcher-block island and leaned against it, crossing his legs at the ankles.

I snorted. A bite that would take me under his spell.

Dillon stalked over and handed me the Taser. "Keep this." Then he went to the refrigerator. "Drink?" he asked Kelton.

"No thanks." Kelton kept his gaze riveted on me. "Good to see you lost the wig."

Good to see he was still persistent as ever. I almost stuck out my tongue then thought better of it since my childish act would only fuel his fire. Which would spread, burning everyone in its wake. Dillon didn't need that. Instead, I placed the Taser in my backpack.

Dillon returned to his seat with a bottle of orange VitaminWater. "Are you okay with him here?" He stabbed his thumb at Kelton.

I was beginning to really like Dillon. He respected me and my privacy.

I shrugged. "That depends. He's here to talk to you, not me." I had a feeling Kelton was here to finish our conversation. "I can leave."

"I'm here to find out the truth, Lizzie." Kelton's voice hardened. "Whether you tell me or Dillon tells me. I'm not leaving until I get answers. Who are you running from?"

"Have you stopped to think for one second that I might be running from you?" I snarled.

Hurt washed over his face before he quickly banked it. "I get that part, but there's something bigger going on. Let's not forget, I haven't done anything to you. I haven't seen or heard from you in seven years." He gripped the island.

Yeah, you did. You loved me. My heart broke into a billion pieces when I moved and left you standing on the street, looking like your world had just crumbled. I've been carrying the burden of that image all these years.

"You did say before he got here that you wanted my help," Dillon said. "Unless he stole from you, which I don't think he did, let us help."

Traitor.

My gaze traveled from Kelton to Dillon then back to Kelton. I guessed it wouldn't be so bad for both to help. I might find Terrance faster. After all, Kelton had an inside advantage since he and Zach were friends.

"He isn't going to leave until he gets his way," I said in a snarky tone, glaring at the blue-eyed Adonis.

"Tell your girlfriend to can the attitude." One side of Kelton's lips turned up.

I chomped down on my tongue, when all I wanted to do was wipe the tantalizing smirk off his face. But if Kelton continued to think Dillon and I were a couple, then maybe he would leave me alone after this conversation.

Dillon capped his VitaminWater. "First, Maxwell, drag the barstool over here and sit down."

Kelton scowled but obeyed the direct order. It was funny to watch him stomp around much like he had when he didn't get his way with Mrs. Nappi in our sixth grade science class.

"Thank you. Second, I'm not going to referee." He turned his attention on me. "If you want him to stay, then no attitude, please. I get you two have history, but let's cut to the chase. I need to pick up Allie and Bee in thirty minutes. And, so we're clear, Maxwell"—his gaze lingered on me as though he was telling me he was sorry for what he was about to say—"Lizzie and I are not dating."

Well, darn. I didn't have Dillon to hide behind anymore. Maybe he thought the same as I did. If we kept pretending, Kelton would keep bugging him, and while Dillon seemed to have patience, everyone had a breaking point.

Some emotion washed over Kelton's face that I couldn't quite make out. Joy. Shock. Fear. Maybe all three.

"Now, before we were interrupted," Dillon said to me, "you were telling me about your sister, Gracie. Let's start there."

Kelton straightened on the stool. It sat at least two inches higher than the bench seating at the table.

Yeah, this was going to be harder than I'd expected. Explaining how my sister died to Dillon was one thing, easy maybe, but to Kelton? His presence alone caused a queasiness to grip my stomach. Kelton didn't even know my parents were dead.

I swallowed the frog in my throat. My current situation didn't have anything to do with my sister. Keeping my eyes on Dillon, I began with, "In the event both my parents died, my dad had set up an estate for me, detailing how their 401Ks, life insurance, and other assets would be handled. He wanted—"

"Wait. Are you saying your parents are dead?" Kelton asked in a staggered tone.

Trying to keep my voice from wobbling, I sucked in a sharp breath. "Boating accident."

He reached out to grab my wrist. I put my hands in my lap. If I was going to tell the story without shedding a tear, I couldn't have Kelton touching me. I'd start bawling then more than likely jump into his arms. Neither of those actions would help to get my money back.

Kelton mumbled something before he asked, "Gracie, too?"

Dillon's face was void of any emotion. So I concentrated on him.

"No. Gracie wasn't with them. Anyway, my dad had outlined specific instructions for the trustee of their estate. Make sure I go to college, and make sure I get a monthly stipend for living expenses while in college. About a month ago, the university contacted me to let me know my tuition payment was overdue. I contacted the trustee, but he never returned my calls. So I went to his place of employment. Gone. I went to his house. Empty. When I checked my bank account, I also found my monthly allowance had stopped. I knew he had a son who was at BU. So I came to Boston in hopes I could find the man who ran off with my money."

Kelton made an odd noise in the back of his throat. "Let me guess. Zach is the son."

Dillon darted his gaze to Kelton, as did I. He shrugged with an I'm-not-an-idiot look.

"Yeah. His father and mine were good friends." I took a swig of tea.

"How much are we talking about?" Kelton hunched forward, his elbows on his knees.

"A million," I said, low.

Kelton and Dillon gasped.

I continued. "Today, Zach informed me that his father is a gambler. He gambled away Zach's college fund." Fury burned within me, hot and bright, causing sweat to bead on my neck. "And now my entire inheritance is probably gone. I have to find him. I owe the university money and rent to a landlord." I could've paid my rent, but the money I'd had left I'd had to use sparingly until I could get this issue resolved. "Or else an angry Latino man will be hunting me down. Anyway, I went to the cops and filed a statement, but there are more deadly crimes for them to investigate. Plus, I can't prove it."

"So you know this dude?" Dillon asked Kelton.

"Zach's my roommate. His old man is a gambler. Mostly poker. High-stakes poker." He lifted his ball cap, combed his fingers through his messy black hair, then placed the hat back on his head.

"And you," Dillon said to me. "That's why you wanted a gun?"

"I planned to hold Terrance Malden at gunpoint until he gave me my money back. Or hold his son hostage." Saying all that out loud sounded more farfetched than it did in my head.

Kelton chuckled. "Terrance doesn't give a shit about Zach."

"Well, Sherlock, you got a plan? You said you had connections. You said you wanted to help." My tone came out way more caustic than I'd intended.

"It's hard to threaten a guy who doesn't have the money," Dillon said.

"Did your father set up one trust or two?" Kelton asked.

I looked at him cross-eyed. My parents and I had never spoken about trusts or wills. After Gracie died, we hadn't talked about death at all, let alone any legal stuff.

He straightened then began bouncing a knee. "You said at the beginning that your parents had 401Ks."

"Um. That's right." I checked on Dillon, who shrugged.

"Last summer, when I worked at a law firm, I learned that 401K accounts could be handled differently. The client has to request a separate trust. Otherwise, upon death, the money is paid out in a lump sum payment to the beneficiary. This client I worked with set up a separate trust for his 401Ks so that his children would be paid in installments when they reached a certain age. If your parents have a separate trust for their 401Ks, Terrance can't touch those. He could only touch the cash in your bank account." He explained all this like a proficient attorney.

Honestly, I couldn't say for sure if my parents had one trust or five. I did, however, know that my father's lawyer had given Terrance a binder of documents. Shortly after the funeral, Terrance and I had met with Mr. Pilkington. He'd gone through the details. The problem was I hadn't listened close enough to remember much, except that I was set financially. It wasn't until a week later when my head was a little clearer that I'd asked Terrance questions. He'd told me not to worry. He would handle college payments, depositing a monthly check into my bank account, and at twenty-one I'd have full access to all the funds in the estate. "You concentrate on graduating college. That's what your parents wanted most for you," he'd said.

"I talked to Mr. Pilkington after I talked to the cops," I said to Kelton. "He said he would contact Terrance, and then call me when he did. I haven't heard back yet." Then again, I'd tried him one last time before I left for Boston. His secretary had said he was extremely busy with a court case.

I wanted to scream at myself for not paying closer attention. At the same time, I wanted to plant kisses all over Kelton. Then I had to get my hands on that binder. Well, binder first then plant kisses on Kelton.

As if he knew what I'd been thinking, Kelton asked, "Do you have a copy of the legal documents?"

"No. Mr. Pilkington had one binder with all the instructions for the Trustee. He said if I needed anything I could always contact him. And since Terrance had been following through on his duties as far as I could tell, I didn't need to question things." I bit the inside of my mouth.

Kelton hopped off the barstool. "Then contact the attorney who drew up the documents. Have him send copies to you. I'll go through them. In the meantime, I'll find out from Zach where his old man is. Dillon, do you know any underground poker joints in Boston or the surrounding states, aside from the casinos? Sometimes the man is in the area without telling Zach. We ran into him once at a concert at a Connecticut casino when he was supposed to be in Florida."

"I can do some digging," Dillon said. "But what do you have in mind when you find him?"

I'd thought of many things to do to the man, but none of them were within the law.

"I haven't gotten that far," Kelton said. "I really would like to see the legal paperwork first. And I want to talk to Zach. He can contact his old man."

I made the time-out signal. "Wait. If you tell Zach everything I just told you, he might tell his father to stay in hiding. How do you know he'll help us?"

"I don't. But Zach has been trying to get his father to quit his gambling habit for years. And I don't think Zach is even aware his old man has been stealing from innocent people. Which begs the question. If your father and his were friends, does Zach know you? Is that why you were in disguise?"

"Zach and I met once, briefly, years ago. I doubt he would remember me. Still, I didn't want to take that chance."

Dillon glanced at his watch. "Whatever I can do to help. Right now I need to pick up Allie and Bee from work." He glanced at me. "Can I give you a ride back into Boston? Or you're welcome to stay here."

I rose, taking my cup of tea to the sink. "I should get back to the hostel and try to call the lawyer."

"What?" Kelton asked. "You're staying at a hostel?"

"Lizzie," Dillon said, opening the fridge door. "Please move out of the hostel and stay here. There's an extra room. Allie and Bee would love it."

"Or," Kelton said as he drew closer, "you can stay with me. You saw the mansion Zach and I are in. That place has five bedrooms."

I volleyed my gaze back and forth like a spectator at a riveting tennis match until my mouth fell open at Kelton's offer. Me stay with Kelton? Not a chance.

He gave me one of his toothy grins. My belly erupted with fluttering butterflies. Nope, not happening.

Dillon laughed. "Yeah, and you two would be fighting like caged animals. Besides, given that Maxwell lives with the enemy's son, not the brightest idea."

I agreed. Not only that, I was tired of the hostel. More importantly, I wouldn't trust myself with Kelton. I'd be the one to slink into his room at night, if only for him to hold me. Yeah, right. There'd be a lot more than holding.

"Dillon asked first, and he's right," I said. "It would be awkward to wake up to find Terrance in the house if he showed up to see Zach."

Kelton studied me with steely blue eyes. The family atmosphere between Dillon and the girls was something I hadn't had in quite some time, and I could use the quietness of my own bedroom to think.

"Good," Dillon said with a smile that warmed my heart. "Use my office in the basement to call the lawyer. I'll be back later." He shifted his gaze to Kelton. "You're welcome to hang." Then he grabbed a set of keys off the desk and slipped out through a doorway at the far end of the kitchen.

Once we were alone, silence hung heavy in the room as Kelton sized me up. Suddenly, my pulse was all over the place. Seven years of separation. Now, six feet. My gaze roamed over him—up then down and back up. When our eyes met—or more like collided—a beam of tingles shot straight to my toes. Need, want, hurt, and confusion were written all over his handsome face.

I cleared the emotion in my throat. "Cat got your tongue?"

He just stared, cocking his head slightly as though he had a thousand questions. No doubt he did. But if he wasn't going to talk, I had things to do. More like I had to regroup. The kitchen walls were closing in on me. At any moment, seven years of my life were about to combust, and I wasn't ready for the aftermath. Not yet, anyway. So I went in search of Dillon's office.

CHAPTER 13
KELTON

Lizzie walked away, her backside swaying, her long, dark hair almost touching the waist of her jeans. Once she was out of sight, I pushed all the air out of my lungs. I was a complete jackass for staring at her as if I wanted to strip her naked. Even if I did, I wasn't there to get Lizzie in bed. No fucking way. What scared me? She and Dillon weren't an item. That door was open. Fucking wide open. I didn't trust myself. I couldn't risk what would happen if I kissed her. Nor could I risk the rejection if she pushed me away. Yet every muscle in me wanted to taste her sweet lips. I also wanted to comfort her for the loss of her parents. I wanted to hold her in my arms and tell her everything would be okay. Like I did when we were kids. It was clear she didn't want pity. I got that. I hated that emotion myself. But my desire to hold her was far from pity. I wanted to protect her. Yeah, alone with her in this house spelled disaster on all levels.

Pulling out my keys, I jogged to my Jeep. The cold was a relief from the heat radiating off me. As I pounded the pavement, I sifted through her story—Zach's loser father, a million dollars, her parents, a hostel, her plan to hold Zach hostage. Holy hell. This was like something out of a movie, only not one with a happy ending. And I thought Lacey's Italian mob grandfather and Russian mob uncle were screwed up.

I growled. A headache was lurking. I was reminded of Kade when he ended up in the hospital from one of his migraines. Not that I was prone to migraines, but fuck. Dillon was right. Confronting Zach's father wouldn't work. He wouldn't fork over the money, especially if he didn't have it. Just like an alcoholic wouldn't give anyone his bottle of booze. Lizzie said she'd already gone to the cops. I wasn't surprised the law was slow to react, if at all. They probably had more urgent cases to solve. Then something dawned on me. She was enrolled in art class. Had she been at BU all this time? *Focus, numbnuts.*

I grasped the back of my neck when my phone buzzed. Leaning against my Jeep, I snagged it out of my jeans pocket. "What's up, bro?"

"Did you talk to Lizzie?" Kade asked. "Are she and her family up to visiting Mom?"

"Uh. I don't think it's a good idea." I didn't think it would be the best for my mom to hear that Lizzie's parents were dead.

"Kel, this isn't about you. This is about Mom. Visiting with Gracie and the Reardons could help close the door on the past."

Or it could blow it wide open in a bad way. I shrugged, thinking we could never close the door on the past. Death wasn't something one got over, not as deeply as it was implanted in my family.

"I know that." I gritted my teeth. "Lizzie has bigger problems at the moment. Her parents died in a boating accident, and the trustee of her parents' estate ran off with her money. And the kicker? The trustee is Zach's old man."

"What the fuck? And Gracie?"

"Not sure." I was still processing everything Lizzie had told Dillon and me. However, she'd said Gracie hadn't been with her parents. If that was the case, then where was she?

"Bro," Kade said, "I know I've been a dick about you not seeing Lizzie. I'm sorry. I panicked. Mom is... You get it. Anyway, what can we do to help?"

"I'm still thinking." Although running out on her wasn't helping. "I have to go. I'll call you later." I righted my ball cap as I trudged back into the house. I had to put aside my own fears. This wasn't about me, and as much as I loved my mother, Lizzie needed our help.

Dillon's house was quiet save for the heat kicking on. I found my way down into the musty basement. As my feet touched the cement floor, Lizzie's voice trickled out of a room directly ahead of me. Butterflies swarmed in my stomach at the way she giggled, bringing back memories of summer, the tree house, and her.

"I'm sorry I didn't tell you," she said. "Sure. It's a date."

I balled my hands into fists. *Cool your jets. She isn't yours.* Tell that to my heart. Walking into the room, I expected to see her sitting at a desk. She was relaxing on a chaise longue similar to the one my mom had in her bedroom, picking at something on the chair. I stopped, drinking in every inch of her. Her long legs were crossed at the ankle. Her boots were off, exposing rainbow-striped toe socks. When she wiggled her toes, I had the urge to rub her small feet and keep going all the way up to explore, massage, and have my way until she was putty in my hands. Man, I was screwed. I cleared my throat before my blood shot south. It wouldn't look good if I stood there like a moron with a fucking hard-on.

Her thick eyelashes swept upward. "I got to go."

The place wasn't exactly an office but more of a game room with a foosball table, a pinball machine, and a dartboard as well as a small home theater with a TV, the chaise longue, a beanbag chair, and a loveseat. The only piece of furniture that could be classified as office material was a glass table with a computer on it against the back wall. Overall, the room reminded me of our boathouse turned man cave at the lake.

I settled against the foosball table. "So you're not dating Dillon? Find another so soon?" *Dickwad. Those questions didn't help her.*

"What about you and Chloe? Why was she crying outside your apartment this morning?" Her tone was light with a sprinkle of sarcasm.

I cocked my head. "Come again? Chloe was crying? This morning? At my place?" Was she looking for me? Did Zach upset her? Or... No, they weren't dating. Zach and I had a friend code. We didn't date each other's exes.

She picked something off her leg. "Didn't you break up with her?"

"Yes." I was about to drill her for more information, but then I shoved Chloe to the back of my mind. I wasn't there to discuss my former girlfriend. I'd ask Zach about Chloe later. "Any luck with the lawyer?"

"He was in court. His secretary said she'd relay the message."

"How's Gracie?" I lost my attitude. "You said she wasn't with your parents. Is she in college?" Gracie would be nineteen now.

She brought her knees to her chest, wrapping her arms around her legs. Suddenly, tears cascaded down her cheeks.

Panic coursed through me. *Please, please don't say something happened to Gracie*. I pinched the bridge of my nose. She tucked her head down and began to cry.

Motherfucker. I ran to her, sat down, then reached out to pull her to me whether she wanted me to or not. Maybe I needed to hug her for my own sanity or my own dire need to feel her again. I gently grabbed her arms. "Come here," I said softly.

She adjusted herself against me without a fight, sobbing.

"Shhh. Everything will be okay. I'm here for you," I whispered as I rested my chin on her head, stroking her hair. Her in my arms felt so right, yet so wrong. At that moment, I was at peace with my demons. But as soon as she left my arms, I would be a complete fucking mess. It didn't matter. I had to help her, even if that meant putting my feelings on the line.

She hiccupped. "I'm sorry." She pressed her hands to my chest and pushed weakly.

I didn't move.

"I'm getting snot all over you."

I whipped off my jacket then pulled up the bottom of my T-shirt and wiped her tears. "You can blow your nose if you'd like."

She regarded me with a fragile smile. "How many girls have you offered your shirt to?"

"Only you." Honest answer. I couldn't handle girls who cried. But with Lizzie it was different, natural. Like she was part of me or had never left me.

She sucked in a breath then shivered before she accepted my offer.

"I can take it off," I said.

"Please, leave it on." Her voice was nasally and strangled. After she patted her eyes and wiped her nose, she adjusted her position, moving to sit cross-legged. "Thank you. I don't mean to dump my life on you."

"I told you I want to help. Do you want to talk about Gracie?"

She shuddered. "Gracie died when she was fourteen. Overdosed on pills."

Fuck. Fuck. Fuck. I had no words other than that. I wasn't sure I was breathing or if blood was even pumping through me.

She waved a hand in front of me.

I blinked.

"She couldn't handle life anymore. She was never the same after that day. We tried to get her help. But medication, therapy, love, nothing got through to her."

Shooting a friend had to be more traumatic than anything I could imagine. Death alone was traumatic. Finding a dead body was traumatic. My mom and Lacey both understood that more than anyone. But accidentally killing a friend and then watching her die had to supersede all else. I stood up, took off my ball cap, and tugged on my hair. Here I was worried about my own fucking feelings. This girl lost her entire family, and loser Malden had stolen her inheritance. I went over to the pinball machine, lost in a sea of what-the-hell. When I turned, she was standing in front of me with doe-like eyes and about to say something. Before she did, I let go of my ball cap and cupped her face in my hands, her soft skin heating my palms. I mapped my gaze from her lips to her eyes before fixating on the gold speck in her left eye. After a long moment, I lowered my head, a thread separating us.

Her long lashes fell, sweeping the tops of her cheeks. As if that was my cue, I brushed my lips across hers.

She whimpered. My stomach flip-flopped. She grasped my hips before she slipped the tips of her fingers inside the waist of my jeans, moving closer.

Sirens went off in my head. My blood boiled in a good way. I yearned to strip her naked. Not here. Not now. Not while she was vulnerable, and not when I was trying to protect myself from getting hurt. So I silently chanted *Patriots, football, Super Bowl*, anything to keep the madman in me from bursting free. But fuck if her hot touch and delicate fingers didn't send the fire straight to my groin.

My chest rose, meeting hers. "You're so damn beautiful. Just like the day I met you." I slowly pressed my lips to hers. Sparks ignited somewhere. Or maybe it was the throbbing in my ears.

She licked her lips. I groaned then nibbled on her bottom lip before easing my tongue inside her mouth. The world crystalized. Gone was the haze that had been clouding me for the last seven years. I buried my hands in her hair, exploring her mouth. She tasted like summer and bubblegum.

She slid her hands around to my back as she sucked on my tongue.

Patriots. Football. Super Bowl. Stop. Break it off now, my subconscious yelled. The problem was my body wasn't obeying. I wanted more of her, mind, body, and soul. Reluctantly I broke away, kissing along her jaw until I settled on her ear.

She pressed her hips into me.

My body hardened, every fucking inch of it. "I love your toe socks,"

I whispered as my hands—almost of their own accord—traveled down to grab her butt, firm yet soft.

She giggled.

A door shut above us followed by voices and *thud, thud, thud.*

She backed away faster than the Roadrunner. A cold breeze whipped through me, my adrenaline dissipating as the voices drew near. Lizzie fluffed her hair as she went in search of her boots. I fell back, gripping the pinball machine, trying to get my system to quiet, my stomach to stop spinning every which way.

Dillon graced us with his presence along with the two girls I'd seen that day on the porch. They bounced over to Lizzie, clearly excited to see her. The one with a ponytail threw herself at Lizzie. The other one, who had hair shorter than mine, waited her turn to hug the girl who had just made my body fire into fifth gear.

"Are you okay?" the short-haired girl asked.

Lizzie nodded, lacing up her boots.

"Dillon says you're going to stay with us awhile. For real this time," the ponytail girl cooed like a high schooler.

Dillon came up to us. "I see you didn't kill each other."

On the contrary, although I might die if I didn't kiss her again. I might die if I did. *Yep, downshift, dude. Take a step back. Regroup. Help her. Keep your damn hands to yourself.* A laugh roared in my head. Not after that kiss. A kiss that tasted familiar, felt like home. For fuck's sake, I was screwed.

"Did she get ahold of the lawyer?" Dillon asked, cutting short the flashes of images of my tongue in her mouth, my hands on her ass, hell, her fingers burning my skin.

I casually rested my hands in front of my groin as I nodded, afraid to speak, afraid my voice would come out strangled.

"You know finding that dude who stole her money probably won't get her money back. We could rough him up pretty good, though." Dillon watched the girls, who were sitting on the chaise chatting away.

I couldn't help but ogle Lizzie. She was smiling. "Those your sisters?" I knew he helped girls off the street, but the girl with the ponytail could pass for his sibling.

"Nope. The one to the left of Lizzie is Bee. The one with the short black hair is Allie. Both were on the streets, trying to survive."

"I admire you, man. I also commend you. None of my business, but why do you get girls off the street?"

"Everyone needs a chance. And no one should be living on the streets, especially young ladies." His voice dropped to almost a growl as if he were pissed about something. "So, lawyer, huh? You got any other lawyer ideas to help Lizzie?"

"Dude, I'm not even in law school yet. But I could talk to one." As soon as I'd said it, I silently berated myself. I should've thought about that in the first place. Jeremy Pitt, Chloe's old man, was a former lawyer. Better yet, I could speak to Mr. Davenport. After all, he was a practicing attorney. If I did, maybe then he wouldn't see me as a naked model but as a valued summer intern who wanted to learn. Which might help my chances of getting the job and, at the same time, help Lizzie with her problem. In the end, though, we still had to find Terrance. For no other reason than to throw the book at him. Although ramming my fists into him several times would certainly feel good.

"You know, man," Dillon said. "Whatever you do, don't hurt her."

"Where did that come from?" I asked. Dillon's attitude had changed from cordial to protective. While I liked his bravado for wanting to protect Lizzie's feelings, I couldn't help but remember them locking lips at Rumors.

"You're a player. And she's not some one-night stand. Or even someone to use as your play toy then throw out when you tire of her."

Lizzie and the girls were deep in conversation.

"Dude, I haven't forgotten that kiss between you two. So I could tell you the same thing." I ground my teeth together.

"Jealous, are you?" he asked, grinning. "Look, we need to work together to help her."

He was right. I threw aside my jealousy. I had a lawyer or two to call.

CHAPTER 14
LIZZIE

Dillon and I had just left Firefly, a restaurant and bar in a shady part of Boston. I had time to kill before art class, and he was meeting with a guy who knew the underground gambling scene in the city. I wasn't about to miss that meeting.

"So this guy, Tommy, will call you if he hears of a poker game?" Tommy had given me the willies the way he'd sized me up.

"He will if he wants me to forgive his debt." Dillon had sold him a gun, and Tommy still owed him for it.

I'd asked Tommy if he knew the name Terrance Malden. His response had been, "I know faces, not names." After I'd described Terrance as blond with hazel eyes and a big belly, Tommy had laughed. "You know how many men in this city fit that description?"

I yawned as Dillon braked at a stoplight. The last two days had been hectic. I'd moved out of the hostel and into Dillon's house. For some reason, I felt like I belonged there. Bee and Allie were so excited, as was Dillon. Even though he didn't express his feelings like the girls did, he did smile every time I entered a room. I didn't pry anymore into his business about his sister. The girls had mentioned he continually searched for her. I wanted to help him but wasn't sure how. Maybe when I got my life back in order I could do something for him. For sure, I would somehow repay him for all his help and hospitality.

"Any word from Pilkington?" Dillon asked.

"No. He's tied up in some big trial. I asked his secretary if she could send me the documents, but she had to get his approval." I'd have jumped on a plane to Florida, but my intuition told me I would have better luck staying close to Zach. And money was tight.

"What about Kelton? Has he talked to Zach?" Dillon gave his Camaro some gas.

"He said we'd talk when he saw me later." Kelton's other task was to contact an attorney he knew for some advice. Maybe that lawyer could help me with Mr. Pilkington. After all, a call from a lawyer might have more clout than one from me. "Can you drop me off at Rumors?"

His eyes wrinkled around the edges. "Isn't Kelton in school?"

"Yeah, but I'm not going there for Kelton. I need a job. I think the manager has an opening for a waitress." I'd called Peyton that morning to ask if her mom had any catering jobs on the horizon. Since she didn't, I'd remembered something Lacey had said when I was in line for the bathroom at Rumors. Kade had been going through résumés for a waitress.

"You know the manager is Kade Maxwell?" Dillon shifted his attention from the road to me. "And if I'm not mistaken, you don't want to get involved with the family."

"True, but I can't live at your place for free." My insides were twisted over seeing the Maxwells. But I wasn't worried so much about the brothers as I was about their parents. Anyway, since Kade knew me, maybe he would hire me. "You know, I recall that when we first met, you didn't want anything to do with the Maxwells because of the mob. What changed your mind?"

"Kade gave me the lowdown that the Maxwells are not involved with the mob or any of their business. And my gut tells me they're good people." After several more stoplights and turns, Dillon parked in the lot behind Rumors. "I'll go in with you."

"Afraid Kade and I might rumble?" I was having second thoughts as we walked up to the back door.

"You don't have to work," Dillon said. "Or are you here to confront your past?" The light breeze blew his shoulder-length hair over his eyes.

"Maybe I want to see what Kade thinks of me after all these years." I believed Kelton didn't blame Gracie or anyone in my family for what had happened. Deep down a small part of me wanted to see if Kade or any of the other Maxwells did.

Dillon pushed his hair out of his face. "Why do you care what Kade thinks?"

"Because I care about Kelton." And Kelton was all about family. If his family didn't welcome me, then a relationship between Kelton and me would never work. Oh my God. I was getting so far ahead of myself. I didn't even know if Kelton wanted a relationship. Boy, that one kiss— slow, wet, tentative, and amazing—had screwed me up. "You're right. Let's go. I don't know what I was thinking."

I was headed back to the Camaro when I heard the click of the door.

"Dillon, man. What are you doing here? Kelton bothering you again?" a deep male voice asked.

"Nah, Kade," Dillon replied.

I almost laughed that Dillon had told on Kelton. I should've thought about that angle. Yeah, that wouldn't have prevented Kelton from finding me or talking to me. I pivoted and met a sparkling pair of copper eyes.

"Lizzie?" Kade kept his gaze riveted on me. "Is that you?"

Damn. I feigned a smile as I sized up a tall and broad-chested Maxwell.

Kade's expression was soft. "I'm sorry to hear about the deaths in your family."

Dillon cleared his throat. "Lizzie and I—"

"I came here because I heard you had a job opening," I blurted out.

Kade rubbed a hand along his jaw. "Forgive me, but there are a ton of places in Boston to get a waitressing job. Why here?"

"It was a bad idea." I glanced at Dillon. "I'll walk to BU from here." I needed to be alone for a while.

"Please don't hurt him," Kade said, pain coating his words. "Kelton will never come back from it this time."

I knew Kade was watching out for his brother. I didn't blame him, but I couldn't help but dig my nails into my palms. "You're forgetting I was thirteen and I didn't have a choice. So don't blame me. And not that you care, but I bawled my eyes out when we moved. It took me a long time to get over Kelton." I wasn't anywhere near over Kelton.

Kade came closer to me. "I'm not blaming you. But I know you're not in town to stay. I'm asking you not to hurt him. As far as my opening, I don't think you working here is a good idea."

I let out a small laugh. "Protecting your brother's feelings now? You haven't changed." I started for the street. "Oh, and you should probably tell him not to hurt me."

Dillon said something to Kade, but I tuned them out as I picked up my pace. Seeing Kade hadn't resulted in the outcome I'd expected. But he did remind me that I needed to keep things between Kelton and me strictly platonic.

❧

THE WALK to BU allowed me to shed some of my anger and hurt before I saw Kelton. I didn't want him to know that Kade had irritated me, but only because I didn't want a brotherly fight. I'd seen a couple of those as kids. They had ended with bruises and blood.

I made it to the art building then found a restroom. I wanted to don my wig and contacts. Mr. Brewer knew me with red hair. I wanted to keep things simple. It was none of his business anyway. I thought about dropping the class since I'd found Zach, but I'd already paid the fee. Plus, a selfish part of me screamed *no. How else will you get to see Kelton practically naked?*

A girl ran in and directly into a stall. I combed through my wig, examined myself in the mirror one last time, then left. As I did, I bumped into Mr. Brewer. "So sorry."

"Hello, Emma," he said, steadying me before we headed toward his classroom. "Did Zach help you with any techniques?"

"He tried, but I wasn't feeling good." It wasn't that big of a lie. I had gotten queasy when Zach told me his father had gambled away his college fund.

"I see. Well, no running out of class early today. I expect to see what you're capable of before the end of class." He called to a student ahead of us as he hurried off.

I spied Kelton out of the corner of my eye not far beyond Mr. Brewer. A short brunette sashayed her wide hips as she came up to him and handed him a piece of paper. He glanced at it, folded it up, and stuck it into the pocket of his jeans.

Quietly berating myself, I stomped down the hall, merging with a crowd of people who were coming out of a classroom. The last time I'd acted like a jealous fool was in the seventh grade. Erika Ames would pass love notes to Kelton in social studies. After a week of five love notes scented with perfume and Kelton smelling them like he wanted to eat the words off the paper, I'd returned the notes to her with the words, *You're ugly, and I hate you* and Kelton's signature at the bottom. Then she cried every time she saw Kelton. I wanted to do something similar to the cute brunette, but I wasn't in grade school anymore, and I had no claim to Kelton. All the feelings of need, want, and desire for Kelton had to be sealed away in a place whose key I didn't have access to. *Keep things platonic.*

The girl laughed at something Kelton said. I tucked my chin to my chest and sped down the hall.

One foot past him, a strong hand gripped my bicep. "Lizzie?" Kelton asked. The deep timbre of his voice nestled into me, awakening the butterflies.

Swear words sat idly on the tip of my tongue. I peered up at him, hoping I didn't have a trace of jealousy on my face. The brunette glided off in a huff.

He pulled me closer to him, out of the way of traffic. A small space separated us. Filtered sunlight from the window above illuminated all that was Kelton Maxwell. Jeans covered his strong thighs. Bright green boxer briefs peeked through a rip on his left thigh. A red shirt stretched tightly over his broad chest, defining the outline of his biceps. To put the cherry on top of a delicious specimen, his face had a five o'clock shadow. There was no way in hell I would make it through art class.

He leaned into my ear, his hot breath sending a shiver all the way down to my toes. "See something you like?"

"Are you too cheap to buy jeans without holes in them?" I blurted out in a voice that was way too terse.

"You know I might be naked today. Can you handle that?" A devilish grin flashed across his face as he cocked his knee, planting his foot on the wall.

Those butterflies busted out of their cocoons. "So did you talk to Zach?"

"What's with the red wig?" he asked. "I already know who you are."

"I'd rather not have to explain myself to Mr. Brewer."

"Mmm." He scratched his chin. "I don't like you with red hair."

And I don't like you taking notes from girls.

The hall became crowded as more classes let out.

"Did you talk to Zach?" I asked again. *If not, I'll take matters into my own hands.*

"I haven't seen him." He sounded annoyed. "He left a note saying he'd be down at the Cape for the weekend. But I do have an appointment with an attorney later this afternoon."

"I'm going with." My tone was stern.

He tapped a finger on my nose. "You don't have to get bossy. I was going to ask you anyway."

His scent of rain made me dizzy for a second. "Will he charge for his time?" I didn't have money to hire an attorney.

"Consultation is free." He pushed off the wall. "Come on. We should get to class." His phone dinged. As he read the text, fun and cocky Kelton transformed into a man I didn't know, stone cold. The light in his eyes went out.

My guess? It was a message from Kade. I didn't have time to ponder that thought. When we entered the art room, all eyes went to Kelton. His indifferent demeanor changed immediately as he plastered on one of his thigh-squeezing smiles.

Heavy sighs chorused around the room, even from the guys in class. Kelton bowed his head like he had just given a superb performance on Broadway.

"Settle down, folks," Mr. Brewer said. "Mr. Maxwell, get changed."

I sat in the same spot I had the week before. Then I took out my sketchpad, praying that I could draw something. During the last class I'd had a problem with the placement of the eyes. Mr. Brewer had given me pointers on positioning the pupils, but I hadn't listened, not with Kelton an arm's reach from me in nothing but a freaking cowboy hat. My pulse began to beat like a drumroll. I blew out a breath, thinking of lawyers, my money, anything other than Kelton.

On stage, Mr. Brewer removed the screen Kelton had been changing behind. Sharp intakes of breath sounded in the room. Heat seared my cheeks. Handing in any artwork today would be impossible. The urge to run sat heavy within me. I squirmed in my seat.

Kelton winked.

Asshat.

I shook off my impure thoughts and set pencil to paper in an attempt to sketch Kelton as he rested against the back wall in nothing but bright-green boxer briefs. His left arm lay casually across his forehead while he pulled down his briefs on the right side, exposing his perfect *V*. The tightness of the fabric accentuated the shape of his manly parts. I licked my lips as I envisioned tracing the colorful lizard tattoo that made an alluring path south.

As I began my quest to bring Kelton to life on paper, I wasn't certain how I was going to walk into a lawyer's office with him that afternoon. The only thing on my mind would be Kelton's penis.

CHAPTER 15
KELTON

Leather furnishings, deep burgundy walls, and an oriental carpet gave the reception area of Davenport Law Offices a luxurious atmosphere. As Lizzie and I waited for Mr. Davenport, sharply dressed men and women breezed by in both directions. Some hurried with folders in their hands while others casually strolled and talked. I hadn't heard back from Mr. Davenport yet on my interview. I thought I might that day.

"Why are you nervous?" I glanced at her from the corner of my eye.

She chomped on a fingernail. "This place looks too rich for my bank account."

"You sure that's the reason?"

Lizzie had had a tomato-red face all the way through art class. Occasionally she'd wiped her brow as she'd sketched me. When she wasn't clearing the sheen of sweat from her face, she was writhing in her seat. Hell, I was trying not to do the same as I posed. I had to keep my gaze on the door as I usually did, repeating my mantra. *Patriots, football, Super Bowl.* Getting a hard-on was impossible to control, especially when I replayed our kiss in Dillon's basement. By the time Brew called time, I was the one sweating like a pig.

In the law office, she kept her focus on the wall across from us where a colorful abstract painting hung. Her delicate jaw was rock solid as she held a nail hostage between her lips. "Yes," she said in a muffled tone.

I leaned into her. "Maybe you're still thinking of me in art class."

Her knee began to bounce.

A man cleared his throat. I straightened, turning my attention to Mr. Davenport, whose tie sat loosely around his neck as though he'd just lost a big case.

"Mr. Maxwell, nice to see you again. Why don't we sit in the conference room right around the corner here?" He gestured to my left, the diamonds on his wedding band glimmering.

Lizzie hopped up. I trailed behind her, watching her swing her hips from side to side. I stifled a groan as we entered the richly designed conference room—oak and leather furnishings—and filed away any and all impure thoughts of Lizzie.

Mr. Davenport pulled out a chair from the massive table then eased into it. Lizzie and I chose two across from him.

After I made the introductions, I said, "Thank you for seeing us. As I mentioned on the phone, Lizzie has a problem with the trustee of her father's estate. We suspect he's taken off with her inheritance. We'd like to know what her legal options are."

She fiddled with the chain of her necklace between her forefinger and thumb. "I've contacted the attorney in Florida who set up my parents' estate, but he hasn't returned my calls. And I'm in Boston trying to find the man who stole my money."

"Do you know for certain he has?" Interest splashed over Mr. Davenport's face.

She sucked on her cheek. "He hasn't deposited my monthly allowance, and he didn't pay my college tuition at the beginning of the semester. When I went to his house, he'd apparently moved out. At least that's what his neighbor told me."

Mr. Davenport mulled something over. Then he said, "Mr. Maxwell, you want a job here this summer, correct?"

I nodded. "This isn't about me, though." I did want to prove that I wasn't just some naked model. But out of the five law firms I'd submitted my résumé to the year before, Davenport's law firm had name recognition and was known for helping clients who lived in other states. Which could help move things along more quickly for Lizzie.

"Tell you what. Prove to me that I should hire you. Research the estate laws in Florida. You can use the law library here. Once you have some answers, then we'll sit down and talk."

"What?" Lizzie's voice was high, grinding like nails on a chalkboard. "Kelton isn't a lawyer. You are. Time is critical here. Why can't you just give me advice?" Her body was rigid. "I need my money."

The law moved slowly, on lawyers' and judges' time. But I empathized with her frustration.

"Ms. Reardon, I wasn't finished." Mr. Davenport gentled his professional tone. "First, my advice today won't get you any closer to getting your money back today or even next week."

A muscle ticked in Lizzie's jaw as her breathing sped up.

"And while Mr. Maxwell is doing his research, I'll draft a letter to the attorney in Florida asking for a copy of the estate documents. I need to understand what's in those." He opened his hands in a dramatic fashion. "Unfortunately, it's not that easy to remove a trustee from an estate. We need facts. The good news is, as a beneficiary, you are entitled to know every detail about your parents' estate. You should also know if the trustee has been complying with his duties set forth in the legal documents. But again, the process will take time."

"So what you're saying is I won't get my money back." Her face reddened.

Mr. Davenport clasped his hands together on the table. "One way to get to the bottom of this matter is to find the man and ask him for the accounting documents on the estate."

Accounting or not, Terrance needed to be removed as the executor. I settled my hand on her thigh, hoping to ease her anxiety before she combusted. "Can we use the library this afternoon?" While my exercise in Florida law wasn't the silver bullet to Lizzie's problem, I wanted her to feel like I was doing something to help her. *I* wanted to feel like I was doing something to help her. I was confident Mr. Davenport was well versed in Florida estate law. He was right, though. We did need to find Terrance Malden.

"Sure." He stood. "I have a client meeting I have to run to. I'll have my secretary show you to the library. Ms. Reardon, please give my secretary all the information on your attorney. I'll get the letter out to him ASAP. And Mr. Maxwell, make an appointment with me for next Thursday. I should have the documents from Ms. Reardon's lawyer by then."

We made a bathroom stop, then Mr. Davenport's secretary, a short middle-aged lady, escorted Lizzie and me to the library.

"My name is Bonnie, and I'm just down the hall to your right if you need anything," she said, leaving us alone.

With a slow shake of her head, Lizzie took in the stacks of bookcases and law books on all but one wall. When I'd worked for Brady, Schlenk, and Schiel, I'd spent the majority of my time in their library, although it wasn't as big as this one.

"How do you find anything in this place?" she asked.

"If it's like the last one I worked in, the books should be organized by the type of law." I wound my way around eight small library tables.

A high-pitched whimper escaped her. "Do you think I'll ever get my money back?"

I combed my hands through my hair, my heart breaking at the sound of defeat in her voice. I had a clawing urge to find Terrance, tie him up, and beat the shit out of him. I just might do that if Zach didn't cooperate. He was our best shot to find Terrance quickly. "One way or another we'll get to the bottom of all this." My gut told me Terrance had probably gambled away all of her money. Unless her dad had a separate trust set up for the 401Ks. Even so, I wasn't certain Terrance hadn't discovered a way to steal that money, too. I scoured the shelves for anything related to estate law. As I did, I asked, "Are you doing anything on Sunday?" Hopefully taking her mind off the problem even for a minute would help reduce her stress level. "I'd like to invite you to Sunday dinner with my family." I'd explained Lizzie's predicament to my old man, including the passing of her family.

He'd taken the news like I had, swearing, pacing, and looking in shock for several minutes before he'd settled down. Then the psychiatrist in him had emerged. "I'll need to speak to your mother's doctor. We'll decide the best route to take regarding how we break the news to her."

I'd wondered why we should break the news at all. We were a family again. Our mom was home. She still had moments of depression, but they weren't severe like they had been, or bad enough for her to return to a mental health facility.

But my father had said, "Since your mom heard Lizzie's name, she continually asks when the Reardons will be here. I believe her wanting to see the Reardons is another step in the healing process. Although, as her husband, I'm just as afraid as you boys are of how she'll react to the Reardons' deaths."

Death—that word again. I'd lived with it for so long—Karen and then Kody's girlfriend. And in a way, Mom living in a mental health facility had felt like she'd died. In a way, she had. We lost her for years, and it was devastating and terrifying. All those emotions were heightened once again. The living, breathing, sexy woman so close to me, yet so freaking far, frightened the fuck out of me. I'd planned to walk away from Lizzie after I'd spoken to her on Dillon's porch. I'd had no plans to build a relationship with her. But for fuck's sake, every moment I spent with her was another moment I wanted to wrap my arms around her and kiss her until we died from lack of oxygen, got drunk off each other's touches, got dizzy off each other's scent. Was another moment I wanted to get so deep inside her I wouldn't want her to leave me for a moment.

I snapped back to the present when Lizzie came up to me.

"You want me to have dinner with your family?" She scratched her head, scrunching up her face.

I couldn't tell if her twisted expression was from my invitation or because her wig was bothering her. Either way, I wanted to burn that wig.

"You sound shocked." I spotted two shelves on estate law and scanned the books, removing one titled *The Florida Probate Guide*.

"I'm sorry, I can't accept the invitation." Her words were clipped.

"Why? It's just dinner. It's not like you've never met my family, and you've already broken the ice with Kade." I'd gotten a text just before art class from Kade filling me in on Lizzie's visit. It fried my ass that she hadn't told me.

She pinned me with a glare. "Are you forgetting the past?"

"My mom wants to see you."

She stuck her hands on her hips, puffing out her chest. "Why? So we can talk about how my sister shot Karen? Sorry, but I'm not up for that. I've been through more bad shit than I care to talk about. And I don't want anyone to take pity on me, especially your family. I saw the look in Kade's eyes."

I dumped the book on the table, the sound exploding around the room. "I get it, okay? I understand the pain of death. My mom may not have died that day, but she did try to end her life and as a result ended up living in a mental health facility for years. Which hasn't been a walk in the park. I also get you don't want pity. And if you haven't noticed, I haven't given you any." I clenched my teeth, itching like a fucker to either kiss her or spank her.

"You mean that kiss the other day wasn't out of pity?" The woman had the nerve to flaunt a smile.

Easy, dude. You're in a law office. One that you might be working at soon. Don't ruin your chances. I quickly checked the exit. Two windows framed the door, but no sign of anyone watching or passing by. "You think that kiss was because I felt sorry for you? Is that what you felt?" I kept my voice low.

She played with her earring.

"Nervous?" I couldn't help but taunt.

She began to walk away. "I need to use the ladies' room and speak to Bonnie."

"Are you running? Is that your MO these days?" I tucked my hands in my pockets when all I wanted to do was rip off that ugly wig and feel the silk strands of her long, dark hair.

"Asswipe," she spat.

"While you're in the ladies' room, take the wig and the contacts off, then throw them in the trash." If she didn't, I would before we left there.

She flipped me the bird as she sashayed her luscious body out of the room.

My chest tightened, and so did my dick. The woman knew how to irritate me and get me so fucking horny I was about to erupt. I grumbled as I sat down then began perusing the probate guide—nothing like a law text to get my dick to calm the fuck down. I jotted note after note on the role of the trustee, the beneficiary's rights and entitlements, and several reasons a trustee could be removed, including not handling the estate properly, death, stealing, and if the trustee no longer lived in Florida.

The door squeaked open. I kept reading and taking notes, not wanting to check if my guest was Lizzie, out of fear that she probably wasn't coming back. We were both trying hard to keep our emotions in check. The operative word was *trying.* I was failing miserably. One minute I was an asswipe, the next minute I was sweet. Then I was angry and irritated. I wanted Lizzie, then I didn't want Lizzie. I wanted to feel her again, but I didn't.

The word *motherfucker* repeated in my head like a song stuck on loop. I had to get my head on straight. I didn't know how to do that with her in my life again. Whether she got her money back or not, she would probably leave Boston at some point. I nodded to myself. I had to keep things between us professional, like a lawyer would.

"Who are you nodding to?" she asked.

Not looking up, I said, "You didn't run, huh?"

"Nah. You'd only chase me." Her tone was light, sexy, and playful.

Jerking up my head, my mouth fell open. She stood in front of me with her dark hair spilling over her breasts. Her baby-blue T-shirt accentuated her eyes, bringing out the blue over the gray. My throat was as dry as the Mohave Desert, and my dick perked up.

"Stop drooling. It's disgusting," she teased.

"You listened to me." That alone had my heart doing somersaults.

"No, the wig was itchy."

"Do you need me to scratch anything?" *I beg you to say yes.*

She threw me the finger again.

"Flip me off again, and I may lay you out on one of these tables." My balls were turning blue.

"I—"

Bonnie stuck her head in. "We're closing the offices. If you don't have everything you need, you can use the library before your appointment next week with Mr. Davenport."

I tore off my sheets of notes then returned the book to the shelf. I did want to do more research before speaking with Mr. Davenport, but I could use the Internet.

After we thanked Bonnie, we made our way to my Jeep. The sun was finally out after a week of gloomy days.

"Did you get everything you need?" Lizzie asked.

"On the legal end, almost. In the meantime, Zach will be back on Sunday night. I'll talk to him then. What were you doing with Dillon at Rumors?" Kade had only texted me that Lizzie had stopped by with Dillon. Then followed it up with another text asking me to call him. After we'd left art class, we'd come straight to Davenport's. With Lizzie in the Jeep, I hadn't had any privacy to talk to Kade. And most of our conversation from BU to Davenport's had stemmed around her questions about the legal system, most of which I couldn't answer.

"Dillon and I paid a visit to a guy he knows. He told Dillon he would call him if he hears about any high-stakes poker games," she said. "Afterward I went to see Kade. I thought he had an opening for a waitress."

"I'm confused. You can't accept my invitation to dinner with my family, but you can ask Kade for a job?" I mentally scratched my head. Not only that, the idea of her waiting on drunk men who would make advances on her dug a hole in the pit of my stomach.

"It was a bad idea. Can we not talk about your family?"

I halted in my tracks as my throat tightened. It hurt like a motherfucker that Lizzie was blowing me off. I shouldn't have kissed her. I shouldn't have gone anywhere near her. I should've bolted the minute Dillon called her name in the club. The pain in my chest, the one I was trying so fucking hard to avoid, was dull but present.

She threw up her hands, stomping back to me. "What's wrong? Mad because you're not getting your way?"

I tugged her toward a narrow side street away from pedestrian traffic. "It's not about getting my way. It's about why you're so terrified to have dinner with my family. And don't tell me pity." There were more layers to peel back to get to her main reason. The question was whether she would let me peel them.

She huffed and puffed then poked me in the chest. "I'm in Boston to get my inheritance back. I'm not here to make amends with my past. I never counted on finding you. I'm still in shock that you live with the son of the asshole who has been gambling away my money." She stuck her finger into my chest again. "I'm sorry about your mom. But I'm not the key to her happiness or her recovery." She glared up at me, water filling her pretty eyes. "Also, I'll confront Zach. This is my problem. I don't need your help." She marched away.

My whole body was ready to convulse at the sting of her words but also at the truth behind them. My family was thinking of Mom and only Mom. We weren't putting ourselves in Lizzie's shoes, thinking about how she would feel, even though she had told me a couple of times now.

Maybe I was using my mom as an excuse, afraid if I asked Lizzie to spend time with me she'd say no. If she did, the sting would feel like a scorpion instead of a bee. Maybe I should have listened to my old man and not lived my life thinking every woman would run from me.

If she rejected me, I'd be fucked up. But for seven years she'd dominated my thoughts and lived in my dreams. At this moment, I wasn't dreaming, not when I could feel a gust of wind slap me in the face. Not to mention that her curvy form was fading into the distance like she had in my dreams. I'd protected my heart for so long. Maybe it was time to let fate take control.

"Lizard!" I shouted.

She came to an abrupt halt.

I ran up to her. Tears poured down her rosy cheeks. *Schmuck* came to mind. I swallowed hard, forgetting what I'd wanted to say, forgetting that a city of people sped past us on the sidewalks and in the streets. Horns blew. Beeps erupted from a vehicle backing up. *Buzz, buzz, buzz* went the heartbeat of Boston's city streets. My heart beat in my ears just as loudly as the sounds around me.

She batted her eyelashes, tears hanging on the edge like I was. I was holding onto some imaginary cliff for dear fucking life, and I was about to fall into oblivion, not certain if she'd be there to catch me.

I searched her eyes for some sign she knew what I was thinking. Or maybe I was too afraid to speak. If I did, I'd scare her off. But when she blinked, the tears dropped, one by one. I went to wipe away her tears. She jerked back as though I was the scum of the earth. Fuck if that didn't cut like a hunting knife right across my wrists. Her hair whipped in the wind as she skimmed her watery gaze over me before she darted into a group of pedestrians.

"Lizard!" I called again, my voice dying on the last syllable.

She hesitated for a split second before she ran, hard and fast. I watched her weave in and around people. I wanted to chase her, but something told me she needed space and time. And I needed a shrink.

CHAPTER 16
LIZZIE

Dillon's Camaro was stuffy. Or maybe it was the fact that I was holding my breath as we got closer to Kelton's house. Dillon had agreed to drive me out to Ashford. For the past forty-eight hours, I'd been replaying both the strain of Kelton's voice when he'd called me Lizard and the desperate plea in his eyes. Like he wanted to say so much but didn't know how. As we stood on that busy street in Boston, the world spun around him, me, us, our childhood, our tragedies. At every blink, breath, and tear, all I could think about was the good times we'd had, the feelings we'd shared, and the dream of him and me forever. I didn't want to relive the past. Seeing Kelton was already taking a toll on me. Seeing his parents would only serve to open wider the wound that I'd closed to the past. Self-pity. Argh! The damn emotion was like a serrated knife, cutting through me every time I was reminded of the good times I'd had as a little girl when I was happy and had a family.

I toyed with the edges of my jacket then bit on my finger as houses, a farm, wooded lots, and a brook slipped by on the winding two-lane country road.

"I think you should turn the car around," I said.

At breakfast that morning, Dillon had counseled me that having dinner with Kelton's family might help to put the past behind me. Maybe so. Maybe I could say my piece and be on my way. After all, I hadn't come to Boston to pine for Kelton or cry myself to sleep. I'd already done that many times over the years. Maybe it was also time for me to face Mr. Maxwell and get rid of the anger I'd been harboring since the accident. Yet the closer we got to the Maxwell house, the closer I was to puking up my breakfast.

"Lizzie," Dillon said so softly I barely heard him above the hum of the tires. "I can turn around smoother than a race car driver, but for your sanity, you need to do this."

"I know," I replied as my pulse pushed against my wrists. I'd already called Kelton. He'd sounded excited. Part of me didn't want to disappoint him. Besides, I was strong. At least, my mom had always told me that when I was crying over Gracie or Kelton. God, I missed my mom so much. Maybe that was one of the reasons I didn't want to come. I'd always adored Mrs. Maxwell, and at times she would remind me of my mom when she'd told me how beautiful I was as a little girl.

"You think you'll have nails left by the time we get there?" Dillon's tone was playful.

"I'm not chewing. I'm nibbling."

He flaunted a smile. "So, I have good news. Tommy called this morning. There's a high-stakes poker game scheduled in mid-March. All the big players will be there."

"And Terrance?" I abandoned my fingers to play with my jacket again.

"Tommy is trying to get his hands on the list of names. All players have to ante up in order to get a seat."

Even though mid-March was three weeks away, I wanted to jump over and kiss him. Dillon was a super-nice guy. Any girl would be lucky to have him. Well, those girls who loved men who wore ponytails. Dillon had his hair tied back in one. "When will he know?"

"Not sure. Once I know, you'll know. Right now, can I give you some advice about this dinner?"

"Sure." He'd been giving me advice all day. I was grateful. Since I'd met him he'd been nothing but sweet, helpful, and protective. But I kept thinking about the poker game, not the dinner. If Terrance was on the list, then I had to be there, especially if Zach wasn't any help before then.

"They invited you. Hear what they have to say. And don't tear Kelton's head off. I'm not a love guru, but the man clearly still has feelings for you, even though he's in denial."

His last statement erased any thoughts of the poker game. "Did you and Kelton talk about it?" I wasn't sure I agreed, although he had put some emotion behind his kiss, and his voice had held an enormous amount of tenderness when he'd shouted out *Lizard.* Part of me thought Kelton was trying to confirm for himself if he still had feelings for me.

"Hell no. The way you two argue, it's clear you both still have feelings for each other. Why don't you just admit it?"

"With our pasts, we could never build a relationship."

"Today's your chance to clear the past so you can see the future. But something tells me you're afraid of more than your past."

I watched the homes zip by. "People I love die." Saying it out loud sounded like a pity party.

He pried my hand from my jacket and squeezed. "That's what you're afraid of? Christ, Lizzie. You can't live with that way of thinking. Do you think you can kill a tough dude like Kelton Maxwell? You even said yourself he's a cockroach that can't be killed."

I snorted. Then he laughed as he wheeled into a long driveway. A two-story brick mansion sat on what had to be ten acres of land. Not that I'd lived in a dump in Florida. My parents had had a modest home in a gated community. But this place was serene, breathtaking, really, with the lake in the background and the sun setting slowly behind the treetops. Or maybe it was the snow covering the landscape that made the property look like it had jumped off the pages of *Better Homes and Gardens*, the Christmas Edition.

Just as Dillon braked, Kelton came out and jogged toward us. When he reached my door, he opened it. "You came," he said. His voice was equal parts nerves and relief.

"Yeah." I drew out the word, hoping I was doing the right thing.

Kelton squatted down, peering around me at Dillon. "Dude, do you want to stay for dinner?"

Dillon and I exchanged a questioning glance. Or at least he did. I made my eyes bug out, prodding him to say yes.

Dillon laughed. "Why not?"

A lightheaded feeling washed over me. I didn't have to face the Maxwells alone.

"Park in the back," Kelton said, taking my hand.

I guessed I was getting out of the car. When I had two feet planted on the driveway, Kelton and I trailed Dillon on foot.

"So, were you waiting like a puppy on the top of the couch with your tail wagging?" I asked.

"Dogs get rewards like petting and stroking when their masters come home," he teased. "Do you want to pet me? I'll roll over for you."

Yes, please. I slapped him on the arm. "Put your tail between your legs."

"I'm glad you're here." He draped an arm around my shoulder.

Goosebumps spread over my body, which helped to dial back my nerve-o-meter from ten to eight.

By the time we'd walked down to the six-car garage, Dillon was leaning against his Camaro. I couldn't help but grin at how he'd removed his ponytail and combed back his hair, making himself presentable. It wasn't that he wasn't before. Ponytail or not, he was handsome, even though his nose piercing and shoulder-length hair didn't exactly match his lumberjack style of a plaid flannel shirt, T-shirt, and jeans.

Kelton ushered us up the stairs of the wooden deck, which led to a sliding glass door. When he opened it, heat and a spicy aroma filtered out.

I hesitated.

"We don't bite," he said. "And you have Dillon and me to make sure you don't get swallowed up by my brothers." He winked.

I wasn't worried about his brothers. His father was the one that drove my nausea. I'd planned what I would say to him. However, at the eleventh hour, all those words I'd had in my brain—gone. Before I could back away or take a step forward, Kade sauntered up with a warm smile that had me walking into the bright and shiny gourmet kitchen.

"Lizzie, I'm sorry if we got off on the wrong foot the other day."

Before I could say a word, two Kelton lookalikes ambled in. One had massive arms filling out his plain black T-shirt. The other was also built but was smaller in the chest than both of the other triplets. Since I hadn't seen them since Texas, I couldn't tell which was Kross and which was Kody. At least with Kelton the scar on his chin gave him away.

Kelton came up behind me. "Kross is the boxer, hence the arms. Kody is the singer, songwriter, and amazing guitarist."

Kody's face lit up with a handsome smile.

"Glad you're staying for dinner," Kade said to Dillon. "Welcome."

After the introductions and a hug from Kody, a young woman I remembered from the gala came in.

"You must be Lizzie," she said. "I'm Lacey." She threw her arms around me. "Glad you could make it."

As soon as she let go, I needed some air. I felt like a celebrity in the middle of the paparazzi.

"Okay, everyone. Stop suffocating her," Kelton said. "She's not a new toy."

I could be for Kelton.

"Kel, Mom and Dad would like to see you and Lizzie before dinner," Kade said in an even tone.

My nerve-o-meter shot to ten. I guessed we should get it over with. Maybe then my stomach would settle enough so I could eat. Dillon blinked slowly as if to say *you got this*.

"Come on, Dillon. We can hang in the theater room in the basement," Kade said, sounding like the commander of an army.

All the guys left except for Kelton. Lacey hung back for a second, angling her dark head as she swung her wide green gaze between Kelton and me. Then I remembered what Peyton had said. Lacey and Chloe were cousins.

"We're not dating." I didn't know why I even said that. I didn't care what Lacey or Chloe thought of me. I did like Chloe though. Which led me to my next thought. Was Chloe okay? I hadn't seen her since I'd found her crying on Zach's porch.

"Mmm," Lacey said. "I'll see you guys at dinner." She whisked out of the kitchen like she had a newfound secret.

"What just happened?" I asked. "Are you in trouble with Chloe? Lacey and Chloe are cousins, right?"

"Let's go see my parents. My mom has been dying to see you." Kelton placed his hand on my lower back. "And, again, I'm not dating Chloe." His fingers pressed through my jacket.

That might be true, but that girl in the hall before art class had given him a note. I tore my jealousy to shreds. It wasn't the time to fret over a girl or note or Kelton Maxwell. We exited the kitchen into a wide hallway that fingered out in three directions. We headed straight toward a seven-foot wooden door with slim glass panes framing the sides. Dusk crawled across the sky in the distance while a soft glow spilled from the room to our left that Kelton was about to enter.

I shuffled behind him, fingering my earring. A bay window, tall ceilings, fabric furniture, a fireplace, and thick carpeting created a rich but cozy atmosphere, especially with the fire flickering from the stone fireplace on the back wall.

Mr. Maxwell rose from the loveseat like an aristocrat, confident and stoic. Mrs. Maxwell sat like a queen, her tiny hands on her lap, her long black hair flowing effortlessly around her, her porcelain skin barely made up, her red lips turned upward. Her blue gaze swung from her son to me. They were both older but still exactly as I remembered.

My heart rammed like a bulldozer plowing through rubble. Memories swept me from the room and back into the past.

"Elizabeth, stop chasing Kelton," Mrs. Maxwell had shouted from her spot by the pool with a laugh in her voice. "He'll wear you out."

Kelton and I had been throwing a football around. When he caught it I would chase him to the back side of his yard, what we had dubbed the end zone. He did run faster than me. It was always fun, though, to chase Kelton. Once one of us caught the other, we would roll around in the grass like two dogs play-fighting.

"Elizabeth." A hand touched my shoulder.

The sunny day faded back into the soft glow of the room. Mr. Maxwell stood before me, reminding me so much of Kade. Despite the age difference, the resemblance was uncanny.

"May I take your coat?" he asked.

I swallowed again as I took off my jacket and handed it to him.

"Please have a seat." He left the room for a mere second, returning empty-handed.

"Elizabeth." Mrs. Maxwell patted the cushion on her left. "Please sit with me."

I glanced at Kelton, who was mesmerized by my breasts or something on my blouse. Surely he wasn't pulling one of his playboy stunts in the company of his parents. I brought my hand to my chest, praying my scoop neck blouse wasn't betraying me, showing my cleavage. Then I realized my half-heart chain wasn't tucked away. I wore it on a long necklace so it wouldn't be visible no matter what I was wearing. Not that I was embarrassed by it. Over the years my friends had teased me for the cheesy charm. I'd always argued it wasn't tacky, not to me. This piece of jewelry had been my rosary. I wasn't Catholic, but my grandmother on my dad's side was. God rest her soul. She'd carried her rosary beads with her at all times.

I inserted my necklace inside my blouse as I went to sit beside Mrs.

Maxwell. Kelton had mentioned his mom had been in a mental health facility. I'd been expecting to see her distraught, not happy. It was stupid of me to stereotype.

Kelton and his dad made themselves comfortable on the sofa across from us.

"Thank you for inviting me," I said.

"It's so good to see you." Mrs. Maxwell's voice was angelic. "You're just as beautiful as ever. More now that you're a young woman."

Kelton beamed with pride, as he always had when his mom complimented me. I was flattered but was reminded of my mom. I hadn't come there to reminisce but to say my piece and, hopefully, move on.

An awkward silence grew as all eyes were on me. I wanted to say thank you. I wanted to slide closer to her. I wanted to feel what it was like to have a woman who I'd considered a second mom at one time in my life put her arms around me, hold me, and tell me everything would be okay. Instead I fidgeted, pushing my back against the armrest, my tongue stuck in place.

"Martin told me about the death of your parents and Gracie. I'm so, so sorry." Mrs. Maxwell studied me like I was on display at the Miami Aquarium. Then tears pooled in her eyes. "My heart hurts for you." Before I had a chance to flee, she embraced me, stroking my hair. "Can we do anything for you? Do you need a place to stay? We have plenty of room here."

I stiffened, not sure what to do. My mind said to let go of the twisted feelings tearing me up inside. My body had different plans. I darted my gaze to Kelton, pinching my eyebrows together so hard it hurt. His eyebrows were deep into his hairline. Of all the thoughts that had run through my head about how my conversation would go, her hospitality had never been on my list. Sure, I'd envisioned her compassion for my plight, but not a warm bed or a place to call home.

She sat back.

I managed to get my tongue working. "Thank you, but I do have a place to stay."

The fire crackled, spitting up little sparks. Or maybe it was my pulse jumping. I started to play with my earring as tears threatened.

A delicate hand covered mine. "It's okay. Say what's on your mind. I'm not going to get upset." She stole a reassuring look at her husband, who watched with a careful eye, seemingly ready to put out any fires. "I've thought long and hard about you and your family, especially

Gracie, over the years. Honestly, I couldn't bring myself to say Gracie's name without pain searing my heart. It wasn't her fault, Elizabeth. What happened was never her fault." Her head moved back and forth ever so slightly.

Kelton dropped his forearms to his knees, burying his face in his hands. Mr. Maxwell continued to watch Mrs. Maxwell and me.

"Yeah, I know. But Gracie didn't know that. She blamed herself." Tears stung. Damn it. I had to be strong. I gave myself a mental shake then focused on Mr. Maxwell. "Why? Why didn't you teach Karen gun safety?"

Kelton jerked up, caution blanching his face.

Mr. Maxwell scratched the back of his head. "I've been asking myself that question for the last seven years." He gazed at the fire then back to me. "I wish I could change the past. Unfortunately I can't. I take full responsibility for what happened that day." Pain and suffering washed over his features and doused his tone. He stood and padded over to the fireplace. "I'm sorry, Elizabeth. For that day. For Gracie. For your parents." His voice shook.

A tear ran down my cheek. I wished I could change the past too.

Mrs. Maxwell rose gracefully. "It's okay, Martin." She reached up with dainty fingers to touch his unshaven jaw.

He angled his chin down from his six-foot height, gazing at her like she was his everything. No doubt she was. Then he wrapped his arms around her. "I love you." He said those three words as though he hadn't said them in years.

More tears poured out as I witnessed so much love between them. I was envious. I hated that I couldn't see my parents embracing each other ever again. I wanted what Mr. and Mrs. Maxwell had—love, a family, someone who would love me back.

In a flash, Kelton was on his feet, skirting the glass coffee table before taking his mom's spot. Then he wiped a tear from my cheek with the tips of his fingers.

I glanced up into cloudy blue eyes. We didn't need to speak. We both hurt. His parents hurt. I didn't want to feel the pain of death anymore. I just didn't know how to make the suffering stop.

"Can I have a minute alone with Elizabeth?" Mr. Maxwell asked.

"I should get the table set," Mrs. Maxwell said. "Kelton, can you help me?"

"I won't be far." He kissed my head before following his mom.

The fire danced, the shadows playing across Mr. Maxwell's drawn features.

"Thank you for saying all that," I whispered. "I've been so angry with you."

He scraped a hand along his chin as he came to sit down next to me. "There are so many things I replay in my head about Karen. She always wanted to be like the boys. I know you won't understand this until you have children, but she was my little princess. I couldn't bring myself to see her with a gun. I know it doesn't make up for anyone's loss." He grasped my hands. "We want to help you in any way we can. Mrs. Maxwell and I always adored you and Gracie. We considered you family. We still do." Immense pain weaved through his tone.

I lowered my gaze to our joined hands, my anger slowly dissipating. A tear dropped, splashing on his fingers. "It was an accident." Even if he had taught Karen gun safety, Gracie still might have shot Karen. "Mrs. Maxwell seems to be taking the news of Gracie's death and that of my parents well." I'd expected her to react a bit differently considering everything she'd been through.

"She surprised me too when I broke the news to her. Again, I'm sorry." He scooted closer and hugged me. I sucked up the strength in his arms much like I had with my father when I'd needed a shoulder to cry on. At that thought, I wept. I missed my mom, dad, and Gracie. I tried not to feel sorry for myself. I tried to think of all the good times, but death had a way of overshadowing all that was good in my life. I cried harder when he tightened his hold. Hopefully Dillon was right. Maybe now I could see a future that included the black-haired, blue-eyed cockroach. Provided Kelton wanted me.

CHAPTER 17
KELTON

I sat at the bar at Rumors, sipping water, wishing it were a strong bourbon or whiskey from one of the bottles in Kade's hands. He was stocking the shelves as I waited for Lizzie and Zach. I'd had every intention of taking Lizzie for a walk the night before down by the lake. I'd planned to spend time with her, making out as if we were teenagers again. But when I'd seen that half-heart charm on her neck, that sweltering day she'd moved away had come soaring back, along with the pain and heartbreak. Sure, it wasn't her fault that she'd moved. To a certain extent, I even understood her reasons for not wanting to stay in touch. Both of our families had been through something far worse than hell. She'd kept asking me all through dinner if I was all right. All I did was nod. In fact, I'd been quiet as everyone had chatted and gotten to know Lizzie again. Even after dinner I hadn't been in a festive mood.

My dad, on the other hand, had been quite relaxed. After he'd had a one-on-one conversation with Lizzie, he'd been a new man. Over dessert, he and Lizzie had talked excitedly about school and her intentions for a degree in marine biology. She'd had him smiling rather than bracing for a sonic bomb to go off. Prior to Lizzie showing up, he'd been wound as tight as us boys, anticipating Mom's reaction to Lizzie. But even Mom was chatting up Lizzie as though the past was a blur. Once she went as far as tucking Lizzie's hair behind her ear, much as she had when Lizzie was a little girl. Deep down I suspected Lizzie reminded Mom of the good old days, and that alone put a smile on her face.

Knuckles rapped on the bar, snapping me out of the turmoil I was in.

"Mom handled the deaths of the Reardons really well," Kade said. "I talked to Dad earlier. He mentioned Mom couldn't stop talking about Lizzie. She hopes to see her again soon."

All of us were pleasantly surprised at how Mom had handled Lizzie and the sad news of her family. When I was helping Mom set the table, she'd been concerned with me putting the fork in the right place rather than with hiding in her room depressed.

What a night it had been. As we'd said goodbye to Dillon and Lizzie, Mom had offered again for Lizzie to live at the house. Then they'd hugged, both women crying. My knees had gone weak. Luckily Kody had been next to me. He'd put a hand on my shoulder, preventing me from collapsing. Yeah, I was one fucked-up dude. All I'd envisioned at that moment was how I wanted to hold and protect Lizzie. Oh, hell. I wanted more than that. I wanted to take her to my room, strip her naked, and have my way with her, and at the same time, I was deathly afraid of the pain that would come when she went back to Miami.

"Do you want to talk about what's bugging you before Zach and Lizzie get here?" Kade asked.

I eyed the liquor then him. "How many times are you going to ask me that?"

"As many times as it takes to get you to talk." He tossed an empty box over the bar. It landed with a slight thud on top of the pile of other empty boxes.

"I'm not ready. When I am, I'll come find you." I had no doubt he would give me great words of wisdom. He was just like our dad in that regard. "Have you thought about following in Dad's footsteps as a psychiatrist?"

He chuckled as he wiped his hands with a towel. "That means I'd have to go to school for years, and that's not my cup of tea. Besides, I give advice every night to people here."

"Yeah, for free."

"How many times do I have to tell you to use that Mensa brain of yours? I listen. They tip me. I give advice. They tip me. I make good money."

"Then why sleep at the club? Get your own apartment." I had no doubt Mr. Robinson was paying him well for managing Rumors, in addition to his tips.

"I'm saving for a special occasion."

"Dare I ask? Is it the *M* word?"

The buzzer to the backdoor rang. He grinned, reminding me of Donkey in *Shrek* as he left to open the door. I admired my brother so damn much. From day one he'd known Lacey was the girl for him. He'd known he would marry her someday. Their relationship hadn't been all chocolate and roses either. Yet their love for each other never wavered. Why couldn't I be like him? Instead of freaking the fuck out over emotional pain? Talk about a pussy. I was the king of that at the moment.

Lizzie's voice floated to my ears, subtle, smooth, and silky. My heartbeat sped up. I swiveled on the barstool when she breezed in. Her hair fell easily over one side of her chest. Hair that I wanted to smell, touch, and play with. Her cheeks and nose were red, from battling the high winds that day, I imagined. One look at her and my body hummed everywhere, wanting to devour her like a madman. I took in a quiet breath. Lizzie deserved to be touched with a feather, caressed with my fingers, and worshipped like she was the queen of the universe, not thrown against the wall to have my way with her, although the latter was certainly appealing.

She sat on the stool next to me. "How were classes?"

"I've been an ass."

Her face lit up. "That's no surprise, but where did that come from?"

I dragged her barstool closer to mine. "You ran from me the other day and didn't give me a chance to say I was sorry." I rested my forehead against hers. "First, when I asked you to dinner with my family, I was only thinking of my mom and not how you would feel seeing my parents again. And then I was a bigger jerk for practically ignoring you at dinner." I fished her necklace out from her shirt and laid the half-heart charm in the palm of my hand, recalling how my world had shifted when she moved away. "I saw the charm and freaked. I mean, after all these years, you're still wearing it."

"I've never taken it off," she said as she pecked me on the lips.

That fact made my brain fuzzy. But I wasn't about to analyze the significance of it. Instead, I cupped her face in my hands and took control, kissing her greedily. She tasted like bubblegum and memories and home. When our tongues touched, my groin tightened. I broke away as I peppered kisses down her neck, absorbing jasmine and a hint of fruit. I was a second away from taking her into the bathroom when Zach's voice shattered the mood. We both straightened like two teenagers caught by her father. She smoothed out her hair as I adjusted myself in my seat.

Zach strutted in. His blond curls were wild on top of his head, his T-shirt was wrinkled, and he was wearing flip-flops in the dead of winter.

"Hey, man," he said as he ponied up to Lizzie and me.

I pointed to his feet. "You know it's thirty degrees outside?"

We exchanged a quick handshake.

"I hate driving in boots," he said as he eyed Lizzie. "Who's the beauty? You kind of look familiar. Do I know you?"

Touch her and you die.

"I'm the redhead you were supposed to tutor for Mr. Brewer. You know, the girl who was at your place when I found Chloe crying on your steps?" Her sarcasm was epic.

The color drained from Zach's face at the mention of Chloe's name.

I hadn't spoken to him yet about why Chloe was even at the condo. We were there to talk about Lizzie's problem, but I couldn't help but ask, "Why was she crying at our place?" I hadn't heard from Chloe since the night of the art gala. Which was unusual. We'd broken up before, and she'd always tracked me down. Maybe she was tired of hoping I would develop strong feelings for her.

Kade came in and circled the bar.

Zach's jaw moved rapidly. "Wait. Why am I here?"

"I'm sorry." Lizzie extended her hand. "I'm Elizabeth Reardon. Your father stole all my inheritance. Tell me where he is." Her tone and body language screamed *don't-fuck-with-me*.

I exchanged an I'm-impressed look with Kade. I was more than impressed. The tough but sweet girl I knew growing up was making my dick grow harder every time I saw the badass side of her.

Zach whipped his head to me, surprise wiping away his confusion. "What is this? An intervention?"

"We need your help," I said. "And this might be your chance to help your old man."

Zach stalked to the stage at the far side of the room, smoothing his hands over his mop of hair as he went. Then he came back. "Let me get this straight," he said to Lizzie. "You disguise yourself then come to my house hoping you can get information out of me on my old man? How do I know you don't want to steal from him?" He turned to me. "You believe this girl? She must be a good lay or something."

I dove at him. Red colored my vision. It was so unlike Zach to be a jerk in front of a lady. My fist rammed into his jaw just before he threw an uppercut. My head snapped back. He'd sparred with Kross once, but the outcome hadn't been good for Zach. He wasn't a fighter, but I had to give him credit. He could protect himself when he had to.

"Stop," Kade said as he pulled me off of Zach.

I wrenched out of Kade's hold. "Not everything in life is about a good roll in the hay. And what's up your ass?"

Kade offered Zach a hand, but he declined as he got up and spewed, "Nothing."

Kade stretched out his arms between us. "Both of you calm down. Zach, Elizabeth is an old family friend. She needs your help. Hear her out. And, Kel. Cool your jets."

I held up my hands and went back to Lizzie, who was watching us intently with her arms crossed over her chest. Zach brushed his hands down his shirt and jeans then sat on the edge of a table a short distance from the bar. Kade went up next to him.

"You don't remember me, do you?" Lizzie asked Zach. "Three years ago you were visiting your father in Miami. You and he were at my house. He introduced us as I was walking out the door." The edge in her voice had lessened.

Zach rubbed the spot where my fist had connected with his mouth. "Sorry. I don't."

"Doesn't matter," she said. "The long and short of it is that your father and mine were best friends. My father made your dad trustee of my inheritance. I'm asking you if you can contact your father and ask him to call me or meet me. He's not returning my calls. Or tell me where he is."

Zach let out a low laugh. "I barely know when he's in town, let alone where in the country he is. Particularly when he's on a gambling binge."

"Look, man," I said nicely. I didn't want to fight with Zach. It wouldn't help Lizzie's case. "See what you can do. Also, a friend of ours says there's a high-stakes poker game going down somewhere in Boston in a few weeks. If you do talk with your old man, ask him if he's playing in it."

"I'm no lawyer, but can't you use the legal system to stop him? Or even the cops?" Zach asked. He'd also lost the attitude.

"We're trying," I said. I'd done my homework on Florida law. I'd had every intention of sharing my findings with Lizzie after dinner the day before. "Death and stealing are two surefire ways to get a trustee removed. Another is if the trustee doesn't handle the estate properly. That one is harder to prove. However, an easier, faster way is to prove that Terrance no longer lives in Florida. Lizzie, didn't you mention that Terrance's house was empty?"

Zach and Kade were listening attentively.

"Yeah," she said. "His neighbor told me a moving truck had been parked in the driveway for two days." She swung her gaze to Zach. "Do you know if your father moved out of Florida?"

"No clue. But given what Kelton just explained, the law should help you."

"The law will help, but things don't work that fast within the legal system," I said.

"The cops haven't been any help either," Lizzie added. "Your father has the accounting records on my estate. I need them." She sounded as though she was on the verge of tears. "I can't say for sure if your father is guilty of stealing my money, but it would be much quicker if he would talk to me and cooperate."

Zach rubbed his temples. "I'll see what I can do. I got to run."

"I'll walk you out," Kade said.

The room fell silent as Zach and Kade left. I set my attention on the gorgeous lady who was chewing on her finger. I wanted desperately to be that finger. *Patriots, football, Super Bowl.* But no amount of chanting my sports mantra was going to tame the beast inside my pants. The more time I spent with Lizzie, the more my dick disobeyed me.

She switched to another fingernail. "Once Mr. Davenport gets my estate documents and analyzes the money trail and my parents' accounts, then what?"

"Mr. Davenport will lay out your options based on Florida statute.

Whatever the next steps are, they'll involve the court. He'll probably recommend freezing all assets in the estate. That way Terrance can't touch it anymore."

She twisted her earring. "It's going to take forever to get to the bottom of my problem, isn't it?"

"Look on the bright side. That means you're not leaving Boston any time soon, and it gives us a chance to get to know each other again."

A body-tingling smile spread across her face. Fuck. I'd risk my heart a million times if it meant that I would see that sparkle in her eyes, just like when we were kids.

"Are you asking me on a date?"

I slid my hands up her thighs, leaned in, and kissed her on the nose. "Only if I can see those toe socks. And if you'll allow me to cook you dinner this week."

She jerked back. "You cook?"

"Chocolate and strawberries to start. I always like dessert before the main meal."

CHAPTER 18
LIZZIE

Dillon pulled up along the curb right outside Fourteen Louisburg Square. Tonight I wasn't thinking about lawyers, my problem, or Terrance. I couldn't anyway. Not when Kelton dominated my thoughts. Although I'd wanted to check in with Zach. But Kelton had said Zach was MIA for the night, and according to Zach, he'd left a message for his father.

"Rich neighborhood," Dillon said, shifting the Camaro into park. "You sure that guy, Terrance, doesn't own this place?"

"Would it matter?" I asked. Zach had mentioned he was housesitting for a friend of his father's, and I didn't get the impression Zach would lie. Nevertheless, if Terrance had spent my money on that place, I couldn't do anything about it right then.

"Can I go in with you?" Bee asked from the backseat. She'd tagged along since Dillon was dropping her off at the mall where she worked.

"Maybe next time," I said, although I could use a wingman. Bee would certainly keep the conversation flowing, which would help to ease the bucket of nerves that was sloshing around in my stomach. I couldn't remember the last time I'd gone on a dinner date, let alone with a guy—Kelton, no less—who was cooking. On the drive there, I'd pictured Kelton standing in front of a stove in nothing but an apron, his bare butt showing.

Bee tapped me on the shoulder. "Let me make sure your makeup is still flawless."

I turned in my seat.

She surveyed her work as though she was smoothing out the final details of a finished painting. "Perfect," she said.

I had to give her credit. I knew how to apply makeup, but not like her. She worked in the cosmetic department at Nordstrom's for MAC products.

Bee wished me luck as I got out, then she crawled into the passenger's seat. With that, I made my way up the steps and rang the bell. Kelton opened the door, wearing an apron that said No Kiss, No Food.

I pointed to his chest. "Does that mean I can't eat until I kiss the cook?" *Please say yes.*

"There are several questions you need to answer tonight in order to get any food." His tone was deep and husky. "First, are you wearing your toe socks?"

I arched an eyebrow. "Seriously?"

Dillon beeped his horn. When his car rumbled to life, so did my stomach. I felt like I was on my very first date ever. My hands became clammy, my mouth became dry, and I had the urge to jump off the porch and chase Dillon down as his car sped away.

"Well?" Kelton's bulging biceps poked out from under his T-shirt as he crossed his arms.

"For me to know and you to find out." I stuck out my tongue. If he wanted to play, I could too.

"Wrong answer." He turned and moved farther inside. "Oh, and be careful with that tongue."

I tripped over the threshold, almost falling flat on my face. Fortunately I caught myself on the edge of the heavy door. When I was safely upright, Kelton was gone. I slinked into the opulent townhome as if I was robbing the place. I giggled at the thought. As big as the place was, I'd bet no one would even hear me. I peeked into the dining room on my right. The shiny wooden table was clear. I guessed we weren't eating in there. He'd said he liked dessert before the main meal. A picture of Kelton licking chocolate off me ignited heat in my cheeks.

"Lizzie," Kelton called.

I glanced ahead. My chin hit my chest. I shook my head once then again. I knew Kelton had said he was cooking, but to actually see him standing in the large foyer whisking something in a stainless steel bowl just didn't jive with his playboy persona.

He strutted up to me. "I'll ask you again. Are you wearing your toe socks?" No grin. No jackass smile. His expression was serious.

"What is it with you and my toe socks?"

"That was the requirement."

"Do you want to inspect me before I go any farther?" Good thing I'd worn my best bra and panties.

He froze, his hooded blue gaze undressing me. He let go of the whisk, dipped his finger into the bowl, then scooped out a dab of white stuff. Before I could clear the cobwebs clouding my brain, he smeared the sugary concoction over my lips. My tongue slithered out, tasting the sweet meringue.

He groaned, then repeated the process. Only this time he eased his finger into my mouth. A fire erupted low in my belly as I sucked on his finger. Not a bad way to start a date.

A ding went off. He slowly removed his finger. "Dessert is almost ready," he said in a hoarse voice. "Come on." He began whisking again.

He wasn't kidding about dessert before dinner. I wiped my mouth with my fingers and removed my jacket, dropping it on a chair next to the *Cinderella*-like staircase before following him into the spacious kitchen. The cabinets were a rich, dark cherry; the appliances large and stainless steel; and the counters white marble. A marble island traveled from one end of the kitchen to the wall of windows in the back. My mom would've been in heaven. She had remodeled our kitchen at our home in Miami not long before the boating accident.

Kelton removed a pie from the restaurant-grade fridge.

"Lemon meringue? No chocolate and strawberries?" I took a seat on a barstool across from him.

"Lemon pie is your favorite." He set down the pie on the island and began covering the top with meringue, concentrating on getting the peaks just right.

In addition to the giddiness making my heart race, shock and awe careened through me. "What else do you remember?"

"Your favorite color is blue. You love the ocean, dolphins, football, and Grimms' fairy tales." He finished adding the topping to the pie then licked the spatula.

Blue because of your eyes. I'm still in love with you, and football because I loved when you tackled me.

"Is this our dinner?" I didn't see any protein or veggies.

He grinned sinfully as he retrieved a fork then came around to sit next to me. "This is where the game begins. For every right answer, you get a bite of pie. For every wrong answer or refusal to answer, I take off a piece of your clothing. You in?" He dragged the pie over to us.

I was wearing jeans, a belt, and a tank top underneath a sheer lace tee that Bee had insisted I wear. She'd said it was eye-catching. "Um. This is how you envisioned our first date?" I had other ideas—a movie, dinner, and good conversation.

"Yep," he said easily.

I shouldn't have been surprised. Kelton didn't do normal. I'd always liked a challenge, anyway. I was also intrigued by what questions he would ask me. And he did go to a lot of trouble to bake my favorite dessert. "But the pie isn't done. You're supposed to bake the pie again so the meringue can stiffen then let it cool for a couple of hours."

"Lizzie. You're stalling. And I know you like it this way."

Darn guy was right. I loved freshly made meringue that I could eat right out of the bowl. "I'm in on one condition. I get to ask you questions too." If we were playing a game of Strip Questions, it was only fair that the tables were turned.

Excitement blazed in his eyes. "Fair. First question. Are you nervous?"

"No." I toyed with my chain.

"Liar. Let's start with your shirt." He grasped the bottom.

I lifted my arms without arguing. I really had to learn to control my nervous habits. He studied me as my sheer lace tee floated to the floor.

"My turn." I wanted to start with an easy one, but as he smirked like an ass, I couldn't concentrate. "What color underwear do you have on?" A lame question, but with the different colors he wore, maybe he wouldn't remember what he'd put on that morning. I puffed out my breasts, trying to divert him from looking down at the rip below the pocket of his jeans.

A mischievous grin emerged. "Black."

"Why do I get the feeling you know the correct color and you're lying?"

"Maybe I want to get naked."

I gulped down air, remembering the outline of his penis as he'd posed in his green boxer briefs.

He raised his arms. "Go ahead, take off my shirt."

I reached over and helped him out of his T-shirt. My jaw hit the floor before the shirt. No matter how many times I'd seen Kelton in art class with barely anything on, I was still in awe as I studied his tattoo. I couldn't help but run my fingers over the colorful lizard—something I'd wanted to do since I'd first seen it. He groaned as my fingers roamed over his shifting abs, making their way down to the waist of his jeans where the head of the lizard disappeared. When I reached his belt buckle, he sucked in his stomach. I giggled nervously.

A primitive wildness glinted in his eyes, making my heart jump and my stomach flip. "Keep going," he said.

I licked my lips. I could, but then we'd both be naked. That wasn't a bad thing, but I was interested in what other questions he had in store. I straightened.

He pouted briefly before he asked, "Are you wearing your toe socks?"

"Yes."

He lifted my leg to rest on his knee. "I have to confirm."

I thought for a second about arguing, but then he wouldn't know if I was telling the truth, and I was enjoying his hands on me. I quickly gripped the island to prevent myself from falling backward.

He untied my boot before pulling it off slowly. He said nothing about my striped toe socks. Instead, he captured my foot between his large hands and kissed the tops of my toes. "You have the cutest feet, especially in these striped toe socks."

I snorted. "You're weird." Good thing my socks were fresh and clean.

Lowering my leg, I adjusted myself on the barstool. My mouth watered as I anticipated the tanginess of the lemon meringue.

He dug the fork into the pie then brought the piece up to my mouth. As soon as the lemon hit my tongue, an explosion of sugar and tart made me pucker. "You've outdone yourself." I closed my eyes briefly, thinking back to a hot summer day when we'd been twelve. Kelton and I had sat on the edge of my pool with our legs dangling in the water, eating a lemon pie my mom had baked.

"You're remembering that day by the pool. Aren't you?" he asked.

My eyes flew open, as did my mouth.

"I think about that day a lot," he said. "That was the day of our first kiss. And not the one where I kissed you on the cheek in the sixth grade and you punched me."

"Care to replay our first kiss?" My breathing prowled up the charts.

"Nope."

My heart severed in two.

He dragged his barstool closer to me. "Describe our first kiss."

I sucked in a breath, trying to loosen the marbles rattling around in my system. "Wait a minute. Is it your turn?"

Spellbound, he watched me. "Yes. Now answer, baby doll. Or else another piece of clothing comes off."

I played with my earring. "It was awful."

"Liar."

"I'm not lying." In part I was.

"Lizzie, you give yourself away every time." He snatched my hand away from my ear.

Darn habit. "You licked pie off my face," I protested. We'd been playing footsy in the pool, swinging our legs out and up while eating pie. My leg had swung up too high, the momentum causing me to fall backward. My plate had landed on my face.

"After that. But before you continue"—he grabbed the bottom of my tank top—"time to remove this," he said in a wicked tone.

I almost argued, but I was eager to see his reaction when I was left with only a black lace bra.

He groaned as he undressed me. Once my tank top was in his hands, he flung it aside. Then he traced a path along my cleavage, over one side then the other.

My pulse kicked up. "My turn." I tapped his hand.

He licked his lips, plastering a shit-eating grin on his face. "Not yet. The truth."

Make him sweat. I stuck out my chest, pressed on his thighs, strong and hard, and closed the distance between us. "It was awkward." No lie. "Your hair tickled my nose. When I started to giggle, you pressed your lips to mine. The kiss was hard at first, then softened as we explored each other." My fingers danced farther up his legs, stopping short of his pockets.

The muscles in his thighs strained in his jeans.

"When our tongues touched"—I swallowed air—"tingles exploded in my belly. And..." I nipped at the scar on his chin.

He made a low noise in the back of his throat.

"...the goosebumps stayed with me for a week after that day. Did I pass?"

The pained expression on his face was priceless. It was as though he was trying not to tear off the rest of my clothes.

He fed me a piece of pie.

After my belly erupted with glee, I asked, "Aside from the meringue, did you really make this pie? And don't lie just so you can take off your clothes."

Gone was the pain on his handsome face. In its place was a sexy smile. "I did. And if you don't believe me, we can call Kody. He taught me. He's the baker in the house." He scooped out a large piece and held it while he eyed me.

"Go ahead. I believe you for now. If I find you lied, then we can duke it out."

He shoved the helping in his mouth. "At the art gala you said I had flaws. Name one. If I agree, you get your reward."

We might be here all night. I tapped my lip. Kelton was cocky and stubborn. He always had been. Fast forward seven years and his cocksure attitude had multiplied. I wasn't a shrink, but my Spidey sense was telling me that he used those attributes as a cover so no one saw the real him. "Your bravado is a shield so others don't see the real you."

He chuckled even though his eyes expressed something else, maybe surprise that I was right. "And you know this how?"

Coolly, I lifted a shoulder. "Woman's intuition. Isn't that why you model?" The Kelton I knew wouldn't show the world all of him. The Maxwells had always been private people. The brothers were picky about who they let into their circle and who they showed their softer sides to. "I'm right, aren't I?"

"Is it that obvious?" He scooped another forkful of pie and inserted it into my mouth.

The sweet concoction melted on my tongue. "What scares you?" Somewhere beneath all the layers of Kelton, he was hiding behind something.

He lowered his gaze to my breasts, his chest rising. Then he jumped off the barstool and went over to the sink. He snagged a glass off the counter and filled it with water. His back muscles tightened as he gulped the clear liquid. When he finished, he turned, piercing me with a pained look.

I couldn't tell what he was wrestling with—keeping his hands off me or something else. "If you don't want to answer, take off your jeans," I teased. He'd made the rules—wrong answer or no answer and an article of clothing came off.

He glared at me as he crossed one arm over his chest and gripped his other arm.

Whoa! "Hey, I didn't ask you to marry me." I got up and made my way to him. I waved a hand to break his trance. "Kelton Maxwell, you're not going to hell if you don't answer the question." My tone was light.

"I'm *in* hell." His tone was hard.

Way to drive a knife through my heart. "So you consider me hell?" A knot formed in my stomach. If I caused him that much pain, then I didn't need to be there. "This is your game, not mine," I snapped. If I stayed any longer, my own heart was going to stop beating.

He homed in on my breasts.

I covered myself with my arm as much as I could as I grabbed my necklace.

"Why are you still wearing that charm?" His jaw clenched.

I held it up. "Is this what you're scared of?" My voice hitched.

He clutched his hair, his eyebrows knitting tighter than a well-made sweater. Then he grunted. "You want to know what scares the fuck out of me?" He scrubbed a hand down his face as he popped off the counter and drew closer to me so that we were an arm's length apart. "I'm afraid of falling and hitting the ground so fucking hard my heart will explode. I'm afraid of you. I'm afraid of what your touch does to me. Of what your kisses promise me. Most of all"—he moved two steps nearer to me—"I'm afraid when you get on that plane back to Miami, my life will be over. I can't handle that kind of pain again. When you moved away I was a fucking mess. Granted, we were kids. Your mom said it was infatuation. My parents said it was first love. Whatever. It still fucked me up. Over the years, I saw how my old man hurt when my mom went into a mental health facility. I saw how Kody brooded and hurt when his girlfriend died in a motorcycle accident. And I witnessed how Kade went through hell in his relationship with Lacey. My brother almost lost her to a crazy murderer." He sighed heavily, almost grunting.

My head spun at his speech, at the conviction in his voice. I tried to process his words, but his last statement sent a shiver up my spine. But I filed it away for another day. Right then, I had to get my pulse to slow. His emotional rollercoaster was because of me. I was the cause of his pain. I was the reason Kelton hid behind his bravado. I was the reason he was a fucking mess. In part, I understood his strife. After all, I was terrified the people I loved would die.

"I refused to let anyone in." His tone softened. "Then you showed up. Every time I see you, touch you, kiss you, I get dizzy, confused, fearful, crazy, excited. And if I'm being honest, the longer you stay in Boston, the more I won't want you to leave."

The room spun slightly, and I smiled—more out of nerves than anything.

He narrowed those soul-stealing blue eyes of his. "You love seeing me act like a guy who just downed a bottle of estrogen, don't you?"

Since he put it that way, I had to laugh.

He backed up to lean against the sink.

Silence grew like a balloon ready to bust. I thought of something to say, but if I said anything I'd start crying. We were on a date. This was supposed to be a good time, not heavy and laden with deep-seated emotions. Conversations like this one were supposed to be for a time after we'd dated for a year. But Kelton and I weren't strangers. Kelton and I still had feelings for each other. Or *I* still did. I'd said my piece with his parents. It was time I did with Kelton.

I cleared my throat. "I'm sorry when I moved away I didn't respond to your emails or calls. I get why you're afraid of me. *I'm* afraid of me. I'm afraid of you. Life. The future. Love." I shuffled up to him then touched his chest. His heart was beating like he'd just finished a quarter-mile sprint. "But as scared as I am, I want to take a chance with you, with us. Your life isn't over when I return to Miami. I guess I don't understand why we couldn't have a long- distance relationship." They usually didn't last, but I would do anything to make us work.

"That's the thing. You walked out of my life seven years ago, and I couldn't let that happen again, even for a long-distance relationship."

I wanted to argue that I'd been thirteen and had had no control over where I lived. And while his adult brain would probably understand that, his feelings drove his decisions. Maybe we needed a time-out to think, process, and regroup. Although I wasn't certain he would want to. I gave a half smile then went in search of my clothes.

"You never answered. Why are you still wearing my charm?" His voice cracked.

I slipped on my tank top. "You don't want to know why. Let's just end the date now." I put on my boot.

"Lizard, please. Tell me."

I shook my head. "You don't want the truth." I doubted he could handle it.

"I just poured out the truth to you. So, yes. I do." He crossed his arms.

I guessed I owed him that much. Maybe if I eased into why I'd never taken off the half-heart charm he wouldn't freak or go into cardiac arrest. *Now I'm probably being a drama queen.* "You're right. What we had as kids was first love. And first loves stay with a person forever. But time has a way of dimming the past. This charm"—I grabbed it out of my tank top—"never allowed my feelings, what we shared, the good times we had, or even the sadness to dim. Then when I first laid eyes on you in art class, the past lit up brighter than a spotlight. I couldn't believe it was really you. I tried to stay away from you, to make sure you didn't notice me. I didn't trust myself, or my heart. My disguise wasn't so you wouldn't notice me, but it helped at first. Then you kissed me at Dillon's. I knew then that I'd never lost my feelings for you. I'm in love with you, Kel," I said, as sure as the sun set every day. My insides, on the other hand, threw up.

His face paled, turning as white as the marble countertop. Not me —my cheeks were on fire, my hands were shaking, and the room seemed to be spinning slightly. In no way did I want him to say it back, especially not out of pity or because he felt he had to. Then I scratched that thought. Kelton wouldn't say anything unless he meant it.

Cold air would be good about now.

Kelton moved toward me. He was about to open his mouth.

I placed my fingers on his lips. "Don't say anything. Those are my true feelings. They aren't going to change when I return to Miami. Nor will they change ever, no matter where I am in this world."

"I was going to say stay and we'll watch a movie and order pizza."

A movie sounded great. Anything to stay connected. "As long as we don't talk about feelings or our past in Texas." I didn't want him to feel awkward that I'd told him I loved him. I was also drained from our game.

"Deal," he said, color returning to his face.

CHAPTER 19
KELTON

I gazed up at the ceiling as the morning light seeped in through a crack in the curtains. I checked my watch. I had a math exam in about two hours. I'd planned to study after my date with Lizzie, but I couldn't even concentrate. Sleep had been impossible too. I'd replayed the conversation between us at least a hundred times. When she wasn't in my life, I was a fucking mess. Now that she was back in my life, I was still fucked up. The blood had drained from me when she told me she loved me, and not because she'd said the word *love* or poured out her heart. No, I was freaking out because if she was expecting me to say it back, no way. Fear gripped me. Fear that when she left for Miami I wouldn't see her again. *Stop being a pussy and commit. Take a chance. You're not thirteen anymore. People have long-distance relationships all the time.* Kade and Lacey were apart while she was in school. They were doing well. So why couldn't I do it? My old man had always been separated from my mom when he was on deployment for the military, and they were still married. *Do something, or you're going to lose her.*

A knock sounded, and the door opened.

"Can I come in?" Lizzie asked in a sleepy voice.

We had fallen asleep watching *Transformers*. I hadn't wanted to drive her back at midnight. She'd seemed so peaceful, sleeping on my lap. So, as much as it had pained me not to tuck her into my bed, I'd carried her up to one of the guest bedrooms.

"Careful you don't trip over my clothes." They usually ended up on the floor when I was half-asleep.

She undressed, taking off her tank top first, revealing that black lace bra I'd wanted to remove with my teeth during our game last night. Then she shimmied out of her jeans. When she bent over, her breasts practically spilled out of the garment.

Motherfucker. *Patriots. Football. Super Bowl.*

She kicked her clothes to the side and scurried to the bed. I thought to move, but I was entranced at her beauty. That didn't stop her. She wormed her way under the covers, trying to push me. When her body touched mine, warm and soft as warm butter, tingles raced down my stomach. I slid over not more than an inch. I wanted her plastered to me, fused so tight I wouldn't be able to let her go.

"Wow, you're on fire," she said, yawning.

Ha. I was an inferno of massive proportions, and not because I was sweating either. "It's a guy thing." I flipped onto my side, shoving my hand under my pillow.

She adjusted herself so we were face-to-face. "How come you didn't wake me to take me back to Dillon's?"

"It was easy to carry you to bed. I did text Dillon, though."

She threaded her leg in between mine. "Are you okay?" Her long lashes fanned out as she dropped her gaze to my lips.

I repeated my sports mantra in my head, fast and furiously. But it wasn't helping. My body was in desperate need to ravish her in every way imaginable. On the other hand, my brain roared *no*. My body had to be in sync with my brain for me to even think about making love to her. Fuck. I'd said *make love*. Usually I *had sex* with women. I didn't make love. But Lizzie wasn't any woman.

"I really am a dickwad, aren't I?" I pulled at her necklace until the half-heart charm was in my hand. The one thing that kept fucking with my head. This charm was the reason I was in a state of craziness. It raised memories, both good and bad, although the bad outweighed the good. I wanted to yank it off her neck and hide it where I wouldn't be reminded of pain and heartache. But I couldn't do that. It was special to her.

"No. You're scared. It's okay to be."

Terrified was more like it.

"Kel, why all the questions last night?"

I dragged my fingers down her cheek. "I was trying to relive the past." The good times we'd had. Maybe then I could move on.

"Maybe it's time to make new memories."

Her in my bed was already a new memory. "So, you love me, huh?" I stared at the charm.

She snuggled closer before kissing my neck. "Yep." Her lips moved up to my chin. "Flaws and all." She moved her hips into me, her soft lips touching every part of my face except my mouth.

My entire body turned to stone, the necklace falling from my hand.

She snaked her fingers down my chest, dragging her nails until she reached the band of my briefs. I wasn't sure if I was breathing. Then she nipped at my lips as her hand covered my dick. When she moaned, I growled, rolling her onto her back. I placed my hands on either side of her head, keeping much-needed space between us. I searched her hooded gaze as my own sexual needs warred with the right thing to do. And that was to wait until I was ready to confess my love. But with every thrust of her hips upward, every touch of her small hands on my body, every sensual noise that she spewed, and every breath of her jasmine scent, I was a fucking goner. I lowered my head until a minute space separated us. She ran her tongue over her bottom lip, spiking every hormone in me to a new height. The room narrowed until I captured her mouth with mine. Then the world tilted, spun, as I swept my tongue over hers, tasting every sinful pleasure she had to offer.

She fisted her hands in my hair, wiggling beneath me, trying to get me to press my body to hers. I wanted all of her. No, I needed all of her. The more we kissed, the more I felt her softness against me, the more I felt her desire for me, the more that steel wall around my heart melted. My brain fired at the last thought. But as she slipped her hand into my briefs, my brain shut down. The only way I was not taking all of her was if I ran out of there, ran away from her. The problem was I didn't want to run. I wanted to feel her physically and emotionally.

I snapped open the front clasp of her bra just as a door slammed somewhere in the house. Footsteps sounded, growing louder.

Her soft body went rigid.

"It's probably Zach just getting home," I whispered. "He won't come in here." Zach knew better. Then I realized I didn't have the Do

Not Disturb card on the outside of my door and it wasn't locked. He and I had made one when we lived together in the dorms. When we'd moved to the townhome, we'd continued the habit even with separate bedrooms, just in case.

Well, fuck. Panic drove intimacy right out the window.

Knuckles rapped lightly on my door. "Kelton, are you home?" Chloe asked.

Double fuck.

Lizzie dug her nails into me. "I thought you broke up with her."

"Don't move." I scrambled off the bed before Chloe could form any idea of barging in. Which she had one time when I'd had a girl in my bed. How the hell did she get into the condo? I'd never given her a key. Unless I'd left the door unlocked the night before.

"Kelton?" Chloe said again.

Stumbling to get in my jeans, I hopped haphazardly to the door. "What are you doing here? And how did you get in?" I asked through the crack.

"Sorry. I knocked. The door was unlocked. I thought you might be in the shower and didn't hear me." Her eyes were red. "I wanted to catch you before class. Can we talk?"

I wanted to scream at her. She always had a way of showing up at the most inopportune time. Instead I said, in a calm tone, "I can't right now. I'm going to be late for class."

She glanced over my shoulder as though she knew I had a girl in my room. "This won't take long."

"Chloe," I bit out.

Lizzie huffed behind me.

"Oh," Chloe said. "Got it." Then she stormed down the hall. Within seconds the front door slammed.

"What's going on?" Lizzie dressed quickly.

I wanted to laugh at how cute she was with her bottom lip sticking out. "No reason to be jealous, baby doll. I seriously don't know what she wanted."

"I should go. You have class."

I also had a growing hard-on watching her shimmying her hips into her jeans. But I couldn't skip my math exam. I'd missed the last one because I'd been sick. I made it up, but not without the professor taking off ten points. I was striving to graduate next year with honors. "Hey, I'm sorry."

"Not your fault." She lifted up on her toes and kissed me on the cheek. "I'll see you at Davenport's at four." She hurried to the door.

"Wait a second." I grabbed her arm. "I want a proper kiss before you leave." Before she had a chance to protest, I captured her mouth, trying to push my tongue past the lips she was pressing tightly together. "Lizard."

She opened, growling.

Okay, I had to say her growl was the sexiest fucking thing alive. My dick agreed. Regardless, I kissed her slowly and tentatively. Otherwise, as irritated as she was, I might find myself with a knee to the groin. She softened before she whimpered. Then I fisted my hands in her hair, peppered kisses down her delicate jaw and her neck, and then back up to her ear. "Thank you."

She pushed away and smiled, but it seemed forced. I knew that jealous look. I hurried into the hall. "Lizzie? Don't pull an Erika Ames on Chloe, okay?" I didn't need two strong women fighting at the age of twenty, particularly Chloe. She was the daughter of a mob boss. I was certain she had torture techniques up her sleeve, not that I'd ever seen any. But I couldn't help but smile at how hilarious it had been when I'd found out that Lizzie had sent Erika hate notes on my behalf in the seventh grade.

Lizzie flipped me the bird as she barreled down the stairs and out the door.

I grinned as I trudged back to my room, despite being sexually frustrated. Maybe a cold shower, or better yet, I should relieve the pressure if I didn't want to walk around with blue balls all day. Then I shook my head. Exam first, then worry about my sexual needs.

After I'd showered and dressed, I collected my backpack from the library, snatched my keys from the glass table in the foyer, and pulled open the door.

Chloe was sitting on the top step. She popped up, gathering her hair in her hands and twisting it. Everyone had a tell, and hers was playing with her hair.

A Mercedes cruised past, the sun gleaming off its shiny black paint job.

"So who was the girl?"

"You came over here to check on who I was sleeping with? Don't answer that. Look, I'm going to be late for class."

"I don't know how to tell you." Her voice thickened. Then she wiped her nose.

Anxiety sank its lion claws into the lining of my stomach.

"We dated on and off for the last three years. You know how I feel about you." Her voice was low.

I lifted her chin. "Chloe, we had a good time together. You're a wonderful person. Any guy would be lucky to have you. I'm sorry I'm not that guy."

Tears rushed down her cheeks, clouding her brown eyes. "I'm pregnant."

My vision flickered. My mouth locked open. If I'd paled at the word *love*, I was a fucking ghost at that. The sounds of the city streets vanished. I sat down and dropped my head in my hands, trying like a motherfucker to breathe. My mind ran back to the last time she and I had had sex, the day after we'd broken up—almost two months before. What was I worried about? I always used a condom. Always. Maybe the one I used had a defect. For fuck's sake, I prayed the whole box didn't. If so, then I might have more women showing up to tell me they were pregnant.

Motherfucker.

My breathing was all over the place. I had to run, to move, to get out of there. The thought of me being a father pried open my guts. I couldn't even tell a woman I loved her, let alone have a baby with someone I *didn't* love. My future whizzed by with snapshot after snapshot of how I was a fuckup. My father taught me to be responsible. I'd just failed miserably. I pulled on my hair, hungering for pain, for someone to punch my lights out. Maybe when I woke up I'd find I'd been in a bad dream.

Chloe called my name. As she did, a harrowing thought careened through me. Her father. Jeremy Pitt, Russian mob boss, was going to lock me in his torture chamber and cut off my dick, my fingers, and my legs, then my arms. By the time he was done with me, my family wouldn't know who I was. I shot straight up, grabbed my backpack, and catapulted off the porch.

"Kelton, where are you going? I still need to talk to you!" Chloe shouted.

"I need a minute." I ran one block down to my Jeep. Then punched the side window, crushing my knuckles. *Breathe, man. Go back. Talk to her.* I had to think first, clear my head, or maybe jump off a bridge. I dove into my Jeep. I was being a complete jerk by taking off. I should have been asking her if I was the father. But somehow my gut was telling me I was. Otherwise she wouldn't be breaking the news to me.

I zipped through the streets of Boston, not knowing where I was going. Blood dripped down my knuckles as I banged on the steering wheel over and over again. As I stopped at a light, my phone rang. I checked the screen. Chloe. My hand shook as I shut off my phone.

CHAPTER 20
LIZZIE

I waited in the reception area of Mr. Davenport's office. Kelton wasn't there yet, but we had another ten minutes before our scheduled appointment. I flipped through a car magazine, landing on a page that displayed a Lamborghini. The headline read A Relentless Force—A Fearless Look. I studied the picture of the expensive automobile, picturing Kelton behind the wheel. Several other words came to mind when I thought of Kelton—sleek, hard, and powerful from the way he'd felt in my hands that morning to the way he'd kissed me. I'd wanted us to keep going. I'd wanted every part of him, but Chloe had blown that moment to pieces. What was she doing there at eight in the morning? I would've asked her when I practically tripped over her on the steps, but I was too irritated, too frustrated, too jealous. Okay, too angry, too, at Kelton for spouting off about Erika Ames. It wasn't so much the name but rather his flippant and amused attitude over my jealousy.

I tapped my foot on the carpeted floor—3:59. No Kelton. I called him. The line went straight to voicemail. "Kel, where are you?"

Bonnie, Mr. Davenport's squat assistant, walked up. "Where's Mr. Maxwell?" She searched the reception area.

"I'm sorry. He must be running late." He'd wanted to be there since he was vying for a summer position at the firm. Not only that, I needed him. He'd done his homework on Florida law. "We can start without him." I prayed nothing had happened to him.

I clutched my phone as we passed by the conference room, law library, and other offices bustling with lawyers and assistants. Phones rang, doors closed, and a young guy with a ball cap wheeled a mail cart past us. I could never see myself in a stuffy office. Working in some type of marine biology job appealed to me far more than any job that required a suit with heels.

"I explained to Mr. Davenport about your appearance," Bonnie said.

I'd forgotten that I'd had my wig on when I met with Mr. Davenport. "Thank you." Bonnie had done a double take when I'd removed my wig in front of her. I'd thrown it in the trash in the ladies' room.

Bonnie gestured with her painted blue nails to the chair in front of Mr. Davenport's desk.

I eased down onto the leather seat, squinting at the bright sunshine beaming through the windows with a panoramic view of the Boston skyline.

Bonnie waited for Mr. Davenport to sign a document. After she'd collected the paper, she left, leaving us in complete silence.

Placing his elbows on his desk, Mr. Davenport twined his fingers together, his bushy gray eyebrows lifting. "So, no Mr. Maxwell." He didn't sound surprised.

"I know he had class. He probably got hung up there." I hoped Kelton had a good excuse. I didn't want to see him ruin his chances for the summer position.

"Very well. I've managed to talk with Mr. Pilkington, the lawyer in Florida, and read through the estate documents. First, Mr. Pilkington has tried to call the trustee, Terrance Malden, on several occasions. Unfortunately, he hasn't been able to connect with him. Second, while we try to locate Mr. Malden, it's wise to freeze the estate assets."

"Kelton found that under Florida law that if we can prove Terrance no longer lives in Florida, then we could get him removed as a trustee immediately. Is that true?"

"It is. But we would need a document or evidence to support that assumption."

"His son, Zach, lives in Boston."

"Is Mr. Malden living with his son?" He picked up a pen and scribbled on a pad.

"Not to my knowledge." I held a fingernail between my teeth.

"And does his son know where he is?"

"He's left a message with his father to call him. Sir, Terrance Malden is a heavy gambler. While I can't say for certain he's taken my money, my gut tells me he has. We have to do something quickly."

"Freezing the assets will stop him from withdrawing any more money. However, it will take time to draw up the paperwork. Then we have to schedule a time with a judge. Mr. Pilkington will issue the temporary injunction with the courts in Miami. I've drafted an affidavit for you to sign. It's not hard evidence, but we'll see if it will pass muster with the judge." He handed me the document and a pen.

It read that I, as the plaintiff, had not received my monthly stipend from Terrance Malden in the last two months. Nor had he paid my tuition fees to the University of Miami. It also stated that after several phone calls, Mr. Malden could not be reached. In addition that the presumption was that the trustee of my estate no longer resided at the address on file. The details were accurate, so I signed the document.

He scanned the paper. "Mr. Pilkington will do his best. Also, since we can't locate Mr. Malden, Mr. Pilkington will petition the court to gain access to tax returns, bank statements, and so forth. It would help tremendously if we could get Mr. Malden to hand over his files on his accounting of the estate. In the meantime, sit tight until we hear from Mr. Pilkington."

Waiting was never my strong suit. I needed to get to the bottom of this faster. The longer it took to freeze the assets, the more opportunity Terrance had to gamble away all my money. And the more he did, the more my future disintegrated. I couldn't even pay Mr. Davenport. I suddenly realized we hadn't discussed his fee.

I stopped sabotaging my nail. "Sir, I don't have any money to pay you."

His dark eyes softened before he held his chin between his thumb and forefinger. "I haven't done much, but let's see where the case takes us. Then we can talk. And I promise if I do charge a fee it won't be anything you can't handle. Is that fair?"

I stood. "I appreciate that. And I'm sure Kelton has a good reason for missing this appointment."

His expression instantly hardened. "A position at my firm is highly sought after, especially for law majors. I was impressed when he contacted me about your case by the knowledge he had of estate law. I also dug into his employment at the last law firm he interned for. They highly recommend him, but not showing up to this appointment doesn't bode well for Mr. Maxwell." He reached for his desk phone. "One more thing, Ms. Reardon. If you happen to speak with Terrance Malden, please let me know."

I nodded as I crossed the room. When I reached the door, I turned back. "Sir, can I bring charges against Terrance if we find he's been stealing?"

"You can bring a civil suit against him. But as the executor of the estate, he's criminally liable. If he is stealing, he can also be found in contempt of the probate court. That would carry a fine and possible jail sentence. But that would depend on the severity of the case. Let's cross that bridge when we get to it."

"Thank you," I said then whisked out of the posh offices.

Once outside on the busy street, I called Zach. It had been three days since I'd talked to him at the club. Kelton had said Zach left a message with his father. Surely a father would return his son's phone call.

"Hello," he said in a curt tone.

"Zach, it's Elizabeth Reardon. Did you talk to your father?"

"This isn't a good time." The phone went dead.

I called again as I squeezed the phone, trying to crush it in two. It rang several times before his voicemail picked up. I hung up then dialed again. Again it went to voicemail. My need to strangle him was greater than my desire to beat his father into submission at the moment.

Instead of screaming at the top of my lungs, I dialed Kelton's number. His voicemail picked up immediately. I tried one more time. Same result. I set my sights on Rumors. Maybe Kelton was there or Kade would know where Kelton was. As I headed for the "T," fear supplanted my rage. My mind went to accident and death. I didn't have the best luck when it came to people I loved. I shouldn't have told Kelton I loved him. The word itself was a bad omen. I was beginning to see why Kelton was so freaked out by it.

CHAPTER 21

KELTON

After hours of driving around Boston, I still couldn't breathe. I turned on my phone as I pressed on the bell to the backdoor of Rumors. I had fifteen messages, all of which I was sure were from Chloe. I was the biggest fucking dick in the world, and not taking responsibility wasn't in my nature. My father taught all of us boys to own up to our messes. We always had, but at the moment, I didn't know how. I needed Kade's advice. He would probably be stricter than my dad. I wanted that. No, I needed tough love. Or better yet, several punches to the face.

I banged on the buzzer again. My hands were still shaking worse than an eight-point-two earthquake.

Finally, the bar engaged, and Kade opened the door. "What the fuck happened to you? Why is your hand covered in dry blood?"

"You alone?" I wasn't walking in if he wasn't. It was late afternoon, and the nightshift would be coming in soon. I'd seen only Kade's truck in the parking lot.

"Kross is here. We were hanging out in the office."

I pushed past him, my excitement surging at the mention of Kross. He would probably knock me out once he heard the news. *Please*, my inner voice shouted. It might help to fire my neurons back into place. Light spilled out from the office into the dim hall. A stale odor penetrated my nostrils. My pulse raced the closer I got to the office. Telling

Kade was going to be hard, and telling Kross was going to be just as difficult. He'd asked me for a couple of condoms. I'd been the one to tell him to be careful. Now look at me.

I crossed the threshold to find Kross lounging on the couch. I wanted to feel as relaxed as he appeared. Instead, my muscles were strung tighter than a violin string.

When he saw me he straightened. "What's wrong? You look like death."

Truth be told, I'd shed a few tears for fucking up my life and Chloe's life.

Kade lumbered in then found a spot on the edge of the desk, projecting his usual persona: I'm listening, then I'll beat the lights out of you.

I began to pace. "I fucked up. Like really." I combed both hands through my hair and down the back of my neck, then punched the paneled wall. My already-bruised knuckles bled again as bones cracked. With the adrenaline running through me, I felt no pain.

"Unless you killed someone, it can't be that bad," Kade said easily.

I whirled around. "Chloe's pregnant!"

Dead silence. Complete mind-hurting silence. I swung my gaze between my brothers. Both had gone pale.

Welcome to my hell.

I slid down the wall until I was sitting on the floor. Then I banged my head against the wall, rocking back and forth like I had when Karen died.

"Is it yours?" Kross asked.

I banged my head harder. I was embarrassed to say I hadn't asked. All I'd done was lose my shit, bolting off the steps, ready to throw myself off a bridge.

"Well?" Kade asked. "Is it?"

"I don't know." I pulled my hair. "I just took off."

"Can I punch him or should you?" Kross mashed his lips into a thin line as he came to stand over me. "How in the fuck didn't you ask that question?"

"Why would she tell me she was pregnant if it weren't mine?" Chloe never came to me for advice. "Not to mention, she would've said so immediately if I wasn't the father. And I freaked, okay? I needed to think." Part of me was afraid to know the answer.

"Did you use a condom?" Kross asked.

"Always. Fucking always." Never had I had sex without one, even when I'd been drinking.

Kross sank down next to me. "I get why you flipped out. But you got to talk to her." His tone had lightened.

Even though I was terrified out of my fucking mind, Kross was right. "I know," I growled.

Kade's vacant stare gave me the chills. I didn't want to disappoint anyone in my family, particularly Kade. He'd taught us always to man up, never to lie. He gave us great advice, although he sometimes forgot to follow his own, and he'd been a good role model when our dad had been on missions.

"Man up," Kade nearly snapped. "And do it before her old man cuts off your balls."

The buzzer rang. With my luck, Jeremy Pitt was at the back door. Kade stalked out.

"That went well," I muttered.

"He'll have more to say later once he gets over the shock," Kross said.

"I've never been more scared and fucked up in my life." I dropped my head to my bent knees.

"I never told anyone this, but do you remember Ruby?" Kross asked.

I lifted my head. "Ruby Lewis? The girl you dated while we were at the Academy?"

"Yeah. Well, she thought she was pregnant. And I reacted like you. I ran for my life."

"Dude, you better land a right hook to my jaw because I'm not sure I heard you correctly."

Silence. Kross stared off into space.

"Well? Was she pregnant?" I didn't know if I was more shocked that he hadn't told us or that he could be a father. A chill sped down my spine. My brother, Kross, the one who took after Kade in so many ways, strong, protective, and cautious, was about to tell me...

Kross hung his arms over his knees. "No, she wasn't. She'd been stressing over practicing for her ballet performance and was late. It was the first and only time I didn't use a condom."

I propped my head against the wall and grunted.

"Is there a chance that you're not the father?" Kross asked. "Haven't you two been dating other people?"

"I have." I wasn't sure about Chloe.

"Regardless, you can't run from this. And I'll tell Kade about Ruby when I'm ready."

The practical side of me knew he was right. "I'm not telling Kade anything." We never tattled on each other.

Lizzie's voice trickled in. "Is he okay?"

I winced. "Shit." I'd forgotten all about Davenport, her, and the meeting. "Don't say anything." I couldn't tell her. Not until I was sure if I was the father.

"Problems with Lizzie?" Kross picked at the wristband of his watch.

"You have no idea." It wasn't that we had problems. I was the one with the problem.

I didn't hear Kade respond to her.

"You guys still have that brother code, don't you?" she asked.

Kade stayed silent.

Kross chuckled. I didn't. I was on a roll letting people down and fucking up so bad that my sanity was on the brink of destruction. I squeezed my temples.

"There you are," she said.

I was afraid to make eye contact.

Kross nudged me. "I'll be in the bar if you need me," he whispered in my ear.

Kade poked his head in. "Kel, make it quick. Then get to the bottom of the problem."

"What problem?" Lizzie asked. "Other than you missed the appointment with Mr. Davenport. Why?"

Three, two, one. I raised my head slowly and found her pretty face wrinkled around the nose and eyes. In fact, her eyes were slits. Yeah, she was angry.

"Please sit down." I patted the spot Kross had been in. It was better if she was sitting.

She hesitated before she joined me. Then she grabbed my right hand. "Why are your knuckles swollen and bleeding? It looks like you might've broken your hand."

A small amount of pain was starting to set in. Between punching the window and then the wall, I would guess she was probably spot on, considering I could barely move my hand. "I'm sorry about not being at Davenport's. I..." If I told her, I would lose her. But I also couldn't lie to her. No matter the consequences, she deserved the truth, whether I came off as an idiot or not. Plus, I wasn't about to let her think I was running from her because she told me she loved me. Sure, when Chloe said those words I'd bolted, although not as fast as I had today. There was no doubt in my mind my feelings for Lizzie were strong, otherwise I would've run last night. Even sitting there with her touching me, my stomach had that butterfly feeling. I blew out a long breath. "Chloe's pregnant."

Her beautiful, rosy cheeks blanched. Her mouth opened and closed. Grabbing her earring, she popped to attention.

The butterflies morphed into raging piranhas. Schmuck, dick, ass, asshat, asswipe, fuckup. They all described me. I wasn't the adult, or the protector, or the cautious one like Kross or Kade or even Kody. I was the one who threw caution to the wind, stomped on it, and then shoved it in the trash. *Live for the moment* had always been my motto. Hell, it still was, but I had to figure out how to temper my infallibility complex so I wouldn't ruin more lives.

Planting both hands on the floor, I grunted when I put pressure on my right hand. Yep, something wasn't right with it.

Tears filled her pretty blue-gray eyes. "That's why she was at your place early this morning, huh?"

When I was on two feet, I lightly massaged my right hand. "I'm sorry." It tore my insides to shreds to see her crying. I reached out to touch her.

She reared back with her hands raised. Regret and sadness washed over her. "I'm sorry too."

Kade stuck his head in. "Chloe called on the club phone. She wants you to call her."

Lizzie pivoted on her heel and brushed past Kade.

My heart plummeted to the floor. "Lizzie? Lizard." I chased after her, something that was becoming a habit. "Please."

She kept walking until she got to the backdoor. Then she looked over her shoulder, tears streaming down her face.

When I was a foot from her, she opened the door and ran.

Fuck me. I punched the wall. More bones cracked as pain shot up my arm like wildfire. I let out a wail. I wanted to hold her and tell her my heart was hers. I couldn't. I couldn't even tell her if I was the father, let alone say the three words that were glued to the tip of my tongue. No, before I went after her, I had to get my shit together. Then and only then could I deal with my feelings for Lizzie. I just hoped like a motherfucker I didn't lose her forever.

CHAPTER 22
LIZZIE

I dashed away a final tear as I glanced up at the Firefly sign. I was done crying. I had to do something to find Terrance. I couldn't wait for Zach or the law to help me, and I couldn't stand to be in Boston any longer. I knew I shouldn't have gotten involved with Kelton. I knew better than to think I could love someone. Kelton wasn't dead, but it hurt to know that I wasn't the one who would be carrying Kelton's baby.

I steeled my shoulders as I entered the restaurant and bar. A whiff of stale beer made me wince as I glanced around the dive. The floor was sticky. A pool table, scratched-up wooden tables, and several booths were scattered about. A handful of people sat at the bar while three booths were occupied by men drinking pints of beer.

"May I help you?" the bearded bartender asked as he flipped a towel onto his shoulder.

I skirted in between two barstools. "I'm here to see Tommy."

"Who's asking?" The bartender pressed his stubby fingers on top of the bar.

"Tell him Dillon Hart."

He eyed my chest. "Princess, I can say with surety that you're not Dillon."

"Is Tommy here or not?" I climbed up onto a barstool.

The bartender smirked, showing crooked teeth. Then he went over to a phone on the wall at the other end of the bar. Two large men three seats over hugged their beers as if they were protecting something of value.

One wearing an orange vest asked, "Can I buy you a beer, darling?"

As much as I could use something strong to drown my sorrows, I needed my wits about me. I was in a shady part of Boston about to meet with a creepy dude who gave me the willies. "Thanks, but I'm not of legal age yet."

"You don't have to be in this bar," Orange Vest Guy said.

I wasn't surprised.

The bartender returned. "Tommy will be right out. Drink?"

"Water."

After he'd handed me my beverage he waited on the other patrons. I coddled my water like it was my lifeline. Customers came in, waitresses waited on tables, and a low hum of music played in the background.

All that dimmed as several images flashed through my mind with the speed of the shutter on a camera—Kelton stroking my hair while I lay in his lap watching *Transformers*. Me telling Kelton I loved him. Kelton and I entangled in his bed. I lingered on that image. It felt so good to be in his arms and feel his arousal, his lips on me. *Stop tormenting yourself. Stop thinking about what could've been.*

Someone tapped my hand. I blinked to find Tommy sitting next to me with his thin lips curled downward.

"Your mascara is running." He attempted to touch my face with dirty fingers.

I slapped away his hand.

He scowled. "Did you and Dillon break up? Is that why you've been crying?"

I wiped my face but then stopped. My appearance didn't matter. "Did you find out yet who's on the list for that poker game?"

"Pete, can you refill her glass?" Tommy asked.

A gust of cold air hit my back as the door opened. Then a hand landed on my shoulder.

I whirled on the barstool and found Dillon.

He took one look at me and growled, "Tommy? Can you give us a minute? Thanks for calling me."

Tommy disappeared faster than the speed of light.

Dillon dropped into Tommy's seat.

Pete came over. "Drink?"

"Beer. Any kind will do. Lizzie, what happened? Why are you here?" His tone was as deadly as his growl.

Pete slid a bottled beer to Dillon.

I must've been daydreaming a long time for Dillon to have had time to get there. "I have to find Terrance. The lawyer is working to freeze my assets, but a judge has to approve it. Which means it could be weeks, and Terrance will have free rein with my money until then. Zach is being a butthead, avoiding me. Oh, and Kelton got Chloe pregnant." Saying all that out loud made bile burn my throat.

He almost spit out his beer. He dragged his hand across his mouth. "I wouldn't tell if you wanted something harder than water." His brown eyes held sympathy.

My tears threatened to fall again.

He covered his hand with mine, warm and comforting.

I sucked in my lips, my tear ducts opening up. I hated to cry, and in a public place no less. Dillon muttered Kelton's name under his breath as he wrapped one arm around me. I turned into him. His chest was solid muscle contrasting with the softness of his musky T-shirt. I desperately needed someone to hold me. I just wished it was Kelton.

He rested his chin on my head. "I wouldn't mind having a go at Maxwell if you want." He sounded so angry.

Fighting wouldn't erase the emotional pain.

"Dillon," Tommy said, his voice close by.

I sniffled as Dillon released me.

"I just got off the phone with my contact," he said. "The date of the poker game changed. It's next weekend at Frank's in the North End. And your boy, Terrance Malden, is on the list of players. If you want in, there's three spots left. The buy-in is ten *G*s per person."

My tears dried up. Terrance would be in town. I had my opportunity. Then nausea doused my excitement at the cost of the buy-in. I didn't have that kind of money. But I had to find a way in. I had an idea.

"Sign me up," I said to Tommy.

Dillon's eyes bugged out.

"No offense, sweetheart," Tommy said, "but do you have ten large? Or even know how to play poker?"

"We can wait until the game is over to talk to Malden." Dillon wore an are-you-serious look.

"I'm not taking the chance we'll miss him or he'll skip town. And I don't care that I don't know how to play poker." The game was all about bluffing anyway. Above all else, if I could get in the game, I would have Terrance's attention. He wouldn't be running from me or skating out of town or ignoring my calls. I eyed Tommy. "Do you know a loan shark I could contact?" I would bet the city was rife with them.

"Lizzie?" Dillon said as calmly as he could. "I can't let you go into a poker game run by the Italian mob. *Or* let you borrow money from a loan shark."

"I do know several of them," Tommy said quite proudly.

"Shut up," Dillon barked at Tommy.

"Dillon, this isn't your fight. My life savings is on the line." *If you had a million dollars hanging in the balance, you would do the same thing.*

"Fuck," Dillon said. "You're not going to listen to me, are you? Don't answer that." He grabbed the back of his neck then glanced at Tommy. "Reserve two spots for Lizzie and me. I'll call in my marker with Duke."

"No way." Dillon had helped me way too much since I'd been in Boston. "I can't ask you to do that. I can borrow the money myself."

"Time is of the essence." Dillon continued to hold his neck. "We need to get on the list and pay the ante before those last three spots are taken. Duke knows me. This will be faster."

I couldn't argue too much with his reasoning. Plus I was desperate. "Then I'll pay you back." Hopefully I would have the money to do so.

Tommy chuckled. "Dude, they're going to eat her alive. You better teach her your tricks of the game." Then he addressed me, but flicked his head at Dillon. "You know, this guy here is one of the best poker players I know." Tommy smirked as he left us with that piece of info.

My mouth dropped open. Not because Dillon knew how to play poker, but because the more I learned about him, the more I realized that fate was in the driver's seat in bringing us together.

"Are you sure about this?" Dillon asked, beer in hand.

"Never been more sure." If I sat around and did nothing, I'd lose all my parents' hard- earned money. "So you're good at poker?"

"Learned how when I was working on the merchant ships."

"And Duke. Is he a loan shark?"

"He is, but he's also my brother."

"What?" Dillon had never mentioned anything about a brother.

"We don't talk much," he said before downing his beer. "But we do help each other out when necessary. Enough about Duke. It's time to focus on preparing you for the game."

I wanted to know more about Dillon and his family, but he was right. The poker game was the priority, and if he didn't want to talk about his family, I would honor that. He would tell me in his own time if he wanted to.

"Let's get started then." I let out a shaky laugh.

CHAPTER 23
KELTON

I trudged downstairs and into the kitchen to get coffee and pain medication. After I'd rammed my fist into several walls and the window of my Jeep, Kross had had to take me to the emergency room, where we'd spent the majority of the night waiting for a doctor. The end result? I'd fractured all my knuckles but the one on my pinky finger.

I took two Advil, and Kross stumbled in with his shirt in hand. "Where's the coffee?"

"You look worse than me. And I'm the one bandaged up." I prepped the coffee pot. "Didn't you sleep?"

"It was tough when all I kept smelling on the pillow was jasmine."

My finger slipped off the power button on the coffeemaker. Lizzie. Yeah, she had no place in my thoughts, not until I got my head screwed on properly. No Lizzie in my life until I knew what responsibilities I had to Chloe. I also wanted to lower the volume on wild Kelton. I wouldn't change my values, but I couldn't be acting out by sleeping around or posing for Brew's art class. I also had to get serious about what I wanted for my future.

"Yeah, Lizzie slept in that room the other night." I stabbed the *on* button again. Within seconds, the coffeemaker gurgled, and coffee dropped into the carafe.

"Speaking of Lizzie. Have you heard from her?" Kross rubbed an eye.

"Seriously, dude? That girl wants nothing to do with me." I pushed away the idea that I didn't have a chance with Lizzie.

"We talked about this last night. Get your life in order. She'll be there when you're ready."

"And what if she's not? What if the baby is mine? What then?"

"Whoa! Slow down, bro. One thing at a time." He shrugged. "So what if the baby is yours? You're not marrying Chloe. You can date Lizzie. You'll just have a kid."

As realistic as that sounded, it was highly unlikely. Lizzie had a jealous streak. She might be okay with the baby, but not with Chloe.

"Call Chloe." Kross pinned me with one of his if-you-don't-I'll-kill-you expressions.

I'd ignored Chloe's repeated calls the day before until I'd gotten my hand examined. By then it had been too late to deal with anything, and part of me wasn't ready anyway. But if I wanted to start my new life, I had to confront my responsibilities. I snatched my phone from my jeans, then texted Chloe to meet me at the townhome that morning if she could.

My phone buzzed with a response. *I'll be there in fifteen minutes.*

"Can you hang?" I asked. "Chloe's on her way. You might have to pick me up off the floor." *Or maybe take me back to the emergency room. This time for a heart attack.*

"No problem. I have nothing going on today." He made himself a cup of coffee. "I'll be in the library. I need to check messages."

I poured myself a cup then downed the caffeine like it was liquor. Then another. The way I was going, I'd be high and jittery before Chloe arrived. I finished the brew.

The doorbell rang.

Not exactly fifteen minutes. Then again, Chloe didn't live but two miles away.

On my way to the door I shook away the jitters, muttering a quick prayer before I let Chloe in.

She was bundled in her parka and didn't appear as distraught as she had the day before.

I could hear Kross's voice as he talked on the phone.

"Would you like to go somewhere more private?" I asked.

"No, this won't take long." She settled down on the bottom step of the staircase. "It's probably good your brother is here."

I couldn't tell if she was sad or scared or both. Usually Chloe would be giving me some clue. Whether that was playing with her hair as she had yesterday, or crying, or raising her voice. But she was content and calm.

"Kelton—"

"Let me talk first." If I didn't, I would explode. I dug my hands into my jeans pockets as I found a spot next to her. My stomach knotted. Whether I was the father or not, I would man up. Chloe and I had history, and while I wasn't in love with her, I wanted to see her happy. She deserved to be happy. "When you said you were pregnant, I couldn't breathe. I panicked. But I will do the right thing." Letting people down was over. I had to be the man my father had raised. I had to be the man Kade had drilled into us. I had to be the man for me. I had law school ahead of me, a life of what I didn't know, but I had to step into my future with pride and determination, taking the chances I deserved, overcoming my fear of relationships. After all, I was a Maxwell, and we protected our family and friends.

A small, sad smile formed on her lips as she angled her body toward me. "I know you don't want to hear this again, but I love you."

Surprisingly, I wasn't running like I had the first time she'd told me she loved me. In fact, it didn't spark any emotion in me, or make me cringe, or want to disappear. Yet, when Lizzie had confessed her love for me, my reaction had been quite different. At first, the blood had rushed out of me. More from my own fucked-up fear of her leaving town. But I was beyond happy that she'd never stopped loving me.

"You're not running again." She pinched her eyebrows together. "Okay, this has to be a monumental moment."

Epic moment was more like it. I was done running.

"And while I love you," she went on, "you're not the father. I wanted you to be. I wanted to lie and say it was yours. But my parents didn't raise me to be dishonest. And that wouldn't be fair to you or the father. I came to you yesterday so you would hear it from me and not Zach."

"Come again?" I gritted my teeth. We had a fucking code. Friends didn't worm their way in on exes.

"Kelton, we were never going to be more than a good time in bed. I did want more with you. But you didn't. Zach was always there for me whenever you and I called it quits." She sat prim and proper and shuddered out a breath. "He's a good man. He loves me, and I love him."

I pushed to my feet, trying to absorb the idea of Zach and her. "If you two love each other, why all the crying? Why ask me to take you to the art gala? Why ask Lacey to talk to me?"

"The art gala was for my father. I wasn't ready to tell him we'd broken up again. He'd always told me you'd break my heart, and I was trying to prove him wrong. Sad, right?"

I'd always suspected Jeremy Pitt didn't think I was good for his daughter. I couldn't say I blamed him.

"Then between having to tell my parents and beating myself up for not insisting on Zach using protection, I've been a basket case. Zach and I have also been fighting about who was going to tell you. I wanted to be the one because I didn't want you to think I'd cheated on you. I never did."

Zach and Chloe together shouldn't bother me, but it did. "Okay, but why didn't you or Zach tell me you two were seeing each other? I've always been honest with you."

"Really? He's your friend, Kelton. We were both worried that you would kill him."

That might be true. I had no say in who Chloe dated or even Zach. I'd never hidden my dates from her. But I'd never dated any of Zach's girlfriends either. My head was pounding as fast as my heart was ramming into my ribs. A slow burn crawled up my chest as relief pushed it down. I glanced up the staircase. I didn't know for sure if Zach was home, but I was about to find out.

Chloe popped up. "Don't, Kelton." She raised her voice and her hands.

Kross came out of the library. "Everything okay?"

I let out an evil laugh. "That's why you said it was good that my brother was here." Kudos to her for knowing me so well. "Chloe, get out of my way." I wanted Zach to man up.

Kross jumped in between Chloe and me. "Bro, turn around. You've punched enough shit in the last twenty-four hours."

Footsteps padded on the landing above.

"It's okay, Kross," Zach said.

"No, it's not," Kross barked. "No offense, but you don't want a raging Kelton in your face."

"We had a code, man," I yelled. "You should've had the balls to at least tell me."

"Then what?" Zach asked, grit in his voice. "What would you have done? Punched the shit out of me like you do to everyone who makes you mad or when you don't get your way? You treated Chloe like shit."

I clenched my good fist. "I never, ever disrespected Chloe." I eyed her. "Is that what you told him? I've always told you up front I wasn't in the relationship for the long haul. I always broke up with you when I felt suffocated or you were trying to get me to commit." I paced. "Unbelievable. Chloe's pregnant, and I'm feeling like I'm the one to blame. You know, you two make a good pair. You were right, Chloe. I probably would've killed him." Then I disappeared into the kitchen, almost dropping to my knees, but Kross caught me.

"Zach's the father." I released all the air in my lungs.

"I got you, man," he said as he wrapped his arms around me.

It was time to take the chances I deserved. It was time to tell the girl with the long dark hair and the gold speck in her eye, the one wearing my half-heart charm, the one that always had a hold on me, how I really felt about her.

⚜

I SMOOTHED out my tie as I waited for my appointment with Mr. Davenport. After not showing up last week with Lizzie, I had to somehow redeem myself. If there was anything I wanted without any doubt, it was the intern position at Davenport Law Firm. I'd never wavered in my desire to become a lawyer. I had one year left at BU, then I was off to law school. I had everything I needed to submit my application to Harvard Law—the necessary recommendations, good scores on the Law School Admission Test. The only requirement left was a summer internship at a law firm. Professionally, I was in a good place. Personally, I had work to do.

For the last week I'd been making significant changes. I moved out of the townhome and back to Ashford. Zach and I weren't speaking, and it was way too awkward living with him. I also quit my job working for Brew. He was disappointed but understood after I explained to him that I was vying for a position at a law firm and posing for his class could hurt my chances of getting the job. After I'd ticked those two items off my list, I'd made an appointment with my math professor to take the exam I missed. In between all that, I'd spent time either hanging out with my mom, who was thrilled to have me home, or going to classes.

"Mr. Maxwell?" Bonnie stood, holding a folder, smiling down at me. "Mr. Davenport will see you now."

With my nerves tight, I unfolded myself, buttoned my suit jacket, and clutched my leather binder.

"I like your tie," Bonnie said.

"Thank you. My mom had it made for me." I was wearing a black suit with a deep-blue shirt underneath and a silver tie that had *KM* and the number five in superscript embroidered in red stitching. It signified my love for math, but more importantly it was my symbol for my siblings, Kade, Kross, Kody, Karen, and me. When I was a kid, anytime I'd doodled I'd always filled up a piece of paper with the initials *KM* to the fifth power. Karen had loved when I'd plastered her walls with my artwork. My mom had chosen the tie. She'd said it would bring me luck. Hopefully it would, but more importantly, wearing it I felt closer to Karen, and I needed to feel like family was with me on this interview.

Bonnie ushered me into Mr. Davenport's office then closed the door. Mr. Davenport stood, taking in the sunny Boston skyline, his reflection showing a pensive expression. "Have a seat, Mr. Maxwell," he said, turning.

I unbuttoned my suit jacket and complied, setting my leather binder on my lap. "I appreciate you taking my call and setting aside time to see me," I began, removing a report I'd put together on Florida estate law. Mr. Davenport was well schooled on Florida law. This was an exercise to show him how detailed and thorough I was. I handed it to him.

His gaze lingered on my bruised hand as he folded himself into his leather chair. "I know you're very astute, Mr. Maxwell." He flipped through the pages of my report, not really absorbing much. "Your level of knowledge is not what stops me from hiring you. It's allegiance to this firm and the job. You missed the appointment last week. That's a red flag for me. I understand that you're helping Ms. Reardon, but a lawyer would never leave their client hanging."

"I'm not about to make excuses. You're exactly right. I assure you I won't let that happen again. This job is important to me. The law is important to me." I swallowed my nerves.

He mashed his lips into a paper-thin line. "I'll take this report and our meeting today into consideration."

Bonnie poked her head in. "Sir, you have an emergency call on line two."

"Mr. Maxwell, Bonnie will see you out."

I rose. "When will you make your decision?" My dad had counseled me to make sure I closed the deal.

"The position was originally for a summer intern. But we recently lost two lawyers, so the person I hire will intern beginning immediately on a part-time basis. Then, once the college semester is complete, it will be full time through the summer. Do you have a problem with that?"

"No, sir." I clasped my binder as tightly as I could with my left hand. I'd taken the bandages off my right hand to let the cuts heal, but it was still sore. "And I quit my job as a model for that art class your daughter is in."

He cocked a bushy eyebrow. "We'll be in touch soon."

Whether my last statement helped to sway him in my favor, I'd done all I could to land the job. When I got down to the lobby, I loosened my tie.

Kross jumped out of a chair. "How did it go?" Kross and I had driven into the city together since he had a meeting with his boxing coach and Kody had borrowed my Jeep. His truck was in the shop for a tune-up.

"We'll see." I hadn't gotten a good vibe, but I did all I could. "On the way back to Ashford, can we make a stop?"

It was time to break down the steel wall around my heart.

CHAPTER 24
LIZZIE

Dillon and I were sitting at the kitchen table playing five-card draw, which was what we'd be playing on Saturday. Once Dillon had gotten the money from his brother, Duke, and we were confirmed players, Dillon had gone to work prepping me for the game, including bluffing, the most important aspect of poker.

"Any word from Davenport on freezing your assets?" Dillon asked as he kept his gaze on his cards.

"Just that the court date for the temporary injunction is next week. Which means Terrance probably used more of my money for the entrance fee for this game." I twisted my earring, chewing on my bottom lip.

"Stop playing with your earring," Dillon commanded. "Remember that any nervous tics will give you away."

"Sorry. Sometimes when I'm deep in thought I don't realize I'm doing it." I was staring at a crap hand of nothing, thinking of the game and Terrance and wondering how Kelton was doing. Those three things had consumed my every waking minute for the last week. I dropped the cards on the table. "I need a potty break." We'd been at it for two hours. I'd wanted to quit an hour before to watch *Magic Mike* with Bee and Allie in the game room.

"We have two days." Dillon crossed to the fridge. "And don't think of sneaking downstairs either."

As much as I wanted to, the time was closing in. I had to keep at it, more to sharpen my skills at bluffing than at playing the game. I stuck out my tongue.

"I caught that," Dillon said, peeking over the fridge.

I giggled as I went into the half-bath in the hall. One part of me hated that Dillon was invested in the game. I didn't want to be the one to strain his relationship with Duke if he couldn't pay him back. But Dillon had said to let him worry about his family. The other part of me was relieved knowing that Dillon would be there with me. If anyone knew Boston's underbelly, it was Dillon. Not only that but each player was allowed one guest. Dillon had Josh and Rafe lined up to have our backs in the event anything went haywire.

No sooner than I'd parked myself on the toilet, the doorbell rang.

Dillon's heavy footsteps sounded as he passed by. Then the front door groaned. "What the fuck? You're not welcome here." Dillon's tone was lethal.

"I don't want any trouble," Kelton said. "I just need to talk to Lizzie."

I twirled my earring in every direction. One week without talking, seeing, or touching Kelton was probably the toughest emotional week I'd had in a long time. I'd barely eaten, slept, or even left the house. I should've been out searching for a job, especially with ten Gs on the line. My dad had always taught me to be ready for anything, which meant I should be miles ahead in the event I couldn't pay Dillon. But depression had set in like it had seven years ago. I was grateful for my new extended family. If it weren't for Bee and Allie and even Dillon, keeping me occupied with cards and movies, I'd be hiding in a corner of a closet, crying.

"Smart not to show up here alone," Dillon said, anger weaving through his tone. "And I told you not to hurt her."

"Is she here or not?" Kelton asked calmly.

Please don't let him in. I didn't want to deal with Kelton or hear him apologize for what could've been between us.

"You're lucky I don't make decisions for Lizzie. However, if she tells you to leave, then leave," Dillon said. "Got it?"

This was one time I wouldn't have minded Dillon calling my shots.

The *thud thud thud* of their footfalls tramped by the bathroom. Then a chair dragged, scraping the kitchen floor.

"Where is she?" Kelton asked. "This won't take long."

My heartbeat shot off the charts. If I snuck out, I'd put Dillon in a tough spot. Or Kelton and Dillon would end up in a fight. I finished my business and washed my hands.

"Kel, Mom is expecting us for dinner."

"Chill, Kross." Kelton's tone was equal parts determination and frustration.

Damn cockroach wasn't leaving. We'd see about that. I steeled my shoulders then walked out and took up a post in the doorway of the kitchen.

"What card game are you playing?" Kross asked.

"Five-card draw," I said as I set my sights on Kelton, sizing him up from head to toe. My stomach went crazy, spinning in all different directions.

He was dressed in a tailored black suit, a killer blue shirt that enhanced the color of his eyes, and a silver monogrammed tie that hung loose around his neck. He'd finally had his doodling turned into artwork. Whenever Kelton had been bored in class he'd scribbled in his notebook, in particular the initials *KM* and the number five. A thread of sadness hit me at how much family meant to him and how I wanted to be part of his. *That won't happen now.*

"Since when do you play poker?" Kelton bore his gaze into me, soft and apologetic.

"What do you want?" I asked, rooted to my spot. I was a second away from throwing myself at him.

As if he knew what I was thinking, he smirked like an asswipe.

"I want to talk to you without you running away," he said.

Like you run from your feelings? "I don't have time. I got a poker game to prepare for." I shoved my trembling hands into the pocket of my sweatshirt.

Kross shuffled the cards expertly, the sound snapping my attention away from the Adonis. "You play?"

"I can hold my own." A fresh scar on Kross's right hand caught my eye as he shuffled again.

"Don't you have to be home for dinner?" Dillon asked in a sarcastic tone, glowering at Kelton.

"Not *the* poker game?" Kelton's sexy grin became cold and intense.

I should just tell him. So he could leave. The longer we bantered, the longer he stayed, breaking through my already-weak defenses. "After talking with Mr. Davenport, it would be quicker to get Terrance to turn over all the financial documents. And since he's hard to find and the lawyers can't even get him on the phone, my only chance is to corner him at this poker game." I knew he wouldn't have my documents with him. But I had to give it my best shot to plead with him to give them to me or at least cooperate with the lawyers.

Fury reddened Kelton's handsome face as he turned to Dillon. "You're letting her go into an underground poker game?"

"If you're here to talk," I said, "then do so. The poker game is not your concern."

Kelton opened the top two buttons of his shirt. "How the hell are you going to play poker when the major part of the game is bluffing? You give yourself away all the time by playing with your necklace and your earring. And by chewing your nails."

I was getting better, thanks to Dillon.

"Say your piece then go," Dillon spat.

"Shut up," Kelton growled.

Dillon pushed off the sink. Kross jumped up from the table just as fast.

I marched over to Dillon and laid my hand on his taut bicep. "Can you give us a minute?"

He shook his head at Kelton. "I'd throw you out with my bare hands if it weren't for Lizzie." He eyed me. "We have work to do. Please make it quick. And there's a Taser in the kitchen drawer."

Kelton laughed as though daring me to use the Taser. I didn't want any violence, and something told me that Kelton didn't either. Maybe it was the contentment written all over his face, a vast difference from when I'd last seen him at Rumors. Fatherhood agreed with him.

Kross said, "Bro, you didn't come here to get into a fight. As Dillon said, say your piece quickly. I'll call Mom and let her know we're going to be late."

Kross disappeared down the hall, but Dillon hesitated before he reluctantly stalked out.

"What's your problem?" I anchored myself to the counter near the fridge. "You said you didn't want any trouble, but you're acting like an asshat."

Kelton gripped a lock of his hair. "Because you're walking into danger with that poker game. I can't let you do that."

Whether I loved Kelton or not, the man wasn't going to boss me around. "You can't tell me what to do."

Calmly, coolly, and evenly, he said, "I can. I don't let people I love walk into danger."

"Why would you... Wait? What?"

He pushed off the island, wiping his hands on his suit pants. "Baby doll." He blew out a breath as he came up to me. "From the moment I saw you in the fifth grade until this very moment standing here, I've never stopped loving you."

My lungs seized. My brain went blank, until I thought of Chloe. I frowned. "But you're going to be a daddy."

He walked away, seemingly irritated all of a sudden.

I counted to ten, hoping my pulse would slow.

"Yeah, about that." He came back, anger washing over his face. "Zach is the father."

I quietly pushed all the air in my lungs out through my nose. "Why do you look like you want to punch something?" Did he want to be the father? Darkness skirted the edges of my vision as my thoughts held steady.

"Friends' code and all that."

The light grew brighter, my pulse kick-starting. Then I remembered Chloe crying outside of the townhome that day. It was all starting to make sense. "Why didn't you tell me when I was running out of Rumors?"

"I didn't know if I was the father then. I wasn't even going to tell you until I knew for sure, but I also didn't want to lie and make up an excuse about why I didn't show up at Davenport's." He tucked my hair behind my ear. "The good news is that I'm all yours if you'll have me."

I nibbled on a nail. Or more like gnawed on it. I wanted him. I wanted us. But a small voice in the back of my head reminded me of our conversation in his kitchen.

"Lizard, please say something. My heart is slamming against my chest, and my stomach hurts."

"You said your life would be over when I went back to Miami. What's changed?"

"I love you," he said.

"You said yourself you've always loved me."

He traced circles around my lips with his fingers. "The thought of you not being by my side scares me. I'm not going to lie. But Kade and Lacey make it work, so why can't we? If our love is strong, we'll survive the long distance."

"You're not telling me what to do."

His finger stopped on my upper lip, searching my eyes. "Oh, baby doll. There will be times when I will, and you will enjoy it."

I opened my mouth.

He stuck his finger in. "Now, will you have me?"

All I could do was close my mouth around his finger. It occurred to me to bite it, but I sucked on it instead.

Groaning, he mashed his body into me then cupped my face in his hands. "Is that a yes?"

"Just kiss me."

His tongue plunged into my mouth, exploring, before demanding I respond. I kissed him back, wild and free, as a storm brewed deep inside me. I gripped his shoulders, trying to get closer to him even though our bodies were already plastered against each other.

He broke the kiss. "I'm so fucking ready to take you right here."

I was more than ready for him to do wild things to me. But not in Dillon's house, and as much as I wanted to find somewhere to show him how much I loved him, I wanted to wait until after the poker game when I wasn't thinking about my bluffing, what hand I was dealt, or Terrance. Kelton deserved all of me, and I couldn't afford any distractions. "Can we make a date for after the poker game? I need to focus."

His forehead touched mine. "I'm not sure I can wait. But I do want your full attention. And when we make love, I want you to be surrounded in flowers, touched with a feather, and caressed with my tongue." His voice was all kinds of husky.

Kross cleared his throat. "Bro, time to get moving."

Dillon came in behind Kross.

Kelton held out his hand to him. "Man, I'm sorry for being a dick."

Dillon checked on me then shook Kelton's hand. "Apology accepted."

"I want in on the poker game," Kelton said.

"Not a good idea," Kross said. "You need to walk the straight and narrow with Davenport's job opportunity on the line."

I couldn't let Kelton ruin any chance he had with Davenport or his future as a lawyer. "We have Rafe and Josh going with us."

"I promise to be on my best behavior," Kelton pleaded.

"Man, you're a hothead. We can't risk it," Dillon said curtly.

"What if I go with?" Kross asked. "I can be muscle and keep this one in line." He stabbed a thumb at his brother.

I wasn't about to intervene or sway Dillon's decision. He was only part of this poker game for me. He'd gone out on a limb, borrowing the money from his brother for me. So if he felt that Kelton shouldn't go, I would support him.

Dillon rubbed the scruff on his face. "I'm only saying yes because I know you wouldn't let anything happen to her, and Kross is better muscle. Plus I don't need my men getting into any trouble."

I hooked my arm through Kelton's. "I'll walk you out." It was better if they left before Dillon changed his mind.

The stars were out but hardly visible. A light wind blew, the chimes on someone's porch singing.

"Are you sure about this?" I asked. "We're dealing with illegal gambling. If Mr. Davenport finds out—"

"I'm not letting you go in without me."

I prayed nothing went wrong, for his sake.

CHAPTER 25

KELTON

We zipped by buildings, restaurants, and people darting in and out of nighttime establishments as Dillon navigated through the streets of Boston toward the North End or Little Italy. Kross rode shotgun while Lizzie and I sat in the backseat of Dillon's SUV. The Camaro was too small for all four of us.

I snaked my hand out to rest on her thigh. "You look amazing." She was wearing a short, black, low-cut cocktail dress. Since underground games didn't have a dress code, I would guess she was trying to use distraction as part of her bluffing. God, I hoped her strategy worked. I worried she wouldn't be able to bluff. Then she'd be out of the game early. Which meant Lizzie wouldn't have the patience to wait to tear Terrance a new one. Neither would I, for that matter. And that would lead to mayhem. Not good when we were guests of the Italian mob, and because of that I wanted to lock her up and prevent her from coming to this mob-infested soirée, but in part I understood her need to see Terrance in person. Zach always had issues getting ahold of his old man.

She smiled seductively.

My heart slammed against my chest. *Boom. Boom. Boom.* Since I'd told her I loved her, my heart hadn't calmed down. All I kept thinking about was her and how every time I kissed her she tasted of bubblegum, the past, and everything I wanted in my future, a future of her and me tangled together. Yeah, my balls were blue, dark fucking blue.

"Everything okay?" she asked.

Patriots. Football. Super Bowl. Inwardly, I laughed. I'd started chanting my mantra days before the big game. I believed on some higher level that Tom Brady had heard me. The Patriots beat the Panthers in the Super Bowl. Of course, that wasn't what should have been going through my head in that moment.

"You remember what we discussed yesterday?" Kross and I had met over at Dillon's to finalize plans. "Use your nervous habits to throw them off. Bite a nail if you have a good hand. Smile when you have nothing. But don't keep using the same habits. Change it up. If you can, don't use any expressions."

"I get it," she said, doubt resonating in her voice.

My hand traveled up her dress, slow and sure, hoping my touch would calm her. She grasped my hand before it got too far then shook her head.

I whispered in her ear. "Baby doll, relax." I was the one who needed to chill. If my brain wasn't thinking what could go wrong that night, my dick was certainly jonesing to have that woman right there and then.

"Let's run through this one more time," Dillon said as he braked at a light. "There'll be ten players. Two tables. Ten guests. Security guards and two dealers. You're out when you run out of money. Afterward, you're allowed to stay and watch. If Terrance tanks before Lizzie and me, then Kross and Kelton, since you're not playing, make sure he doesn't leave. And remember, this isn't a casino. You can't cash in your winnings if you want to leave early. Also, Lizzie, as much as you want to have words with Terrance, keep things civil during the breaks. Otherwise, you'll be thrown out."

Quietness kept us company for two more turns and three more lights until Dillon parked across from Frank's.

My body tensed. "You sure you're ready?" I asked Lizzie.

"One hundred percent," she said with no hesitation, puffing out her chest.

I stifled a groan. *Now is not the time to be thinking about sex, moron.*

As soon as I stepped on the sidewalk, all thoughts of my steamy plans for Lizzie and me dissipated. My nerves began jumping around like a pogo stick. I'd rather have pinned Terrance down at a legal casino, not a mob-infested underground game. I'd suggested to Dillon and Lizzie that I could reach out to Jeremy Pitt for help in snagging Terrance from this game. After all, he was the Russian mob. But Dillon had told me that the game had been set up by the Italian mob. Which would only spark a fire between the Russians and the Italians, and I didn't want to be the one to start that war, especially when I knew how much Pitt hated the Italian mob. After all, he'd been instrumental in rescuing his niece, Lacey Robinson, when her grandfather, head of the Italian mob, had kidnapped her.

We checked in with the security guard at the door, who scanned the list of names. Once cleared, we entered the narrow hall of the brick building only to be stopped by two more security guards. I watched intently as Lizzie slipped off her jacket, revealing her body to the guards. My muscles hadn't loosened, and they wouldn't until I was comfortable she was out of this place and safe. They went about their business, sizing her up instead of searching her. She couldn't hide any weapons with that dress. The garment barely fell to her knees, the spaghetti straps were angel-hair thin, her hair was up, and her sandal-type heels had no room to store even a razor blade. They sifted through her jacket before they waved her through. I went next, then Kross, then Dillon. We were all in jeans and button-up shirts, and we'd left our jackets in the car.

We made it through easily before we were escorted by another guard down a set of stairs and into a basement that smelled of piss and other unpleasant things. I kept my hand on Lizzie's lower back as much as I could. Just before the guard opened the door into a room, I whispered to her, "Last chance to back out."

"No way," she said, smiling at me.

Son of a bitch. The woman was determined as hell, which made me love her even more. But she didn't know what she was walking into. None of us really did. I didn't want to jeopardize my law career, but I couldn't let anything happen to her. I would never recover if I lost her again.

CHAPTER 26
LIZZIE

Cigar smoke choked me as we entered a dungeon-like room: cement walls, cement floors, a bar that appeared to have been wheeled in, and a cluster of metal folding tables. The lighting was dim, except over the two poker tables. The room hummed with mostly middle-aged men. It took me a second to orient myself, and I blew out air through my nostrils.

Kelton guided me forward with his hand on my back. "You'll get used to the smoke in a few minutes."

I didn't know about that. The haze was thick and suffocating. But no amount of cigar smoke would deter me from the reason we were there. Plus I was actually excited to play poker.

Heading to the bar, I scanned the crowd. All manner of men—tall, short, skinny, hefty, fat, bald, hairy—mingled. A handful of women, mostly short in stature, chatted as though they were long-lost friends. But no man resembling Zach with a big belly.

A bartender with a buzz cut was serving a beer to a large man with a comb-over when we joined the group. The other bartender, a female who had biceps as big as Kross's, served a lady with short brown hair.

We hovered near an empty table away from the other people in the room.

"Drink?" Dillon asked us.

"Water," Kross said.

I wouldn't have minded a shot of tequila to calm my nerves. It wasn't like I couldn't have one, either. After all, everything there was illegal. Kelton and I declined. Better to keep my wits about me and my bladder empty. Dillon had schooled us that a poker game could go on all night. And I wasn't sure how many breaks we'd get.

"Are those two men the dealers?" I asked Kelton.

Two men, one short, one tall, both dressed in black suits and red ties, stood between the two round, felt-topped poker tables, talking.

"Probably," Kelton responded as he eyed the room with mechanical precision, reminding me of a robot.

Dillon brought over two glasses of water. Kross plucked one from his hand. Dillon sipped on the other.

"Terrance here?" Dillon asked.

"No," I said, my voice cracking. Then something depressing popped into my brain. "What if he doesn't show?" With Zach and Kelton not on speaking terms, maybe Zach had warned his father of our plan. We'd told Zach about the poker game, although he didn't know we were playing in it.

"Then we still play poker," Dillon said. "We paid the money. Might as well see if we can win seventy thousand dollars."

Yeah, that would be the icing on the cake. I could pay back my debts and have money left over. I dismissed the thought, as exciting as it sounded. I'd only learned the game a week before. Unlike some of the people playing that night, who I imagined had been at it for years.

"This is all wrong," Kelton said. "I got a bad feeling. Particularly with the frightened look on Lizzie's face."

My muscles tightened. "I'm good."

Kross set his water down then pushed up his shirtsleeves, revealing a rattlesnake on his forearm. "Make them believe you have something you don't. It's like boxing. During a match, I always throw a left hook when my opponent thinks I'm going to throw a right."

"I know, bluff." Habits were hard to break, especially with frayed nerves.

The tall dealer with slicked-back hair announced, "Five minutes. Last chance to use the facilities until the scheduled break."

People scattered. Some darted to the restrooms located in the far left corner while others casually made their way to their seats at one of the two poker tables. As the area thinned out, the door opened, and in strutted blond-haired, big-bellied Terrance Malden with a short platinum-blond woman at his side. He glanced around. I couldn't say for sure if he would recognize me. Bee had done my makeup. Allie had coiled my hair off my shoulders in a fancy twisting up-do. Anytime I'd met with Terrance, I'd been plain Jane—no makeup and hair down, wearing shorts, a T-shirt, and flip-flops.

"That's him," I said.

Kelton agreed. "He's looking quite haggard these days."

I'd forgotten that Kelton knew him.

"You know, maybe if we hit him up now, we could get the hell out of here," Kelton said.

Dillon shook his head. "That will only start a shit-storm. Remember, no trouble. Let's stick to the plan."

We couldn't waver from our plan since Dillon and I had money on the line.

"Mr. Malden," the tall dealer said. "Nice to see you." They shook. "Why don't you take your seat? We're about to begin."

Terrance nodded then kissed the short woman before finding his spot. Those exiting the restrooms claimed their seats.

"Is it assigned seating?" I asked, hoping that I was at the same table as Terrance.

"Yeah." Dillon focused on Kelton and Kross. "You two strike up a conversation with the blonde. See if you can find out where he's staying in case we can't get anywhere with Terrance."

At least someone was thinking of all the angles.

Kelton drew me to him. "Remember: bluffing is the game here. And"—his lips feathered over mine—"kick some ass."

Laughter escaped me, skittish and high-pitched, as anger and fear crashed in tidal waves through my stomach. Dillon grabbed my hand and ushered me to the tables. The players seemed to be in their own worlds, checking their phones one last time or lighting up fresh cigars.

Beads of sweat began to form on my forehead. I took in one breath of cigar smoke then released it. Then I repeated the process as I found the tent card with *Reardon* typed on it. I was at the same table as Terrance.

The butterflies in my stomach perked up as I took my seat. On my left sat a large man with a comb-over and body odor, whose name card read Oscar. The brunette with short hair from the bar sat on the other side of Oscar. I couldn't see the name on her card. Next to her was Dillon, followed by Terrance, who sat across from me. He was reading something on his phone. I straightened in my chair, glancing past him to the bar where Kross and Kelton were, though the light above us made it difficult to see them.

The tall dealer walked up to stand next to me. "Okay, let's begin. Each of you has a tray of poker chips with twenty, fifty, and hundred-dollar chips. We'll begin by dealing first to Ms. Reardon." The dealer motioned to me with a flip of his hand.

At the mention of my name, Terrance whipped up his head. His hazel eyes went wider than the poker chips. I kept my expression impassive—at least I hoped I did—and pictured kicking him under the table, handcuffing him until he confessed, sticking out my tongue, screaming at him, or even punching him square in his hook nose.

My imaginary fun was shattered when the dealer continued. "The game is five-card draw. Once the cards are dealt, the bet will begin with Ms. Reardon. You can't replace more than three cards unless you have an ace. Breaks will be on the hour. Once your money is gone, you're out. Any questions?"

"I have a problem with Ms. Reardon," Terrance said, his voice gruff as though he'd smoked one too many cigars. "She doesn't belong here."

The dealer glanced at me then back at Terrance. "Her money is as good as yours."

"She can't be but twenty." Terrance's jaw flexed.

The man knew exactly how old I was. He knew more about my life than anyone else at the table.

I narrowed my eyes. "And you don't need to be gambling my money away."

The dealer studied me for a long minute. "Do you have an ID?"

"Are you kidding me?" The gambling age in Massachusetts was eighteen. "He's just afraid I'm going to take his money." I lifted a shoulder. "Which I am." *Don't get cocky, girl.*

"You tell him, honey," the brunette said.

Terrance glared daggers at the woman, who reminded me of Halle Berry.

"Milt," Terrance said to the dealer, about to stand.

Dillon put his hand on Terrance's shoulder. "What's your problem? We're all here to play."

"In an underground illegal poker game, no less. Therefore my age doesn't matter." My tone was neutral, even though I was shaking inside.

"Again, her money is good," Milt said. Then he dealt the cards.

Terrance scowled.

When all five cards were in my hand, I fanned them out close to me. I had the two of spades, three of diamonds, seven of hearts, ten of diamonds, and three of clubs. I had nothing.

"Ms. Reardon, pass or bet?" Milt asked.

I slowly lifted my gaze to Terrance. He still had a dirty look on his face. Might as well make him sweat. The game was about bluffing as much as it was about the hand that was dealt. I could start us off with a bang by betting half of my money—make a statement. That might serve to show them I was crazy, and I did want to be taken seriously, be professional, and handle my situation like an adult, not like some lunatic.

I counted out ten black chips then pushed them to the middle of the table.

"Bet is a thousand," the dealer said.

Oscar, the Halle lookalike, and Dillon each bet a thousand. Studying me, Terrance stalled before dumping his thousand into the pot. I didn't have an ace, but I only discarded two cards—the seven of hearts and the two of spades. I was left with a pair of threes and a ten of diamonds. I wanted to keep my highest card.

When everyone was ready, Milt dealt the appropriate number of cards to each player. Perspiration coated my underarms. As I picked up the two cards, placing them behind the others, I willed my hands to stop shaking. Then I checked the cards one by one.

"Ms. Reardon, it's your bet," the dealer announced.

I had three tens and a pair of threes—a full house, which was the fourth best hand to have outside of a four of a kind, straight flush, and royal flush. Since I'd started off with a bet of a thousand, I continued with that amount, placing my chips in the pile. In my mind, it wouldn't be appropriate to lower the bet. That would infer I didn't have anything or that I'd screwed up by getting rid of the wrong cards.

Oscar folded. Halle matched my bet. Dillon folded. The bet was to Terrance. He checked me, then his cards, then looked at me again, his expression blank.

"I'll see your thousand and raise it by two thousand." He counted his chips before plunking them into the pile.

"Ms. Reardon, the bet is to you," the dealer said. "Two thousand to stay in the game."

Oscar lit up a cigar. Dillon's eyebrows furrowed. Terrance sat back, plastering a smug grin on his face. Everyone at my table watched me intently as the room dropped into a thick silence.

I wanted to check on Kelton, but I didn't want to be distracted. Nor did I want people to think I was seeking help. So I stared at my cards, thinking. The pot totaled ten thousand dollars. Twelve if I matched Terrance's bet. I had a full house. Three other poker hands topped what I had. Terrance had more experience than me, and I had eight thousand dollars remaining to play more hands. So I wasn't in any danger of running out of money yet. But if I could come out of the game as the big winner, I'd win seventy thousand dollars provided I didn't make stupid decisions. A wild laugh broke out in my head. Sitting there was a stupid decision. No, it was a desperate one. *Leave now. Get up gracefully and walk out the door. Let the legal system take care of Terrance. But if you win, the money will help you get on your feet until the courts resolve your case.*

"Ms. Reardon," the dealer prodded.

I glanced at Terrance.

"You don't belong here, Elizabeth." Terrance looked down his hooked nose at me.

I bent the cards as a desire for vengeance overtook the impulse to leave. I peeked at Dillon. He shook his head with the barest movement. Whether Terrance was an expert at the game or not, at that moment, nothing mattered except revenge. Sitting across from him, seeing his condescending mug, remembering my dad and how he'd admired Terrance, I wanted to physically harm him. He was betraying my dad and the tight friendship they'd had. That thought alone made my blood boil.

"I'm all in." I slid all my chips to the center.

Gasps, chokes, and guffaws chimed around the table and from the audience at the bar. The brunette, who was waiting to bet, threw her cards down. Dillon drilled his gaze into me.

"Are you sure you know what you're doing?" Terrance asked. "Your father was stupid like that, too."

"Come again?" The hairs along my arms stood at attention.

"I'm not repeating myself. And that was an amateur move."

God, I was a fool to think Terrance would help me. "And you think you're not stupid? Do you think stealing all of my inheritance was wise? Do you like taking from a woman who just lost her parents?" I planted my hands on the table, ready to attack him.

Dillon cleared his throat.

Yeah, no trouble. I got it. But this jerk had laid down the gauntlet. No way in hell was Terrance getting away with anything. So much for being nice, calm, and professional. Fuck all that. "My father did have a fault, and that was trusting you." I locked my jaw so tight I swore my teeth were about to crack.

Kelton stalked over. The dealer snapped his fingers to a hulk of a man standing at the door who I hadn't noticed before. He left the room, probably to get reinforcements.

When Terrance laid eyes on Kelton, his chair flew back as he vaulted out of it like a jack-in-the-box. His gaze searched the entire room.

"Don't worry, Mr. Malden," Kelton said nicely. "Your son isn't here. But I'm sure he would want you to know you're going to be a grandfather."

"Pardon?" Terrance placed a hand on the back of his chair.

"That's right," Kelton continued. "In fact, I think you'll like getting to know the baby's other grandfather, Jeremy Pitt."

Dead, scary silence filled every nook and cranny in the place.

I stomped around the table to stand next to Kelton. Kross hung back close to the door. Dillon joined me.

"You mean *the* Jeremy Pitt?" Something far worse than fear washed over Terrance as sweat beaded on his upper lip.

Everyone seemed to be paralyzed, even the dealers. Dillon had mentioned the night before that it wouldn't be good for Kelton to involve Jeremy since he was the Russian mob and we were in Italian territory. But the mere mention of Jeremy's name held more weight than if he had been there. Reality bloomed. I was in a world I wanted no part of—a world that reeked of thugs, guns, danger, and all kinds of bad shit.

Terrance glowered at me. "So is this your way of getting to me? Threatening me by flouncing the name of Jeremy Pitt?"

"Is it working?" I couldn't help but ask.

He scrubbed a hand over his mouth.

Milt broke out of his trance and said, "Either sit or all of you will be escorted out." He eyed the door.

"Me?" Terrance sneered at the dealer. "These kids don't belong here."

"We need to go," Kelton whispered in my ear. "That dude at the door went to get men and guns."

I should have been fazed, but I'd come there to find out why Terrance stole from my dad. More importantly, to get him to cooperate in handing over any documents he had on the accounting of my estate. I silently swore at the last thought. The man was a gambler and a thief. He wouldn't be filling out tax returns or following the law. I should've thought about that before I borrowed thousands of dollars from a loan shark and put the guys into a dangerous situation.

A wave of cigar smoke filtered up my nose. I coughed.

"Come on." Kelton cupped my elbow.

I wasn't leaving yet. Dillon placed a hand on my back.

"Sir," I said to Milt. "May I have a few words with Mr. Malden? Then we can resume the game." My tone was firm but polite.

"You have two minutes before the security team storms in," he said.

"Then hold them off," Kelton barked. "Or take one of those scheduled breaks."

The short dealer at the other table spoke up. "We'll take a five-minute break." He started in the direction of the bar with his phone to his ear.

With the exception of two players at the other table who went to the bar, no one moved.

"Are you about to read me my rights?" Terrance asked, sarcasm dripping from his tone and sweat sliding down the sides of his face.

"Why did you steal from a man who adored you?" Each word burned as though I'd downed a nasty glass of moonshine. But once the question was out there, a warm feeling danced down my chest. Hours upon hours of worry, frustration, anger, rage, and anxiety lifted off me.

"He's addicted." Oscar's gritty voice cut through the tension. "Like the rest of us with this habit."

Not all of us had a gambling problem, although I could see how one could become addicted to the high of betting, playing, and bluffing. Regardless, I wanted to hear Terrance own up to what he'd done. His confession wouldn't change the past, but it would help me sleep better.

"You need help," I said, jutting out my chin, my hands fisted at my sides.

Terrance let out a roar of laughter. "You think you can save me?"

"I'm not here to save you," I said. "I want to know how much of my money you threw away. And why."

Kelton's hand touched my lower back before pressing into my spine. He tapped his fingers as though he was trying to send me a signal in Morse code. Dillon left to stand near Kross.

Terrance darted his gaze to Milt then back. "Fine. If it gets us back in the game." He ran fat fingers through his hair. "A man like me should never have been given access to large amounts of money."

The door flew open. Four men in black stormed in, pointing guns in every direction. Milt held up his right hand at the men.

So much for no trouble.

"Hurry the fuck up," Kelton said. "Tell her now."

Dillon and Kross held fast as they both gave us a nod. No doubt telling us to hurry up.

"I tried at first to do the right thing." The guns didn't seem to faze Terrance.

On the other hand, Kross and Dillon shifted on their feet, as did Kelton. I crossed my arms over my chest, not nearly as antsy as they were. I'd been waiting for this opportunity for months.

"I stayed away from gambling for years. But when I started to sift through your father's bank accounts, I told myself I would only play one game." Terrance wiped his forehead.

"How much?" I asked, holding my breath.

"All told, there's only two hundred thousand left." Terrance held his condescending tone until the last half of the sentence, when his voice cracked.

I didn't know whether to be happy there was money left or angry he'd gambled away most of the million dollars.

One of the guards said, "Sir, cops are on their way."

At the mention of cops, chaos erupted. Poker players grabbed their chips and rushed for the door. The dealer and the guards made their way toward the exit as well. Kelton pushed me in that direction.

"No," I snapped as I tried to hold my ground. "I'm not done talking to him."

Kelton wrapped his arms around me from behind and lifted me off the ground. "We have to go." He merged into the melee of the panic-stricken crowd.

"Hurry!" someone shouted.

"Get out of my way," another snapped.

Kelton stumbled forward. I went down, twisting my ankle before I was plastered to the floor. I tried to get up, but a stampede barreled over me. A high heel dug into my hand. I screamed.

"Lizzie!" Kelton shouted. "Lizzie!"

Someone tripped over me, landing in the group ahead.

"Kross!" Kelton said from somewhere. "Where is she?"

I tried to scramble upright, but someone else knocked me down. Then a hand gripped my arm, helping me to my feet. People were yelling at one another to move. The person behind me gently used his bulk to push me out the door. Before we reached the stairs, I quickly checked to see who my savior was.

"Keep moving," Oscar said.

A gravelly voice ahead of me warned, "Cops are in the stairwell."

I had nowhere to go but up, since the hall was narrow and a quick scan around showed no exit signs.

I couldn't lose sight of Terrance. But I couldn't breathe. I could barely walk in my damn heels. Blood pooled on the back of my hand, my body throbbed, my brain was frozen, and I didn't know where Kelton, Dillon, or Kross were. My only option was to climb the stairs into the hands of the cops who were cuffing people as they reached the landing. Even if I'd wanted to run back down to the poker room, Oscar's big stature wouldn't have allowed me to. I could've pushed him out of the way, but then he would've become a human bowling ball, knocking down those behind him.

I trudged upward into the hands of the police. The night hadn't gone anywhere near how we'd planned it, and I was to blame.

A beefy cop waited on the landing, handcuffs in hand. Cuss words shouted in my head, lots of them. All I could do at that point was accept my fate. After the cop cuffed me, he escorted me out of the building into the freezing cold night. I laughed, otherwise I'd start crying for fucking up the only plan I'd had to get Terrance's attention.

"Watch your step," the beefy cop said. My ass was hanging out of the cocktail dress and my breasts were practically on display.

I climbed into the police van and took a seat on a bench. Fortunately, my long hair had come undone, spilling over my breasts.

Not far behind me was Oscar. He grunted as he tried to get his large body into the van, then he dropped beside me. I leaned my head back against the metal wall. *Fuck.* Kelton didn't need to get arrested. Dillon was probably furious with me, and poor Kross. He'd only tagged along to keep Kelton in line when he should've tried to keep me on the straight and narrow.

"How come we're the only two in this van?" At least a handful of others had flown out before us.

"There's another vehicle in front of this one." Oscar didn't sound surprised by any of it.

The van had no windows, so I couldn't see anything outside except the two cops standing guard at the open back door. Beyond them, the street was empty of traffic. It was midnight or so. "You seem to know the ropes. Are cops always called at games like this?"

"My guess is that someone in that room was an undercover cop trying to infiltrate the Italian mob. Maybe they saw it was about to get out of hand and called in support."

All because of me.

"Put him in this one," a male voice ordered.

Terrance came around to the back side, arms cuffed behind him. His mop of curls was wild, reminding me of his son. He got in and sat on the bench opposite Oscar and me.

We stared at each other for the longest time. All I could think about was my dad and what he'd seen in Terrance as a friend, why he'd trusted him.

"What did you mean when you said my father was stupid like that, too?" I'd never known my father to gamble.

"Why do you think your parents always took the boat to the Bahamas? Your father had the bug. He loved the casinos there."

"For the nightclubs and dancing." My parents had loved to dance.

"Maybe at first." Terrance sighed as he lost his snarky attitude. "But after he won his first craps game, he was hooked. He was a good man."

I wanted to yell at him and hurt him for what he'd done. But the despondent look on his face when he talked about my father led me to believe he missed him, too. Whether he did or not, Terrance had to pay for what he'd done. No matter the consequences.

"My dad trusted and respected you. He'd be disappointed and furious to know that you broke that trust."

He lowered his gaze to his shiny shoes.

"Stop disappointing the people who love you. You're going to be a grandfather, Terrance. Get help. Reconnect with Zach." Family was so important. "You have a great son." I hardly knew anything about Zach. On the surface he seemed mad at the world, but he gave me the impression he wanted his father's attention. "And I envy him. He still has a father." Tears pricked my eyes.

Oscar placed his hand over mine. "I'm sorry for your loss."

A lone tear fell, and I latched onto Oscar's stubby fingers. I should've been demanding Terrance give me all my money back, not grieving and playing psychologist. But my dad would have done the same, trying to make Terrance see reason. Yet all the reasoning in the world wouldn't return the lost money.

Terrance stared out the door.

"I can't force you to do the right thing," I said. "But the courts can. So it's up to you. If you cooperate, I'll consider not pressing charges." Mr. Davenport had said I could bring a civil suit against Terrance.

"Close this one up." A cop came up to the open door.

"Wait," a female voice said. "Throw this one in." The petite officer came into view with Kross at her side.

His white shirt was bloody. His hair was disheveled, and anger was stamped in his blue eyes.

I let go of Oscar's hand and got up.

"You're not going anywhere," the female cop said. "Sit back down."

"Where are Kelton and Dillon?" I inched closer to the door.

Kross shook his head. "Not sure."

"I said to sit your ass down," the female cop ordered in a tone that made the hairs on my neck rise.

Kross's blue eyes prodded me as he climbed in, forcing me backward and into my seat.

"Are you okay?" Kross dropped beside Terrance.

I nodded and shivered at the same time. Maybe they'd escaped. That would be great. Kelton had that job on the line. And Dillon. Well, he was always trying to stay under the law's radar. Thanks to me, not anymore.

The two cops that had been standing watch outside hopped in. The female officer closed the doors, and the sound made me shiver again.

CHAPTER 27
KELTON

The van bounced along the city streets, jarring my body. I didn't know if Lizzie was in the other van or not. When someone had yelled "Cops!" I'd tried to get the fuck out of there. But people were frantic, rushing toward the exit. Someone had pushed me from behind. Lizzie had gone down. Then fucking Terrance had practically thrown me out of the way. I'd tackled him to the ground. I'd wanted to unleash all the frustrations I had for this man for not only stealing from Lizzie, but for how he'd treated Zach. Sure, Zach and I weren't on speaking terms, but we were friends. Zach wanted his father in his life. He'd always told me how envious he was of my relationship with my old man. Unfortunately, I hadn't gotten to wield my fists. Dillon had grabbed me, and we'd found an exit tucked away in the far corner of the poker room. It hadn't helped though. The cops had been waiting in the alley. I wasn't even sure where Kross was.

The driver banked a hard right, and my shoulder knocked into Dillon. The van was packed with at least ten of us from the poker game.

"She's probably in the other van," Dillon said.

Motherfucker was clamoring in my head over and over again. My life was flashing before me. I was on my way to jail. My career as a lawyer could end before it had even begun. Davenport's question played in my head in between the cuss words. "Have you ever been in trouble with the law?" Where was Jeremy Pitt when I needed him? Three years before, he'd been instrumental in keeping Kade, Hunt, and me out of jail for a brawl that had broken out among the three of us and two of our high school enemies. That night a gun had gone off and someone had almost died. Luck had been on our side, particularly since Jeremy Pitt was in bed with the Boston Police Department. No such luck tonight.

"Man, I hope so," I murmured. My heart beat like a stampede of cattle. It wouldn't settle until Lizzie was in my arms. Fuck, if this was how my life would be, constantly worrying about her, then I definitely needed to hire a shrink. I was beginning to understand why Kade was always a mess whenever Lacey wasn't with him. Whatever. I would take the erratic heartbeat, the pacing, the ripping out my hair, and every other thing if it meant that I had her forever.

A burly cop sat on my left. "About eight people got away," he said to his partner across from him.

Dillon nudged me.

Please, please, let Lizzie and Kross be two of those eight. Kross didn't need to get in trouble either. Not with his boxing career in full force. He was trying to sign with a big boxing promoter.

"Who called the cops?" I asked the officer next to me.

"Anonymous tip," he said.

I couldn't say for sure what the laws were specifically on illegal gambling. However, what I did know was that they hadn't read us our rights, which meant they had nothing to book us on. Not yet, anyway. Although they could hold us for twenty-four hours, and that wouldn't be good either. Jail was jail. If Davenport found out, I could probably kiss my internship good-bye.

The van came to a stop in an underground garage. From there we were escorted up an elevator. When we got off, we were steered toward a set of interrogation rooms. The burly cop deposited Dillon and me inside a tiny, sterilized room with Terrance and the fat dude who'd sat next to Lizzie at the poker table. The room was devoid of any furniture but was filled with a strong scent of body odor coming from one—or both—of the two men.

The cop unleashed me but not fast enough. I choked at the stench then covered my nose. Dillon did the same as we scrutinized Fat Dude and Terrance.

I rubbed my wrists. "Where's Lizzie? Have you seen her?" I narrowed my eyes at Fat Dude, then at Terrance.

Both wore placid expressions as though they'd been through the police drill a hundred times before.

"Your girl was with us in the van," Fat Dude said. "Lovely lady. Sad that she got herself into this mess. But a Detective Rayburn took her and a guy who looks like you for questioning."

I leaned against the two-way mirror. I'd hoped that Lizzie and Kross had gotten away, but it was good to hear she wasn't far.

"They can't prove anything," Dillon said as he stood next to me.

"Maybe not." I closed my eyes. "But what about the money you put up for this game?"

"We wouldn't be here if it weren't for Elizabeth," Terrance spat.

My eyes flew open. "Are you for real?" I balked. "Maybe if you hadn't stolen her money." I pushed off the window, not caring that someone had to be watching us.

Dillon held out his arm. "Easy. Karma will prevail."

Fuck karma. My fists were ready to show Terrance what karma was all about.

"The cops will probably question us if you beat his ass." Dillon pointed at Terrance. "Then they *will* have a reason to throw you in jail tonight."

I growled.

Fat Dude piped up. "Don't worry about the money. The rules of the house stipulate that when the game is stopped due to reasons beyond the house's control, they keep twenty percent of each player's entrance fee. So you're only out two thousand."

Dillon slumped next to me. "My brother said something about that, but I wasn't sure. At least now I don't have to kiss his ass." He laughed.

The door opened, and in waltzed Lizzie, with her hair messy around her face and a smile that sent heat to grip my nuts. She was wearing a leather jacket that fell to her knees and carrying her heels. She smiled as she came barreling at me. When I locked my arms around her, I swore I heard violins play. My dad was right. I did see the world in a whole new light, and that light was Lizzie.

"I'm sorry," she said. "This was my fault, the cops showing up. I shouldn't have let my anger get to me."

I let go of her. "Where's—"

Kross swaggered in, laughing with a man dressed in jeans, a T-shirt, and a shoulder holster housing a Glock twenty-two. I guessed that was Detective Rayburn.

"I saw one of your matches three months ago," he was saying. "My brother dragged me to one. I was impressed. You knocked out your opponent in three rounds." The detective placed his hand on the doorknob.

"I have a bout next month," Kross said.

"Let me know date and time," the man with the Glock said.

Dillon and I exchanged a wide-eyed look.

"They started talking about boxing," Lizzie added.

I'd gotten that. What surprised me was that they acted like buds from high school. Maybe Kross's minor-celebrity status boded well for us.

Kross flicked his head at me. "That's my brother."

"I see the resemblance." He chuckled. "I'm Detective Rayburn." He pointed at the fat dude. "You, go with Detective Bensen."

A female detective dressed similarly to Rayburn settled in the doorway.

Fat Dude pushed off the wall and came up to Lizzie. "I hope everything works out for you."

"Thank you, Oscar," she said. "And stay out of those poker joints."

After Oscar and Detective Bensen left, Rayburn walked over to the two-way mirror and knocked on it. Then he said to Dillon and me, "I already questioned Kross and Elizabeth. I suspect if I question you two I'll get the same responses. And we don't have anything to hold you on. Besides, we're after bigger fish at that poker game anyway." Rayburn looked at Terrance. "You, on the other hand, I do want to question."

The blood drained from Terrance's face. "You turned me in?" he asked Lizzie. "I thought you said that if I helped you, you wouldn't press charges?"

"I said I would consider it, although I already went to the cops in Florida weeks ago. They have my statement."

"According to Ms. Reardon, you know one of the dealers from that poker game," Rayburn said. "I don't have anything to hold you on either, but I do want to hear more about the dealer."

"Oh," Terrance muttered.

"But don't think for a minute that I can't call down to Florida and talk with one of my brethren. So if I were you, I'd do the right thing." Detective Rayburn waved his hand toward the door. "Let's go."

Terrance shuffled past us.

Lizzie grabbed his arm. "My attorney here in Boston is Robert Davenport at Davenport Law Firm, and you have my number. I hope to hear from you soon."

Detective Rayburn pinned a look on all of us. "Stay out of illegal poker joints. I don't want to see any of you in here again." Then he shook Kross's hand. "You have my card. Give me a heads up on your next fight. And someone will be by in a moment to escort all of you out."

When it was just the four of us, I let out a heavy sigh. We weren't going to jail. My future as a lawyer wasn't ruined. Most of all, the woman who had my heart in the palm of her hand was safe. It was time for flowers, feathers, and foreplay. Lots of foreplay.

CHAPTER 28
LIZZIE

I walked into a posh hotel in the Back Bay of Boston to meet Kelton. Large vases of fragrant lilies dotted the lobby tables as I crossed the shiny white floors on my way to the elevators. I inhaled the sweet aroma—a definite upgrade from the cigar smoke at the club the night before.

I stabbed the up arrow for the elevator, thinking of Terrance. I had hoped he'd call. During our conversation in the van, I'd thought I'd rattled a nerve or two, talking about his son and my dad. But maybe I'd read him wrong. Or maybe Detective Rayburn threw him in jail for some reason. Aside from all that, Dillon had confirmed with Duke that all but twenty percent of our money would be returned to us. Apparently, Oscar gave Dillon a heads up on that piece of info. At least I wasn't out ten thousand dollars, only two.

But I stowed away my problems. For that night, Terrance, money, and everything else didn't exist. I pressed the button again. Then I checked the text message Kelton had sent me earlier with the room number. *Ding.* The doors whooshed open. After a couple filed out of the elevator, I hopped in and hit number twenty-five. When the car began its ascent, so did my pulse. Our first date hadn't gone so well. We'd both been on eggshells. We were still getting to know one another. Only tonight would be on a whole new level.

The churning in my stomach kicked into high gear as I got out of the car. I laughed as I looked in the mirror that hung on the wall right outside the elevator.

"No reason to be scared," I said out loud. Despite the drizzle of rain I'd trudged through on the way from the "T" to the hotel, the little makeup I had on was intact. My cheeks were pale and my hair draped around me, but my eyes weren't as red as they had been earlier from lack of sleep. I smiled at my last thought. *I probably won't get much sleep tonight either.*

I made my way to room twenty-five twelve, which was two right turns off the elevator. After a long trek down the hallway, I arrived at Kelton's room. He'd instructed me to meet him at 9:00 p.m. I rapped on the door with a shaky hand and nausea ready to rise. We'd been through our first kiss, first touch, first eye contact, first fight—lots of firsts, but never had we been intimate with each other.

As I wiped my damp hands down my jeans, the door opened with a light click, revealing a shirtless Kelton with his colorful lizard tattoo snaking out of sight into his jeans. I wiped my hands on my legs again and again. The way I was going, I was about to start a fire. Or maybe I was *on* fire.

He opened the door wider. "Hey." His lopsided grin made me squeeze my thighs together. As he held onto the door, his left bicep flexed, causing his serpent tat to move as if it was slithering up his arm.

Then again, I was probably dizzy. I grabbed onto my necklace as I padded deeper into the room. Waiting for Kelton to close the door, I took in the scene. Candles peppered the desk, dresser, and nightstands. The city lights spilled in through the floor-to-ceiling windows. A faint, flowery fragrance hung in the air, and the bed—or should I say the elephant in the room—was inviting with its comforter folded down and the pillows fluffed to perfection.

Kelton came up behind me and pressed his body into mine, gently helping me out of my jacket before he swept my hair to one side. Then his lips touched the spot of skin just below my ear. I jumped as tingles exploded from head to toe.

"Easy, baby doll."

He smelled clean like fresh air, sparking memories of our summers together in my backyard as we'd lain on the grass in the rain. I sank back against him, tilted my neck, then reached up to cup his smooth-shaven face. He turned into my hand, his tongue snaking out to trace circles on my palm. My body instantly erupted in another wave of tingles, and this time I didn't jump. Instead, I dropped my head against his chest as he grasped my hips then trailed his hands up under my sweater. He brushed my breasts as he continued his slow ascent until he whispered in a husky tone, "Raise your arms."

I obeyed. He removed my sweater then tossed it aside. I shuddered at the coolness in the room but was quickly rewarded with warmth when his strong hands found their way to my waist and he guided me around to face him. His blue eyes appeared darker, like sapphires in an expensive ring, as he lowered his head then stroked my lips with his thumb.

I closed my eyes, my limbs languid as he moved to caress my neck, working his way down to my breasts. Moaning, I gripped the waist of his jeans before reaching for the button.

"Not yet. *Slow* is the key word tonight."

I pouted as I opened my eyes, meeting the most insanely blue and intense gaze. His black hair was messy. The scar on his chin—a reminder of our past. I went to feel the ridges of his six pack, but he grasped my hand.

"This way."

We bypassed the bed, heading to the bathroom. My pulse was erratic as I tried to control my breathing. He pushed open the door. Curls of steam floated out as he tugged me inside. Before I could do anything, he lifted me up by the waist and set me down on the long counter opposite a bathtub surrounded in candlelight. In quick moves he removed my boots. Then he raised my legs so my feet were planted on his chest. I held onto the counter. He glanced at me then at my toe socks and grinned, a little amused, a little feral. He hadn't told me to wear them that time.

"What is it with my toe socks?" I wasn't complaining, but his fetish was kind of weird.

He gripped my right foot between his hands, pressed his thumbs into my heel, then massaged. "They look sexy on you."

I purred my approval as I closed my eyes, feeling the relaxing sensation of his magical hands.

"They'll look even sexier with your jeans off." He lowered my legs.

I planted my hands on the tiled counter as he worked to unbutton and unzip my jeans. As he pulled them down, I raised my hips. He sucked in a sharp breath when I sat in only my pink lace bra and thong and my socks. He sized me up slowly, smoothing his rough hands over my thighs and stomach before settling on my breasts.

"So fucking stunning." He traced the outline of my cleavage, his hand slightly shaking. He appeared to be using every ounce of energy not to rip off my bra.

I poked out my chest, hoping he would replace his hands with his mouth. Instead he took off my socks, gripped my waist, and set me on my feet. Then he had me face the mirror as he positioned our bodies in front of the un-fogged spot in the middle. We peered at each other as his hands roamed freely over my body, his eyes heavy. The image of us heated me and made me want to cry. Never in a million years would I have thought I'd be standing in Kelton's arms.

"You're everything I imagined, everything I dreamed of." He nibbled on my ear.

I rested against him, soft to hard, before I snaked my hands between us, feeling his arousal straining through his jeans.

He flattened a hand on my stomach then dipped his fingers inside my thong. He growled, pushing his hips into my hand. When his fingers landed on my bundle of nerves, I let out a soft moan, squeezing him tightly. He flipped me around and unhooked my bra, practically tearing it off. My breasts fell free. He hedged back, drinking me in. I wasn't going to last if he didn't do something soon. Nor was he, with that large bulge in his jeans. As desperate as I was to move things along, I also wanted to enjoy every second, every touch, every kiss, every noise, and every look between us.

As he continued to study me, the light in his eyes dimmed, his eyebrows knitting. I had a sudden urge to cover myself or wrap my arms around my chest. I hardly shied away from anyone, especially Kelton.

I did a mental shake to rid myself of any self-doubt then shimmied out of my thong, watching him the entire time. He licked his lips as I stood naked in the bathroom, surrounded by candlelight, flowers floating in the tub, tension hanging in the air, and steam and lust swirling around us. I clutched the half-heart charm as my nerves perked to life.

I inched closer to him, hoping he wasn't having second thoughts about us, about his love for me or mine for him. Or was he rethinking the long-distance relationship?

I hooked my fingers in his belt loops. "I love you, Kel."

Without so much as a warning, I was in his arms and he was lowering me into a warm bubble bath filled with jasmine flowers. I squealed as he knelt down outside the large oval bathtub, his pensive expression never wavering.

"What's wrong?" I asked as I picked up a flower.

"It's not what's wrong. It's what's right. For so long I closed off my heart, afraid of what would happen if I let someone in. Even when I told you I loved you at Dillon's, I truly didn't grasp the strength of the feeling until now." His hand disappeared under the water. "You deserve the world, Lizard, and I want to give it to you. No matter if you're in Miami and I'm here, we'll work it out. And"—his hand coasted up my thigh—"I just want this night to be perfect." His confident tone, the love in his eyes, and his smile erased any reservations I'd had about what he would do when I flew back to Miami.

Tears pricked my eyes. "Are you getting into this bathtub with me? Or are you going to talk all night?" Not that I didn't want to hear what he had to say, but actions were always louder.

He chuckled as he quickly stood, shucking his jeans. My mouth dropped open, heat pinching my cheeks as my gaze lingered on his erection, imagining how he would feel inside me. He grinned like an ass as he climbed in—all six feet of hard ridges, tight abs, colorful tattoos, toned thighs, and impressive package.

I scooted forward as he eased behind me. When he was situated, he pulled me back to him. Then he snagged the soap from the tray and began lathering my body, concentrating on one breast with the soap and the other with his hand. Warmth slithered down my stomach. Excitement soared up. The night was just beginning.

CHAPTER 29
KELTON

My fingertips were shriveled, and the water was lukewarm at best. For the past thirty minutes, Lizzie had been mush in my arms as I'd lathered her body, feeling her perfect breasts in my hands, kissing her ears, her neck, anywhere I could as we sat in the tub. I took my time, not wanting to rush the evening. Although when she had first arrived I'd wanted to throw her on the bed and release the need that had been building since I'd first seen her again after seven years. Even more when she'd been standing naked earlier with a shy look, curvy hips, long legs, and those soul-stealing eyes with that square pot of gold shining brightly. Hell, the gold speck was one of her attributes that had snared me from the moment I'd met her in the fifth grade. My mind reeled at the fact she was there with me. I wanted to make new memories with her. I also wanted to cherish those that we had from the past. Good or bad, those times had defined us.

I snaked my hand down, found her sweet spot, and began to move my finger in circles. She whimpered as I teased her awake.

"Baby doll, I'm going to get out. But I don't want you to move." I wanted to get a couple of things in place before I laid her on the bed and worshipped her.

"Hurry up. The water is getting cold." She shivered.

I climbed out and toweled off. "Two minutes."

Her gaze traveled like a race car over my body until she put on the brakes, skidding to a stop on my painful hard-on. Yep, I had been rock hard since she'd walked into the hotel room. But I didn't care about the pain. The pleasure would come soon enough. Besides, this night was about her, about showing her how much I loved her.

I darted out of the bathroom, grabbed my bag, removed a large purple feather, and placed it on the nightstand. The woman at the flower shop had thought I was nuts when I asked her if she sold feathers. I'd had to repeat myself a couple of times before the shop owner came out from the office. I wasn't about to explain why I wanted it. Luckily, the shop owner had some left from a flower arrangement she'd made on a special request.

I dove back into my bag, grabbed the condoms, and set them next to the feather. Then I arranged the pillows from the headboard to the side and tore the comforter from the bed. I checked the candles around the room. All flickered. Satisfied, I hurried back into the bathroom, snatched a towel from the rack, then stretched out my arms. "Your chariot awaits," I said.

She rose, carefully easing out of the tub. I followed every droplet of water as it slid down her body. More blood rushed to one place. I stifled a groan as I bundled her up, then I hoisted her in my arms. As I carried her, she sucked on my ear. In that second, my knees nearly buckled. Fortunately, my legs brushed the side of the bed.

I let her down as gently as my shaky arms allowed. "Head on the pillows."

"Demanding still, I see." She moved up, the towel falling and exposing her naked body.

My gaze was riveted to her. My pulse sped up. My mouth was bone dry. Pure, raw hunger gripped me. The fire coursed through me like a slow burn, and at any moment the door would burst open, the backdraft sending me over the fucking edge.

"Are you going to stand there gawking?" she asked.

All night if I couldn't get my legs to move. My gaze wandered lazily upward from her navel to her breasts. Her nipples were calling to me. I blew out a breath, but the knots in my stomach didn't loosen. I was never this nervous when it came to women and sex. *Hey, moron. You're not having sex. You're making love to the most beautiful fucking woman you've ever laid eyes on. The woman who always had the superpowers to unlock those feelings you stowed away forever.*

She cupped one of her breasts and squeezed. My body jolted. Oh, hell no. As much as her touching herself was a turn-on, those babies were for me. I moistened my lips, yanked the towel from her, and flung it behind me.

She blushed seductively, her body outstretched, her hair messy around her. The half-heart charm fell between her breasts. A surge of warmth spread through me. That piece of jewelry was a testament to the love she had for me.

I reached for the feather then crawled up on the bed beside her, propping up on my elbow. "Hands over your head."

Concern glimmered in her eyes. "You know I'm ticklish," she said in a breathy tone.

I ran the feather lightly over her face. "I know." The feather wasn't meant to tickle her. "Trust me?" Her entire body was all mine, every satiny inch of it was mine to do with as I pleased. My dick jerked at that thought. I'd lain awake the past several nights, imagining the feather dipping in between her legs but never touching the spot she would eventually beg me to touch. I wanted to see her wiggle, see her facial expressions, and hear her moan. I wanted to feel every emotion with her as I tortured myself in the process. Because in the end, the high would be like no other fucking high in this world.

I started my assault on the tops of her feet, slowly dragging the feather up one leg, all the while watching her. She sucked in her bottom lip, her chest rising, her nipples hard. As I approached the apex of her legs, her eyes fluttered closed. I switched to the other leg, doing the same thing, then ran the feather over her shifting abdominal muscles, between her breasts, along her neck, her arms, and her legs. When I was anywhere near the tops of her thighs, she raised her butt off the bed, trying to guide me toward her core. Beads of sweat broke out on my body. I wasn't sure I'd be able to stick to my plan.

"Kel, I love the sensation, but I need to feel you all over me," she whined.

I groaned. The need to be inside her bellowed through me like fucking wildfire. "Foreplay," I said in a strained voice.

"Don't you think the last hour or so has been enough foreplay?" She captured one of her nails in her mouth.

Fuck. The first second after I'd opened the hotel door had been enough. "You're not ready to scream my name." I leaned over and captured her lips with mine, pushed my tongue through, and took, tasted, and got lost in her, in us, in our past. Seven fucking years of dreams of her, of pain that wouldn't go away, of memories, of wondering every day where she was and if she was okay. Now the only pain I had was a throbbing erection. But her needs came first.

She curled into me, moaning as she returned the kiss. When our tongues met in a heated frenzy, sparks shot off inside me like a cannon. I growled and abandoned the feather. I needed to taste more of her, all of her. I adjusted us so I was poised with my legs between hers, my hands pressed into the mattress on either side of her head. We continued to kiss as she gripped my butt, trying to tug me down.

I broke away, both of us breathing heavily. Her hands were all over me, and yet nowhere. She opened her legs, and my dick brushed the inside of her thigh. She rocked her hips upward, wiggled, did everything she could to fuse us together.

Control, control, I chanted in my head. What control? We both wanted each other badly. I grasped one wrist then lifted her arm over her head. "Leave that one there," I said in a hoarse voice. "I promise I won't tickle you."

"I'm not going to last," she said. "I need you. I've dreamed of this moment. My foreplay started years ago, Kel." A glow of pink stained her cheeks.

"Baby doll, you have no idea how many times I've imagined this moment. But I promise in the end your dreams will be answered more than you imagined." I slid down, capturing a nipple as my hand covered her breast. I sucked lightly then nipped. She writhed as I lifted her other arm over her head. Then I ran my fingers down her body, careful not to tickle her sides.

She watched me with a quiet but lazy intensity, her body relaxed, her skin glistening in the soft candlelit room.

Perfection came to mind as I settled on her other breast. She moaned her approval as I began dragging my lips slowly down her shifting abs, circling the outline of her belly button before landing on the inside of her thighs. I kissed the inside of both legs then glanced up at her, silently seeking permission. With her arms still over her head, she blinked.

Fireworks went off in my stomach, causing my heart to beat out of control. I lowered at a snail's pace, torturing myself as I did. I wanted to take my time, but my body was telling me to speed up the process so I could be inside her. When I captured her clit between my lips she let out a squeal, gripping the sheets above her. I licked lightly, up then down, before falling into a steady pace. Her breathing grew shallow. I reached up with one hand and found her nipple. When I pinched, her hips shot up as she screamed my name. I didn't think I could be any harder, but fuck. When my name fell from her lips, it was all I could do not to become a madman. Instead I continued to suck lightly, wanting her release to last. When her body finally softened, I reached for the condom, tearing the hell out of the packet. In two seconds flat I rolled the condom on and crawled up her body, my biceps shaking like a motherfucker, until I was completely over her.

Her face glistened as she smiled through hooded eyelids, her gold speck shining like a beacon.

I rocked my hips and barely pushed in. Her eyes widened as she gasped.

I stilled. "Open for me." I was a millisecond away from exploding.

She wrapped her legs around me.

I glided in deeper. "You okay?" She felt like heaven, fitting perfectly around me.

"Better than okay." She dug her fingers into my biceps.

With our gazes locked, I drove in far and deep, wild and free, savoring the feeling of her around me, beneath me, and with me. She kept up with my rhythm as we melded together effortlessly as though we'd made love to each other before. She made soft breathy noises with each thrust, sending me closer to the one place I'd never thought I'd experience with her.

She kissed my mouth, hungry and heated, tethering her hands in my hair. I pumped harder and faster as I devoured her lips. Then I rolled us over without breaking contact. I needed her on top of me. I needed to absorb all of her, from the wildness of her hair, to the love in her eyes, to the way she moved on me. She swept her hooded gaze over my chest as she planted her hands on my tat.

"The lizard has blue-gray eyes." She was holding her lip hostage, seemingly lost in my tat.

"Like you, baby doll." I grasped her hips, guiding her up and down before she pressed her breasts into me. We moved together, kissing, my hands dancing rough and wild in her hair, until the fire morphed into an inferno. I flipped us one more time, taking control, thrusting faster, our bodies slick as we moved.

She screamed my name for the second time that night, and when she did, my heart fucking exploded with glee. I pumped harder, not wanting any of it to end. Desire flared to an impossible high that I hadn't even known existed. Tingles, heat, and suddenly, the room disappeared. I growled my release, my body shaking then stiffening, laboring for breath, the adrenaline pounding in my ears. "I love you, Lizard." I kissed her nose then smoothed back her damp hair.

Her eyes welled up.

"What's wrong?"

Her hand cupped my face. "Can we do that again?" She giggled.

"Fuck, yeah." My dick was already getting hard inside her again. "But why the tears?"

"I don't want to leave Boston. My heart can't handle being away from you."

Those words were a symphony to my ears. I wanted to pick her up and swing her around and shout out my happiness to the city of Boston. "Then don't. We have great schools here. We can get an apartment together."

"What? Naked model Kelton wants to settle down with one woman?" Her mouth curled on one side.

I was as shocked as she was, but I was also dead serious. She was the missing link in my life. "Lizard," I said in warning. "I will tickle you with that feather." I didn't want to lose her. I didn't want her to go back to Miami. Although, as rough as it would be for me to be away from her, I would deal if I had to. I loved her that much. Deep down I always had. If it weren't for Terrance Malden stealing her inheritance, I wouldn't be there with the one girl who wasn't getting away from me again. "Better yet." I squeezed her sides.

She squirmed faster than a rattlesnake. "Okay, I won't tease."

"Seriously. Think about it. I know you still need to get your inheritance worked out, but I can't keep living at home. The commute is too far. And I don't want to live with Zach. His gig babysitting that house ends when summer starts anyway. I don't want to go back to the dorms for my senior year at BU. Aside from all that, I want to make new memories with you."

She traced the scar on my chin. "I'll think about it. For now, can we have a repeat of tonight?"

"Hell yeah." I climbed off her then extended my hand. "Let's go. The shower awaits."

CHAPTER 30
LIZZIE

Kelton and I were sitting in Mr. Davenport's office, waiting for him to get out of his meeting.

I gazed out at the city skyline, the March sunshine glinting off the buildings. I played with my earring as I sifted through the events since I'd arrived in Boston. My sole purpose had been to find Terrance Malden, get my inheritance back, and return to Miami and school. Never had I imagined I would find Kelton along the way—or Dillon, Bee, and Allie either. I had some decisions to make once I resolved the legal part of my inheritance. Miami was home to me. All the memories of my parents were there. I was enrolled in a great marine biology program, and I had access to the tropical waters off the coast of Florida.

On the other hand, it was time for me to stop shutting people out of my life. I'd been doing that since my parents died, afraid that I would lose anyone I loved, and while I'd taken that chance exposing my feelings to Kelton, I was still deathly afraid that all the good that had come out of my time in Boston would vanish in an instant. More importantly, I would be a complete wreck if I left Kelton behind. I couldn't ask him to leave his family or school. He was taking every step to get into Harvard Law. I refused to ask him to give up his dream for me. But my dream was to finish my degree in marine biology and build a life with Kelton.

After our amazing night together that past Sunday, I'd had to time to think. I'd remembered from when I was researching colleges a couple of years before that BU had a great marine biology program. However, before I made that decision I had to ask Kelton one more time if he was serious about his offer for us to get an apartment together. I believed he was, but people did say things in the heat of passion. Since we'd had time to think about us, I didn't want to assume anything.

I glanced at Kelton, who was bouncing his knee. He hadn't heard from Mr. Davenport about the job offer yet. And given that we'd ended up at the police station, I was somewhat nervous for him.

"Do you think Mr. Davenport got wind of you at the police station?" I had an inkling as to why I was there. The lawyer in Florida, Mr. Pilkington, had had the meeting the day before with the courts for my temporary injunction to freeze my assets, which I was praying the courts approved.

He shrugged a muscled shoulder. "I hope not."

I snagged his hand, twining my fingers in his. "Maybe we'll both get good news."

"Did you think more about staying in Boston?" Kelton asked, trepidation pooling in his blue eyes.

The door opened, followed by the voices of Mr. Davenport and another man. The hairs on the back of my neck rose. Kelton and I turned our attention to not only Mr. Davenport, but to Terrance Malden.

My mouth dropped open. Kelton and I exchanged a smile.

"Let's all sit over here." Mr. Davenport waved at the small conference table behind us as he held folders in his other hand.

Terrance carried his briefcase as he crossed the floor to a chair at the table. He was dressed in a business suit, and his hair was combed back. He appeared fresh and ready for battle.

My stomach heaved as Kelton helped me to stand. Sure, I was happy Terrance was there. To me his presence signified that he was willing to help. But I was also apprehensive. He'd said there was only two hundred thousand dollars left in my bank accounts. However, if he hadn't done any accounting on the estate, the remaining funds might be slotted for unpaid bills.

Mr. Davenport didn't give me a chance to think or speak. No

sooner than he'd sat in a chair at the head of the table he said, "Ms. Reardon."

I swung my gaze from Terrance to Mr. Davenport as Kelton and I took two chairs across from Terrance.

"I called you here today to discuss the outcome of the temporary injunction that took place yesterday," Mr. Davenport said. "Before I get to that, I want to address the reason Mr. Malden is here."

I pinned my gaze on Terrance. He flashed me a tentative smile.

Mr. Davenport flipped open a folder. "Mr. Malden has handed over all the documents on your estate. And for the last three hours, I've had the opportunity to go through them."

The churning in my stomach settled for the moment. I wasn't about to get my hopes up. Kelton reached under the table and rested his hand on my thigh. I placed mine on top of his. For so long I'd been on my own with no one to turn to, and while I could fight for what was mine, his love, his presence, and his strength were a balm to my frayed edges.

"It appears from these documents that Mr. Malden has been draining the estate of cash. He's failed to file any tax returns. He's failed to pay any debt of the estate, and he's also failed to provide Ms. Reardon's living expenses." He glanced at Terrance. "Under the law, I have no grounds to have you arrested. However, Ms. Reardon has a right to bring a civil suit against you, which we will discuss in a minute. The Florida courts can also hold you in contempt. But you wanted to say a few words."

Terrance bobbed his head at Mr. Davenport before setting his apologetic gaze on me. "After our conversation in the police van, I thought long and hard about what you said."

Kelton gripped my hand tightly. I glanced at Mr. Davenport. He studied Kelton for a moment before writing something down on a piece of paper. Yeah, he knew.

"Your father and I were great friends," Terrance continued. "I'd have done anything for him. But when he asked me to watch over you if something ever happened to him and your mother, I was speechless. I told him I wasn't the right person. He'd said he didn't trust anyone else, not even the little family he or your mother had." He lowered his gaze briefly. "I've never been a good father. I put my kid through hell. I stole from him too. Gambling is an addiction that's hard to break. I cursed your father in his grave. I'm still angry with him for dying and for thinking I was the right person for this job. I was supposed to be on that boat with them that weekend." Tears formed in his eyes.

I was supposed to have been on the boat with my parents as well. I had to sympathize with Terrance. I was also angry that my parents were taken from me, but that wasn't anyone's fault. Habit or not, sympathy aside, he stole from me. *He has a disease.*

"I'm sorry, Elizabeth. I'm not proud of what I've done. You made me see that I need to make vast changes in my life, especially now with a grandbaby on the way. So I'm entering a rehab facility. But I will do what I can to cooperate with the attorneys and the courts to make this right."

"How much have you gambled away?" I asked.

Mr. Davenport pulled a piece of paper out of a folder. "Roughly six hundred thousand dollars has been depleted from the bank accounts. Is that correct, Mr. Malden?"

"Yes. But there's the two hundred thousand that's left in the bank account, and I have three hundred thousand in winnings from recent poker games that I'll return immediately."

"How can I be sure I'll get that money?" Once Terrance walked out, he could very well disappear.

"Terrance and I have already started the paperwork for the wire transfer," Mr. Davenport said.

I let out a quiet breath.

"That's the cash part of the estate," Kelton chimed in. "But what about the rest, the 401Ks or any other monies her parents had?"

"Fortunately, her parents had set up a separate trust specifically for the 401Ks," Mr. Davenport explained. "And that trust hasn't been touched. Mr. Malden couldn't touch it anyway. The details outline there's two point five million in 401Ks. When Ms. Reardon finishes college, she will be paid a portion of the monies from the 401Ks on an annual basis, leaving the balance to grow and adjust with market fluctuations."

My breath caught in my throat. I remembered Mr. Pilkington telling me after my parents' funeral that I'd be set for life. I also recalled something about a million dollars, but I hadn't paid close attention during that meeting. I slumped in my chair, gripping Kelton's fingers, holding back tears of joy that the majority of the money was tied up in 401Ks and Terrance hadn't had access to those accounts. But I wasn't out of the woods yet. Mr. Davenport explained that Terrance hadn't filed any tax returns or paid any bills associated with the estate. I couldn't be certain, but I guessed the IRS would want their share regardless of a trustee's theft of the money.

"Ms. Reardon?" Mr. Davenport said. "Are you okay?"

I blinked away a lone tear. "What bills need to be paid against the estate? And how much do I really have when everything is paid?" Since I didn't have access to the 401Ks until I graduated college, I needed to live, pay for school, and pay back my own debt, though that wasn't much in the grand scheme of things. I owed a landlord for back rent, which totaled three grand. I'd bet he'd already packed up my things and rented out the apartment. I had to settle my score with him if I wanted my furniture and the rest of my clothes.

Mr. Davenport's bushy eyebrows lifted. "Until we work up the tax documents, it's hard to say. The good news is that the lawyer in Florida was able to get the temporary injunction approved to freeze the assets. Mr. Malden will not have access to any of your money. The next steps are to get the accounting straight, remove Mr. Malden as the trustee, pay any outstanding debt, and name a new trustee. You also need to decide if you would like to bring a civil suit against him."

I wanted retribution. I wanted for all this to end. I wanted to move on, and above all I wanted control of my life. If I did take Terrance to court, that would be more money out of my pocket. In the end, it was a crapshoot whether I would win. Not to mention, if I did, how would he pay me?

Kelton rubbed the backs of my fingers as he leaned into me. "Whatever you decide, I'm with you," he whispered in my ear.

Terrance was cooperating, and I'd told him I wouldn't press charges if he did. "No civil suits." I pinned a glare on Terrance.

"I'm sorry for everything, Elizabeth," Terrance said. "I truly am."

Behind Terrance's gambling habit, he wasn't a bad man. I'd never known him as well as my dad had, but I knew my dad would have done whatever he could to help a friend turn his life around. "You need serious help. I pray rehab works for you."

"Thank you," Terrance said.

"Good." Mr. Davenport glanced at Terrance. "I appreciate you coming in. If I need anything else, I'll be sure to call. I'll walk you out." Then he eyed Kelton. "I need a word with you and Ms. Reardon."

Kelton stiffened his chair.

Terrance and Mr. Davenport left the office.

"I'm so screwed. Did you see how he looked at me when Terrance said *police van?*" Kelton's voice wobbled.

Mr. Davenport came back in. For one beat, the room was silent. Then Mr. Davenport cleared his throat. "Before we get to the matter of your résumé, Mr. Maxwell, care to explain the events of last Saturday night? Mr. Malden mentioned how all of you ended up at a police station for illegal gambling."

Kelton's knee moved.

I would've reached out to comfort him, but even I was jittery. I knew I should leave. I had no business being part of Kelton's job interview. I couldn't let Kelton take the rap for what had been my fault though. If I hadn't gotten angry, we wouldn't have found ourselves in a police station.

"It's my fault," I said. "I figured it was the only way to get Terrance's attention. Kelton tried to talk me out of it."

"Is that true, Mr. Maxwell?" Mr. Davenport asked, his finger resting under his chin.

Kelton sat up stoically. "I knew the consequences of my actions when I accompanied Elizabeth on Saturday night. And as much as I want to be a lawyer, Elizabeth is more important to me than the law. So, thank you for your interest in me." Kelton started to stand.

No way Kelton was jeopardizing his one dream of being a lawyer for me. I opened my mouth to speak.

"Sit down, Mr. Maxwell," Mr. Davenport said in a hard tone. "First, I admit that I was skeptical of your qualifications until I spoke to Brady, Schlenk, and Schiel. Then I was impressed when you contacted me about Ms. Reardon's case. Then you didn't show with Ms. Reardon for our meeting, so I thought you were irresponsible. However, you did surprise me by making a follow-up appointment to try and salvage your screw-up. I get that you're dedicated and that you want this intern job. But I was serious when I said that any trouble with the law will not be tolerated in this firm." His gaze fell to a sticky note on the outside of a folder in front of him.

While he did, the silence was deadly.

"After Mr. Malden explained the events of Saturday night, I made a call to a Detective Rayburn." Mr. Davenport switched his gaze from the note to Kelton. "He said you kids were in the wrong place at the wrong time. Apparently his undercover agent, who he wouldn't name, said Ms. Reardon and a friend of yours, Dillon Hart, were the ones playing poker. Regardless, Mr. Maxwell, none of this gets you off the hook. But..." He ran a finger over his eyebrow. "My gut tells me you will be a great lawyer. And we need great lawyers. So you get one shot with me. If you pull a stunt like that while working here, you'll be fired on the spot. Are we clear?"

"Yes, sir," Kelton said as he stood and held out his hand. "Thank you."

I was about to explode, but I didn't want to come off as a crazy person by jumping into Kelton's lap. So I smiled as wide as I could.

Mr. Davenport pushed to his feet and accepted Kelton's hand. "You will show up on time. If for any reason you can't make it, you will let me know immediately. In the meantime, work with Bonnie on your class schedule and what days you're available to work. And you won't be working on Ms. Reardon's case. If you two are in a relationship, that would be a conflict of interest."

As long as Kelton got the job, I didn't care if another intern was working my case.

"No problem. Thank you so much. I will not disappoint you," Kelton said with his head held high.

"I have every confidence you won't." Then he said to me, "We've made long strides today. I'll fill in Mr. Pilkington. In the short term, I'll need you to stay in town in case I need you to sign any documents, if that's okay."

More than okay. Kelton and I had some unfinished business.

CHAPTER 31
KELTON

I was dying to scream, shout, and swing Lizzie in my arms. But I had to wait until we were out of the building so I wouldn't come off as unprofessional. We made it down to the lobby, and I was just about to pick up Lizzie when Zach and Chloe rose from the lobby chairs. Zach took Chloe's hand as they made their way to us. I hadn't spoken to Zach since the day Chloe had told me he was the father. Even when I'd moved out, he hadn't been around, and since I wasn't modeling for Brew anymore and Zach and I didn't have any classes together, I hadn't bumped into him on campus.

"Hey, man," Zach said. His hair wasn't messy, he was clean-shaven, and he was dressed in tailored pants. The dude appeared as though he'd shed years of worry.

"What are you doing here?" Lizzie asked, swinging her gaze between Zach and Chloe.

Chloe beamed. Gone were the puffy eyes that had seemed to become the norm for her. She stuck out her small hand to Lizzie. "I'm Chloe. I know we met when you had red hair, but since then we haven't really met." She laughed.

It was good to see Chloe happy.

Lizzie shook hands with her. "I'm Lizzie. Congrats on the baby."

Chloe blushed at Zach.

Okay, this was way too awkward for me.

"We came with my dad," Zach said. "I wanted to thank Lizzie and apologize to both of you." He let go of Chloe. "My dad told me what happened. He said Lizzie made him realize he needed to get his head screwed on properly. Well, not in those words." He chuckled. "Anyway, I wanted to thank you. I also wanted to say how sorry I am. I was an ass to Lizzie at Rumors that day, and to you, Kelton, for everything. I should've told you Chloe and I were dating. I know we had a friend code, and when I put myself in your shoes, I get it. I would've been equally as pissed. I value our friendship, man."

I wasn't one to hold grudges. He hadn't slept with Chloe while she and I were dating, at least that was what Chloe had said. I'd never known her to lie either. Therefore, no one cheated. The only problem I had was Zach breaking our friend code on dating ex-girlfriends. But seeing how happy they were together, concerns about that friend code disappeared. I couldn't fault either of them for wanting happiness. Hell, I was over the fucking moon with Lizzie in my life.

I pulled Zach in for a man hug. "Congrats, daddy." I laughed as I stepped back.

Zach beamed from ear to ear. "Dude, thank you."

"Where is your father, by the way?" Lizzie asked.

"He went to get the car," Zach said. "He doesn't want Chloe walking five blocks to the garage."

"We got to run." I had some private celebrating to do with my girl.

After we'd said our goodbyes, Lizzie and I headed to my Jeep. As soon as we were on the busy streets of Boston, I swung Lizzie in my arms. The only piece of news left that would make this great day complete was her decision about moving to Boston. Sure, Mr. Davenport wanted her to stay in town for the short term. But fuck short term. I itched to start hunting for an apartment right away.

She squealed as I twirled us one more time. People passing by didn't give us a second glance.

"So." I laced my fingers in hers. "We were interrupted when I asked if you'd made your decision." She'd had days to think about it. "Boston or Miami?" I'd thought about moving to Miami if she decided that Boston wasn't the place for her. But I had a year left at BU. I also had my mind set on attending Harvard Law. I couldn't disappoint my parents. My mom was beaming with pride that one of her sons was going to be a lawyer. Yet Lizzie was my future, too.

We started walking.

"Do you still want to get an apartment together?" she asked. "I mean, you did ask right after sex."

I came to an abrupt stop. A lady bumped into me. I pulled Lizzie into the doorway of a yoga studio.

"You think I asked because we had mind-blowing sex?" I held my emotions in check. I got how people did or said things in the heat of the moment. "Baby doll."

Her blue-gray eyes met mine.

"Do you know how difficult it was for me to say the words *I love you*? I've never been this crazy for any woman."

"I just had to be sure. I don't have anything to go back to in Miami. BU has a great marine biology program. But..." She bit her lip, looking down.

My insides took a nosedive. With my fingers, I guided her chin up. "What? Is it the money? I've been saving, and with the intern job, we'll be fine." I'd pick up a high-end modeling job if it meant she would move to Boston. Of course, nothing naked that would ruin my career.

"No." She sighed. "I didn't think of this until now. What about your family? How will they feel about you and me living together? I know they offered me a place to stay. But will me being around your mom all the time be too much of a reminder of the past? Will she relapse?"

It was a logical worry. "She can't stop talking about you or how much she wants to see you. You're good for her, Lizzie. We're good for her. I believe we bring out more of the good memories for her too. And seeing her sons happy makes her happy. Aside from that, we both need to be closer to campus." My stomach wouldn't settle until she said yes.

She wrapped her arms around my waist. "I want you and me to be happy too. I choose Boston."

"Don't mess with me," I teased.

She lifted up on her toes then softly kissed my chin. "I can't live without the other half of my heart."

I devoured her mouth as my own heart beat a wild cadence. At that moment, all I could think about were Lacey's words. "When you do find that special girl, you'll never be the same. Or maybe you'll be less of an ass."

She was right on the first account, but I'd always be a lovable ass. Even more so now that Lizzie was by my side.

EPILOGUE

KELTON

Oranges and deep reds colored the trees surrounding the lake. The fall weather was warm with the sun beating down on us.

"Okay," Kody said. "I'll throw the ball to Kelton. He's the fastest. We only need one more touchdown to win."

Since March, I'd looked forward to our Sunday gatherings at my parents' house. Not that I hadn't liked spending time with everyone before Lizzie had re-entered my life. But now that sense of family I'd always had inbred in me had multiplied tenfold. My mom beamed with happiness every time Lizzie showed up. Even more when she saw us together. That alone made me as giddy as a schoolboy.

Kody, Dillon, Josh, Zach, Allie, and I were on one team. Kade, Kross, Rafe, Lacey, Bee, and Lizzie stacked the other.

"Break!" Kody clapped his hands.

We fanned out into position, which was wherever we wanted to be. I made a point of facing off with Lizzie. I stuck out my tongue as I readied my stance to run.

"You plan on using that?" she asked as she rolled her eyes.

Kody yelled hike. I took off, sidestepping her then raising my left arm in the air, signaling to Kody to throw the ball to me.

When the football landed in my hands, the spectators, consisting of Mom, Dad, and the very pregnant Chloe, shouted for me to run. I hesitated, watching Lizzie pump her legs, her hair blowing in the breeze. I grinned as she got closer, debating whether to stay put so she could tackle me or run for the woods where she would chase me. Then I could have my way with her.

Out of the corner of my eye, I spotted Zach.

He sprinted, catching up to Lizzie. "Run, you ass," Zach shouted at me.

Lizzie was two feet from me when I tossed the ball to Zach.

"Go!" Chloe yelled as Zach hugged the ball, heading for the end zone.

Lizzie dove hands first into me, knocking me backward. Before I fell, I reached out and grasped her wrists. No way was I going down without her. I landed in a pile of leaves with her on top of me.

She giggled as we tumbled around like two dogs play-fighting.

I bit her ear. "I do plan on using my tongue when we get back to our apartment tonight." We'd found a brownstone in Boston that had three bedrooms and was close to BU. Since we couldn't afford the rent on our own, Kade and Kross had stepped in as roommates. Kade was stoked at the idea of not sleeping on the couch at Rumors. And now he had a place for when Lacey came home on weekends. As far as Kross, he trained constantly in Boston. So he was happy not to drive back to Ashford after a hard workout. We'd asked Kody if he wanted to get in on the roomie action, but he preferred home for the time being. He'd said he needed the solitude to write songs.

Chloe walked by us to hug Zach, who'd scored just before the others tackled him.

"Is it weird to see your former girlfriend pregnant?" Lizzie asked.

I jumped to my feet then held out my hand. "No." It wasn't a lie. I wanted the best for Chloe.

She took hold of my hand. "What if I was?"

I almost dropped her hand. "Come again?" My heart left my chest. The music from the trees' leaves died. I hadn't even thought about starting a family. We both had school. She'd registered at BU once Terrance had returned the three hundred thousand dollars, and she'd paid her debts, including the money owed from her trust to the IRS. "Don't mess with me," I said, holding my breath.

She pressed her body into mine. "You don't want kids?"

"Baby doll, I want tons of kids with you. But we have school. Then there's the money thing, or lack thereof."

"You know I'll be a rich woman when I finish college."

True. I'd accompanied her to Florida. The judge had decided that Lizzie could manage the trust with Mr. Davenport's supervision. But she couldn't touch the 401K funds until she graduated, which was what her father had outlined in the trust. Considering that most of the cash she'd had available went to pay debts, she had just enough left to pay for college.

"Lizzie," I warned, enfolding her in my arms. "Are you?" My hands shook as I wracked my brain about how she could be. She was on the pill, but shit could happen.

She frowned. "Nah. But you're right. We need to finish college."

I blew out my nervous energy as I squeezed her. "Hey, we'll have rugrats running around someday."

"I know. It's just when I see Chloe glowing and happy, it reminds me of my mom. She would show Gracie and me pictures of her pregnant, and she said it was a glorious time in her life. I want that."

"You're everything to me, baby doll. But let's enjoy each other. We have seven years of catching up to do." I wanted to make her happy. I wanted to give her the world. But right then, we needed to focus on building a foundation.

"Let's head in for dinner," Mom said. "All of you get cleaned up."

Zach marched up to us then slapped me on the back. "Great game."

Since we'd made amends, Zach and I were back to our old selves as friends. "The best part of the game is when Lizzie tackles me for no reason." I kissed her on the head.

Chloe came up beside him. "I wish I could've played."

Lizzie hooked her arm around Chloe's. "You will eventually." They started for the house. "How are you feeling?"

I tuned them out as Zach and I trudged behind the girls.

"Have you told the family?" he asked low.

"I will at dinner," I said.

"I've been meaning to ask you. Would you be my best man?" Zach asked.

"Fuck yeah. Is your old man going to be there?"

"We haven't set a date yet. But if he's out of rehab."

The court in Florida had decided that they wouldn't hold Terrance in contempt for two reasons. He had cooperated with them and Lizzie, and any court proceedings or jail time would cost the taxpayers far more money than what Terrance had stolen. She'd also been happy with their decision. She wanted him to get help. She'd said her father would've wanted that. As for me, I hoped for Zach's sake that Terrance would come out of rehab a new man.

Voices buzzed as we walked into the kitchen. Mom was filling glasses with water from a pitcher. Lacey, Allie, and Bee were huddled near the stove, laughing. My dad, Kade, Kody, and Kross were talking with Rafe, Josh, and Dillon in the hall just outside the kitchen. Lizzie darted over to my mom and swiped the pitcher away to help. Zach pulled out a stool for Chloe.

I stood near Chloe and Zach at the end of the island and cleared my throat. With everyone in one room, it was the perfect time to announce my news.

The voices died as everyone looked at me.

Zach nodded. I'd only told him. Lizzie had never been good at keeping secrets when we were kids. I wasn't sure if that had changed, and I wanted to see the surprise on my family's faces.

Lizzie set down the pitcher of water then glided to my side. "What's going on?" Her eyebrows were mashed together.

I grabbed her hand. "I have some news I'd like to share."

Mom swung her blue gaze from me to Lizzie. The men gathered around the island along with everyone else. My dad angled his head, hesitation flaring in his copper eyes.

I kissed Lizzie on the back of her hand.

"No way you're getting married before me, bro," Kade chimed in, standing next to Dad.

At Kade's side, Lacey slapped him on the arm. "Seriously? If Kelton is about to tell everyone he's getting married, you should be recording this."

Kade raised an eyebrow. Bee squealed. She was always bubbly and excited at any surprises.

"Kel?" Lizzie said. Her voice was shaky.

"Everyone take a breath," I said as my heart dropped. Lizzie probably did think I was proposing.

Zach was laughing. Kody and Kross wore nonplussed expressions. The rest of our extended family waited anxiously.

"I got my acceptance letter into Harvard Law." I focused on my dad.

He immediately started to push through the crowd toward me.

"Oh my God!" Lizzie cheered. She tried to jump into my arms, but Mom came up to us.

"I'm so proud of you," Mom said.

A hand landed on my back, then my dad pulled me away. Tears clouded his eyes. "Congratulations, son." He hugged me tighter than he ever had. "You did it. Talk about proud." He choked on his last word. "A lawyer."

Kody and Kross ponied up, hugging and punching me.

Then it was Kade's turn. "So damn proud. You're on your way to living your dream." He glanced at Lizzie before embracing me. "And you've even given love a chance," he whispered in my ear. "Love you, bro."

My heart burst with so much love. I was grateful for everything in my life, but nothing more than showing my dad and Kade that I was the man they'd both raised.

After several handshakes and kisses from everyone, I homed in on Lizzie. She had a huge smile on her face. I stalked up to her and buried my hands in her hair. "I'm sorry I might've given you the wrong impression. I didn't tell you about the acceptance letter because I remember you weren't all that good at keeping secrets. But when I do propose, you will be the first to know, and it will only be you and me."

She blushed two shades of red. "I did get a tad nervous until I thought back to our conversation earlier about building a foundation. We're not ready for marriage."

"But we are ready for feathers, flowers, and foreplay. How about tonight?"

"Let's make a new memory," she said as she tugged on my belt. "Let's celebrate by sleeping in a tent down by the lake. No roomies. Just you and me under the stars."

"Anywhere as long as you're under me." I kissed her forehead.

So many things had gone right since Lizzie had showed up in Boston. My mom was in a better place thanks to Lizzie. My dad had shed years of grief after his talk with Lizzie. If it weren't for her, I would still be walking around with the guilt that had haunted me for seven years. Even Lizzie had grown, letting go of the anger she'd harbored for my dad for so long. Best of all, I had my best friend back. She was my girl with the bright gold speck in her left eye—the only girl who would hold the other half of my heart for a lifetime. She was my Lizard, and I was the luckiest fucking dude alive.

DEAR READER

I had a blast writing Kelton's story. He definitely challenged me with all his hidden emotions. Don't be afraid to open your heart for that special someone.

Other books in the Maxwell Series
Dare to Kiss - Kade and Lacey
Dare to Dream - Kade and Lacey
Dare to Dance - Kross Maxwell
Dare to Live - Kody Maxwell
Dare to Breathe - Final book on Kade and Lacey. Coming in 2018

Dare to Kiss and Dare to Dream should be read in order.

However, Dare to Dance, and Dare to Live can all be read as a stand alone.

Dare to Breathe should be read after reading Dare to Kiss and Dare to Dream.

Also, if you have moment to spare, I would super appreciate a short review. Your help in sharing your excitement and spreading the word about the Maxwell brothers would be greatly appreciated.

TITLES BY S.B. ALEXANDER

To read samples and find out where to purchase all books visit:
http://sbalexander.com/books

To read samples and find out where to purchase all books visit:
http://sbalexander.com/books

The Maxwell Series:

Dare to Kiss - Book 1

Dare to Dream – Book 2

Dare to Love - Book 3

Dare to Dance - Book 4

Dare to Live - Book 5

Dare to Breathe - Book 6

The Maxwell Series Boxed Set – Books 1-3

Dare to Kiss Coloring Book Companion

The Vampire SEAL Series:

On the Edge of Humanity – Book 1

On the Edge of Eternity – Book 2

On the Edge of Destiny – Book 3

On the Edge of Misery - Book 4

On the Edge of Infinity - Book 5

The Vampire SEAL Collection - Boxed Set

A Stand Alone Novel

Breaking Rules

ACKNOWLEDGMENTS

I want to thank my fans, readers and bloggers. Without you guys I wouldn't be writing. You motivate me, you support me, and you encourage me. I'm humbled by all the reviews and messages I've received along the way. Hugs and kisses to each and every one of you for taking the time to take this journey with me and sharing your excitement.

To everyone in Maxwell Mania, I love the crap out of you. Thank you for loving the series, and the Maxwell boys. Most of all, thank you for spreading the word, your excitement means more than you know.

The team at Red Adept Editing is without a doubt the best editing team in the industry.

An enormous thank you to the talented Hang Le for her creativity and book cover design. You're absolutely amazing.

Marketing a book is one of the hardest aspects for an author, and I'm so lucky and overjoyed that I'd met Marissa at JKS Communications. She had a vision for Dare to Kiss, and she has an even bigger vision for the future of my books. To Marissa, Angelle and the entire team at JKS, thank you.

The publishing industry changes constantly, and without Katey Coffing's inspiration and coaching I wouldn't have come this far without her. Love you, girl.

Wendy Kupinewicz, you are a superb lady, a great friend, and poet. The poem you've written is perfect. Much love and thanks.

Kylie Sharp, thank you for all your support, feedback and advice. Love you.

Cassie Schlenk, not only are you the Future Mrs. Kade Maxwell, you are a dear friend. I love your excitement, energy, insight, and feedback, and how you dedicate your time to helping authors succeed. You've gone above and beyond in helping me to spread the word about the Maxwell Series. Love you!

Tracy Hope, you are my super fan. You've read my drafts and every line I've ever written, even when it was rewritten fifteen times. You're honest in your feedback when something isn't working. You kick me in the butt when I need it. And you've brought my books to life with your creative vision and superb producing skills of my book trailers. Love and hugs!

Finally, to the man who stole my heart. I love you more than you know.